APR − − 2016

Also by Chitra Banerjee Divakaruni

Before We Visit the Goddess

Chitra Banerjee Divakaruni

Simon & Schuster

New York   London   Toronto   Sydney   New Delhi

Simon & Schuster
1230 Avenue of the Americas
New York, NY 10020

First Simon & Schuster hardcover edition April 2016

SIMON & SCHUSTER and colophon are registered trademarks of Simon & Schuster, Inc.

For information about special discounts for bulk purchases, please contact Simon & Schuster Special Sales at 1-866-506-1949 or business@simonandschuster.com.

The Simon & Schuster Speakers Bureau can bring authors to your live event. For more information or to book an event, contact the Simon & Schuster Speakers Bureau at 1-866-248-3049 or visit our website at www.simonspeakers.com.

Interior design by Joy O'Meara

Manufactured in the United States of America

10 9 8 7 6 5 4 3 2 1

Library of Congress Cataloging-in-Publication Data

Names: Divakaruni, Chitra Banerjee, 1956- author.
Title: Before we visit the goddess : a novel / Chitra Banerjee Divakaruni.
Description: New York : Simon & Schuster, 2016.
Identifiers: LCCN 2015041714
Subjects: LCSH: Mothers and daughters—Fiction. | East Indians—United States—Fiction. | Families—United States—Fiction. | Families—India—Fiction. | Domestic fiction. | BISAC: FICTION / Family Life. | FICTION / Contemporary Women.
Classification: LCC PS3554.I86 B44 2016 | DDC 813/.54—dc23 LC record available at http://lccn.loc.gov/2015041714

ISBN 978-1-4767-9200-2
ISBN 978-1-4767-9202-6 (ebook)

To my three men:

Murthy, Anand, and Abhay

Yatra naaryasto poojyantay, ramantay tatra devata.
(Where women are honored, there the gods are pleased.)

—Manusmriti 3/56, 100 CE

Everybody lives two ways. The first is simple, the second less so.

—"Fire Dreams," Jean Thompson

Contents

Fortunate Lamps: 1995

Somewhere in the dark, jackals are howling. They like it when storms bring down the electric lines in the village, leaving only broken bits of moonlight. Maybe they have a blood-memory of how it was before humans came and pushed them to the edges.

By now Sabitri is usually asleep. The doctor has warned her that she needs to keep regular hours. Her heart isn't doing too well, and there's the blood pressure, too. Did she want to be bedridden and force-fed barley water? Did she want him to phone her daughter in Houston? Or Bipin Bihari Ghatak, her business manager who lived in Kolkata?

No, she did not. Bela would rant, which was her default state when besieged by guilt, and Bipin Bihari, who was her oldest friend, would go silent with worry because he hadn't ever wanted Sabitri to move back to her ancestral village, so far from Kolkata, in her retirement. The savage lands, he termed it.

She sets out pen and paper on the rickety dining table next to the kerosene lamp. She takes care not to wake Rekha, snoring on her coir mat in the alcove, because then she'll start scolding, the way longtime servants feel they're entitled to.

The evening had started well, with her perched on the windowsill, watching sheets of rain blotting out the world. Gashes of lightning tore open the sky. Behind her Rekha wrung her hands. *Let me shut the window. The rain will make all the bedclothes damp, the quilts will turn moldy, you'll get the pneumonia again, and then what will we do?* But Sabitri refused. She loved the smell of night rain: wet earth, darkness, but also something else, nameless and a little frightening. When she was young, no one could keep her indoors at times like this. Even now, after she had grown brittle and creaky, the storm tugged at her insides. Ah, but Bipin Bihari should have seen her tonight!

The phone rang. She wasn't going to pick it up. That's what she had bought that fancy expensive answering machine for. But then there was Bela's voice, ragged. She'd been crying. What is it about children? An old need twisted in Sabitri's chest. *Protect, protect.* She lunged unwisely across the dark and banged her knee; pain shot down her leg like a fire.

"What happened?" she called into the receiver, her voice sounding rough and angry, though she had not meant it to come out like that. Even now Bela had this effect on her.

But Bela, preoccupied as she often was by her own drama, didn't seem to notice. She rushed into her tale. Tara was thinking of dropping out of college, they had to stop her, she'd only completed one semester, it would be the worst mistake of her life, the girl refused to listen to Bela, she never listened to anything her mother said nowadays.

Sabitri hid her concern. Sympathy would only make Bela cry more.

"I'm sorry to hear this." But how cold and unfeeling she sounded.

"You've got to write to her, Ma! You're the grandmother. If you stress the right things, point out the dangers of her stupid choice, perhaps it'll stop Tara from ruining her life!"

Sabitri wanted to remind Bela that she had tried all of the above with her. What good had it done? Besides, Tara had never even seen Sabitri. Every time Sabitri had asked Bela to bring her to India, Bela had an excuse ready. Almost as though she—or maybe that husband of hers, that Sanjay—felt Sabitri would be a bad influence.

The years had taught Sabitri to keep such thoughts to herself. She said, instead, "What made Tara want to drop out? She's such a good student."

When she didn't receive an answer, she continued, "Has Tara's father talked to her about this? There's a better chance of her listening to him than to me. Aren't they really close?"

Silence at the other end, more distressing than any amount of weeping. Then Bela said, "Tara isn't talking to Sanjay at the moment."

Something else was wrong, something worse than Tara aborting her studies, which in America, Sabitri had heard, could easily be picked up again. Sabitri suddenly felt much older than her sixty-seven years. She didn't have the strength to question Bela. What was the use of questions, anyway? Already she knew the most important thing: if her daughter—proud, stubborn, so like herself—had had anyone else to turn to, she would never have called Sabitri for help.

She wrote down, carefully, the college dorm address that Bela dictated. She promised to take a rickshaw to the post office early tomorrow morning. She promised to send the letter by express delivery.

Now she sits at the table that has been with her for decades, running her fingers over a gouge that Bela had hacked into the wood after they'd had a fight. What can she write in her rusty English to change Tara's mind? She cannot even imagine her granddaughter's life, the whirlwind foreign world she lives in. All Sabitri has is a handful of photos. The child Tara in a costume, brandishing a broomstick, celebrating some odd American festival, the point of which Sabitri could not figure out. A teenage Tara at a special party called a prom, alien and glamorous in a strapless dress. Sabitri had been intimidated by her glittery cheekbones, the sophistication of her plucked eyebrows. How different from the photo she kept in her drawer, under her sari-blouses: baby Tara in Bela's arms, peering from under a woolly blue hood, a foggy orange bridge floating in the distance.

That had been the first photo. Sabitri still remembers the pang she felt on receiving it because she had so wanted to be present at Tara's birth. But she hadn't been invited.

Push away the past, that vessel in which all emotions curdle to regret. Start the letter.

❧

> *Dearest Granddaughter Tara,*
>
> *I am sure you are surprised to receive this, since customarily we write to each other only to send Bijoya greetings. Your mother informs me that you do not wish to continue with college. I am very sorry to hear this and hope you will reconsider. Without education, a woman has little chance of standing on her own feet. She will be forced to watch from the sidelines while others enjoy the life she has dreamed about—*

Wrong, wrong, all wrong. An entire hour wasted. She balls up the sheet and throws it to the floor.

> *Dearest Granddaughter Tara,*
>
> *You do not know how lucky you are to be sent to college. So many families are too poor to be able to afford such an expense. It would be a criminal waste if you do not avail yourself of the opportunity life has given you.*

She hates what she has written, prissy, stilted, schoolmarmish. Tears it up. Her mind wanders, again, to the photos. Her favorite one, which she keeps on her dresser, is of Tara at the swimming pool, taken when she was nine. Dressed in a pink two-piece swimsuit, she balances on the edge of a board, about to leap into the water. Her face is filled with terror and elation.

How well Sabitri knows that feeling.

Sabitri's own leap began, as so many things in Bengal do, with a platter of sweets. She has forgotten many things from that time—just a few years after Independence; she was only seventeen then—but the platter she remembers clearly: heavy, made of solid silver, with a sharp, raised edge that cut into her fingers as she carried it down a mud path behind her mother, Durga, who held a similar platter. Durga's back was bent. As she walked, the knobs of her backbone bobbed up and down under her worn sari-blouse. She was the hardest worker Sabitri knew. But for her, their household would have fallen apart long ago, for her father was the kind of man the world routinely took advantage of. Sabitri felt a churning inside her as she watched her mother, a mix of sadness and anger and love.

The platters belonged to the Mittirs, the wealthiest family in the village. Their names were etched on the rims to discourage theft, or perhaps as a kind of proclamation. Mittir's wife Leelamoyi had ordered the sweets from Durga for a luncheon. The Mittirs had their own cook, a brahmin imported from Kolkata, but Durga's sweets, famous through-out the village, were far superior to anything he could have concocted. And Leelamoyi had to have the best.

Sabitri hadn't wanted to come. Leelamoyi, who lived in Kolkata and only visited the village under duress during festival time, was known to have a sharp tongue, unpredictable moods, and an elevated notion of her own importance. She would surely remark on how tall Sabitri had grown and how, if her parents didn't act fast, they wouldn't be able to marry her off. But there was no one else to help Durga. Sabitri's sister was too young. Her father was at the temple, where he was a part-time priest. And even if he had been home, he would have reminded them in his mild, surprised way that this wasn't a man's job. So here was Sabitri, sweating and irritated and trying not to step in cow dung.

Inside the Mittir home it was cool and misty, the windows covered with damp rushes. Two maids wielded large palm-leaf fans. Leelamoyi, surrounded by a gaggle of gossips, had spread her considerable bulk over a flowery silken sofa. She must have been in an expansive mood, because she tasted the desserts, pronounced them satisfactory, and handed Durga a stack of rupees without counting them. Then she looked Sabitri up and down.

"What's your daughter's name again?" she asked Durga.

"Sabitri, Rani Ma."

"Ha! Ambitious, aren't you, naming her after the mythic heroine who snatched her husband from the clutches of Death himself. Well, you'd better find her a match fast, else she won't have a husband at all."

Sabitri hid her fury and tugged at Durga's sari, trying to get her to leave, but Durga said, "Sabi doesn't want to get married, Rani Ma. She wants to go to college. Wants to become a teacher. She's smart. Stood first in the matric exams in the Girls School. But we don't have the money."

Sabitri's face burned. *Go through life with your head held high,* Durga had taught her. Why, then, would she humiliate herself—and Sabitri— by exposing to a rich, spoiled woman the tender dreams that Sabitri had entrusted to her? Dreams as impossible as sprouting wings. She would never confide in her mother again!

Sabitri thinks: If only one could erase the years—just long enough to say, *I understand.* But by the time she realized how much it had cost her mother to speak those words—Sabitri was a mother herself then, and alone—Durga was dead, beyond the reach of all apologies.

"Really?" Leelamoyi raised disbelieving eyebrows. Gold weighed down her arms. Just her bracelets would have paid for Sabitri's college twice over.

Sometimes the unfairness of the world made Sabitri feel like she might burst. She pushed her way through the entourage toward the door.

Behind her Leelamoyi spoke sharply. "Girl, did I say you could leave?"

Sabitri considered disobedience, but an angry Leelamoyi could make their lives more miserable than they already were. She couldn't do that to her family. She stopped, though she did not turn around.

"Tell you what, Durga," Leelamoyi said, her voice indolent once more, "if your impatient daughter is as smart as you claim, if she manages to get into a Kolkata college, I'll pay her fees and let her stay in our home while she studies."

The sycophants jostled around Leelamoyi, jealously exclaiming at this goddesslike generosity, so much more than Sabitri deserved. Sabitri stood frozen in disbelief until Durga pulled her forward and told her to touch the Rani Ma's feet in thanks.

The pure chill of marble against her forehead. Her thoughts whirling like a flock of startled birds. The drab dead-end wall of her future had just become a golden door. *Thank you*, she thought fervently, ashamed of her misjudgment. Leelamoyi's voice, booming from above, did sound like a goddess's. Sabitri could not decipher the words, though she heard the women titter in response.

A lifetime's worth of impatience, days slow as cattle grazing in a parched summer field. Then she was in front of the Mittirs' Kolkata home, peering through the wrought-iron gate, clutching a painted tin suitcase in a sweaty hand. She had expected grandeur. Still, she was taken aback by the hugeness of the mansion, three stories tall, the shuttered windows like heavy-lidded eyes. Under an enormous portico gleamed a motorcar. The brick walls surrounding the compound were topped with broken glass to keep out intruders. A gatekeeper, thick-mustachioed as a bandit, banged his lathi on the paved driveway and shouted in his terrifying voice for her to move along. When she said that Leelamoyi had invited her to live here, he sneered in disbelief and tried to snatch away the letter of confirmation the Mittirs' manager, Sarkar Moshai, had sent her.

How the matter would have ended she did not know, but right then a young man emerged from the house. "What's all the commotion?" he asked.

His shirt blazed in the sun, blinding her. She had never seen anything so white. Later she would ask him what kind of soap the Mittirs used. But his life had not taken him anywhere near the washing area of the house, so he did not know.

She gathered her courage, pushed past the gatekeeper, and held out the note with desperate, trembling fingers. The young man gave it a brief glance and ordered the gateman to send her in to Sarkar Moshai. "Make sure someone gives her food and water," he added. "Can't you see she's exhausted?"

Before Sabitri could thank him, he stepped into the waiting car.

Later she would say, "You didn't even read that note, did you?"

"No," he said. "But I read your eyes."

"Eyes can lie."

"Not yours," he said.

~❧~

Useless, these rambling memories. Focus on the letter, the one thing that might make a difference in the future.

> *Granddaughter, people look down on a woman without education. She has few options. To survive, she is forced to put up with ill-treatment. She must depend on the kindness of strangers, an unsure thing. I do not want that for you—*

~❧~

Even the most startling adventure, sooner or later, must become routine. So it was with Sabitri. Each morning she took the tram to the women's college, where most of her classes were held. For science and mathematics, she walked to a nearby men's college with a small group of girls. They sat in a nervous clump on a back bench because they had never had male classmates. The professors addressed only the men. Sabitri was mostly grateful to be ignored. The village school had not prepared her adequately; it was only with frantic effort that she managed to keep up.

After classes, she studied in the library with two girls who were also from distant villages, sharing textbooks since none of them had enough money to buy them all. Sabitri received a monthly stipend from Sarkar Moshai, but it was barely enough to pay her fees and her tram fare, and she was too shy to ask for more. In between homework, they spoke of their families, how much they missed them. The girls stayed in a run-down women's hostel, six to a room. Once they went with Sabitri to see where she lived and stood staring at the mansion. Struck dumb by their amazement, Sabitri couldn't tell them how unhappy she was there.

So many things run together in her head nowadays. But this she remembers: On the day of her arrival, Paro, Leelamoyi's favorite maid, had taken her to the second floor. Leelamoyi sat on a four-poster bed carved with massive lion paws, playing cards with three friends. Sunlight dazzled an oval vanity mirror that stood, tilted, on a mahogany stand. On the wall was a clock unlike anything Sabitri had seen. Even as she stared, it struck the hour, and a little wooden bird popped out with a series of squawks, startling her so that she jumped. And the windows—with their shutters thrown wide, they were as big as doors. Through the bars, she could see hosts of treetops dancing in the breeze. It was like living in a leafy ocean. If this was Sabitri's room, she would have sat on the windowsill all day, staring into the sky. But these women didn't even glance out.

Paro gave a small, apologetic cough and Leelamoyi looked up, frowning.

"Who's this?" she said.

Sabitri had prepared a careful speech about appreciation and gratitude, but when she realized Leelamoyi had forgotten her, she grew flustered. Her words ran into each other as she tried to explain her presence.

Leelamoyi raised her hand to cut her off. "Ah, yes, you're that sweet-maker's daughter. Study hard now, and stay out of trouble." She turned back to her cards, and Paro pinched Sabitri's arm, indicating that she had been dismissed.

Paro showed her where she would stay, a musty ground-floor room with a tiny, barred window set too high for Sabitri to look out. A weight pressed down on her chest—she can feel it even today. Their mud hut in the village had been rudimentary, but there was dappled light, the bright emerald of lau vines climbing up a wall. She knows now that Paro could easily have given her a better room—many lay empty in that mansion. But Paro had taken a dislike to her. Perhaps she resented her because she did no housework and yet received food and lodging. Sabitri wept that night for her mother, for the lost moon. For her own folly in believing that Leelamoyi's benevolence had been something more than a moment's caprice.

It took her some time to understand her complicated position in the household's hierarchy: neither servant nor master. She was of a higher caste than the servants, but they made the important decisions: what she would eat, where she would bathe and hang her clothes to dry. They hesitated to ill-treat her because she was the daughter of a temple priest; but it was a small temple in a faraway village, so they did not feel compelled to treat her well. Someone would put her morning meal, a thala of rice with a dollop of dal thrown over it, a grudging piece of fish dumped on the side, in the passageway outside the kitchen in the mornings. She sat on the floor by herself and ate before leaving for college. The aroma of the dishes being cooked for the Mittirs—jackfruit curry, mutton kurma, biryani—assailed her. She hungered also for the bits of conversation floating from the kitchen: a moment of laughter, a raucous fight between the cook and the bazaar-servant. Her stomach ached with the longing to be included. At night she was afraid to arrive too soon for dinner; she didn't want the servants to think she was greedy. By the time she sat down to her meal, the rutis were leathery, the vegetables dry. Dinner was when she missed her mother the most. At home they had eaten together, Durga listening with fascinated admiration to Sabitri's recital of her day.

One evening, gathering her sari from the clothesline at the far end of the backyard, she noticed a narrow winding staircase, rusted in places. She climbed it—perhaps from a desire to escape. It led to a terrace, empty except for water tanks marked with pigeon droppings, a place where no one came. She made it hers. Each night after dinner she escaped to it, careful to ensure no one saw her. She looked at the stars and imagined them shining on her family. She finger-traced words onto the twinkling vastness of the sky, the things she would have written to her mother had Durga been able to read. Sometimes she wrote things she needed to believe: *I'm lucky to be in Kolkata, getting an education. How many girls get this opportunity? Soon I'll get a great job. I'll earn enough money so my family will never be hungry again.* Sometimes she whispered into the dark the saying Durga had quoted before bidding her goodbye: *Good daughters are fortunate lamps, brightening the family's name.* There was a second part to the saying, but Durga had left that out. When she said goodbye to her daughter, her eyes had glittered like broken glass. To send Sabitri to Kolkata, she'd had to fight all their relatives, who warned her that she was sending the girl to her ruination. Remembering that gave Sabitri the strength to go down to her cheerless room for another long night of study.

~✦○

Granddaughter, this is the truth: if you are uneducated, people look down on you. To survive, you are forced to accept crumbs thrown from a rich man's table. How can such a woman ever brighten the family name?

~✦○

One morning when Sabitri came to the passageway, there was no food. She ventured through the door to find out why. The kitchen was in an uproar. Leelamoyi had ordered the cook to make rasogollas for a luncheon, and so he had. But something had gone wrong. The soft round balls that should have been floating in syrup had exploded into hundreds of pieces. There was no time to make another batch. How shamed Leelamoyi would be if the guests had to be served store-bought sweets! Cooks had been fired for less.

"I won't be going alone," the cook was shouting. "I'll make sure you all come with me." He transfixed Sabitri with a terrifying frown. "What do *you* want?"

Don't meddle, her wiser side warned. But she heard herself saying, in a small voice, that maybe she could fix the problem. The cook glared at her effrontery, but then he waved her in. Her hands shook as she boiled milk, sweetening it with jaggery syrup. She shredded the exploded balls into tiny pieces, remembering how her mother did it. She added them to the milk, along with ground cardamom and chopped pistachios. She was late for college already. But the mixture needed to be stirred, constantly, gently, so it would not stick to the bottom of the pan. She could not abandon it.

By the time she got to the college, she had missed her first three classes. Even in the others, she was distracted. Her friends joked that it was because of the new Maths professor. Their regular professor was in the hospital with a lung infection, and the university had found a substitute, a recent college graduate, a lanky young man with an Adam's apple that bobbed up and down when he got excited about what he was teaching. Sabitri didn't pay her friends—or him—much attention. Was Leelamoyi angry because her menu had been changed? Or did she like the new dessert? If she did, the cook would probably take full credit for it.

But how Sabitri had enjoyed cooking! At home she would grumble while helping Durga. This morning, though, when the milk had thickened perfectly, no ugly skin forming on top, she found herself smiling as she had not done since coming to Kolkata.

"Look at her grinning," her friends whispered. "Ei, Sabi, are you in love or what?"

Upon her return, she was summoned by Leelamoyi. She climbed the stairs with some trepidation. One never knew what pleased the rich, what affronted them. But Leelamoyi, reclined on her bed—did she ever do anything else?—chewing on betel leaves, was all smiles. The guests had loved the dessert. Even her husband and son had asked for second helpings.

"From now on when I have company," she said, with the air of conferring a great favor, "I want you to make the dessert."

Though she hated herself for it, Sabitri's heart ballooned at Leelamoyi's approval. But what about her studies? She had copied her classmates' notes today, but she had not understood them well. If this happened often, how would she pass her classes?

Leelamoyi gestured to Paro, who walked over to the mahogany almirah with a face like she'd just bitten into a bitter melon. From the bottom shelf she removed two saris and handed them to Sabitri. Sabitri held her breath, marveling at the slip-shiny feel of the silk, trying not to show her excitement. She had never owned a silk sari. And these, though not new, were far more expensive than anything her family could afford to buy her.

"Rani Ma wants you to have them," Paro said with her bitter-melon mouth.

In her room, Sabitri tried on the saris, wishing she had a mirror. The first was pomegranate-red with a border of green parrots. She would wear it to college tomorrow, even though she knew it was too showy. The second sari was more expensive, evening-sky-blue with a thin gold border. Where could she wear it? Certainly not to the kitchen, where no doubt Paro was fanning the waves of resentment by telling everyone of these undeserved gifts. But she couldn't bear to take it off. It was smooth as water against her skin, lighter than she had imagined a sari could be. She decided to go to the terrace.

Once there, she walked up and down the way she imagined a great lady would, steps tiny and elegant, the sunset breeze rustling the silk. She became a rich heiress who possessed two entire almirahs of saris like this. Her diamond nose ring sparkled as she promenaded.

But she was not alone! In a corner behind a water tank stood the young man who had helped her upon her arrival at the Mittirs', smoking and watching. Leelamoyi's son. From overheard kitchen gossip she knew his name: Rajiv. He was studying to be a doctor so that he could take over the family business, a hospital. There was a smile on his face—derision, no doubt. She rushed back to the staircase.

"Please don't run away!" said the young man, and when she didn't listen, "Stop, I insist!"

~✦~

*Granddaughter, at that, I stopped. Perhaps a part of me believed
that, charity case that I was, he had the right to command me. But a
part of me wanted to stay because he was young and handsome and
had been chivalrous. My heart beat unevenly as I turned to face him,
and not just out of fear.*

She looks down at the page. What made her write this foolishness? She crushes the sheet in her fist, as though to crush the memory. Then she smooths the paper out again. She is not equipped to advise Tara, she knows this. But perhaps, if she shares her life, the girl might see something there. For the first time, she feels hopeful.

~✦~

How long did they speak that time, and the next, and the next? And of what? Later she would only remember fragments, torn clouds drifting in front of the moon. When she told him, shyly, why she was in Kolkata, he listened with careful attention. Then he talked about himself, disarming her with his self-deprecating honesty. He hated medical school: the stink of illness, the pus and the vomit, the dark, jaundiced urine of the patients. But it wasn't something he could tell his parents, who were counting on him. The terrace was his escape, too. He loved playing the flute. Would she like him to play for her one night? But already she knew he would never do that. They could not risk anyone finding out.

Days passed. How many? It is hard to keep track of such mundanities when one is balanced inside a fairy tale. After some time, he brought up an old red quilt, so they could sit in comfort as they spoke. One moonless night, he lay down on it so he could point out the constellations to her. Here is Kalpurush with his shining, here are the seven wise rishis. She was impressed. She hadn't thought a city boy would know the names of stars. Maybe that was what made her lie down next to him on the worn malmal, though her mother's warnings buzzed in her ears like mosquitoes. She told him her dreams: she would dress in a starched sari and teach history to schoolchildren, stories of conquerors and despots. Her students would be obedient; she would never need to cane anyone. She would become a principal with tortoiseshell glasses, the entire school standing at attention when she entered the assembly hall.

He nodded. She would make a great principal, he said with conviction. He wound a finger softly around a lock of her hair, which he had persuaded her to unbraid. That was what made her fall in love, finally: his belief in her, and his gentleness.

But even as she confessed her dreams, they were changing.

That first night, their conversation, so hard to break off, had continued beyond safety. She rushed to her room to change the magical sari that had summoned her prince for an old cotton one. She was frighteningly late for her meal. But no one noticed. They were chattering about how the young master had been tardy to dinner. Leelamoyi had scolded him severely when he finally showed up. She demanded to know where he'd been. He wouldn't tell her, though. The servants guessed it was at some nightclub with his no-good friends. Didn't he look like he'd had one too many to drink? The older retainers decried today's youth, their lack of filial respect. The younger ones grumbled because now everyone would have to stay up late. Sabitri could barely swallow her food as she listened, her throat dry with guilty excitement, her heart hot and swollen with a secret power.

～•○

*Granddaughter, when you are poor and ill-educated, how
unequipped you are to read the world. All you know is your place in
it: down near the bottom. You believe you are meant for better
things, but how will you ever climb out to get them? The first
opportunity that appears, you grasp at it to pull yourself up. You
don't check to see if it can bear your weight.*

～•○

She wore her red sari to college and was roundly teased by her friends,
especially when, in Maths class, the young professor dropped his books
while setting them on the table. *You're distracting him, Sabi!* She laughed
it off, but as he was leaving, in a spirit of mischief she looked him in the
eye, with what she considered a sultry smile. He dropped his books
again. Later her friends said they thought they would die from holding
in their laughter.

It was as though she had entered a golden time. She woke early and
heavy-eyed and rushed to the kitchen to prepare desserts: mihidana and
malpua, pithay made from sweet potatoes, fried and dipped in thick
syrup. Leelamoyi's friends loved them all. Even the young master—
who had never had a sweet tooth, Leelamoyi told Sabitri—asked for
two helpings of rice pudding. He told his mother that whoever had prepared it was a treasure. Make sure you don't let her go, he said.

Sabitri wrote all this in a letter to Durga, along with elaborate de-
scriptions of the sweets, which she had adapted to Leelamoyi's citified
taste. She did not mention her missed classes, how she was falling behind in her schoolwork. On the envelope, she wrote a line asking her
father to please read the letter to her mother. Perhaps the letter was lost,
because she never received a reply.

Late at night, after the terrace (they had decided it was best to meet
post-dinner, when everyone assumed they had gone to bed), she tossed
and turned on her pallet, longing to tell her mother about Rajiv. Her

secret cramped her belly like indigestion. If there had been a chance to see Durga face-to-face, she would have done it. Durga would have been shocked. Maybe she would have slapped her. But because she loved her daughter, she would have finally come around.

On the terrace, Rajiv told her how in the operating theater he felt he was drowning in the blood, horrifyingly bright, that sometimes pulsed out over his hands. She shuddered and held him close, her lips in his hair.

"Thank God I have you to talk to," he said against her collarbone. "Otherwise I would kill myself."

This, then, was why he loved her. She was his confessional, his absolution.

Yes, she thought. She had never felt so necessary.

He took her face in his hands and looked into it as though it were the moon. When he buried his own face in her breasts, desire, dangerous as a sparking wire, traveled down her body into the pit of herself until she thought she would break apart.

"I wish this moment would last forever, Tri. That it would become my whole life."

Yes, yes.

She loved the way he shortened her name, made it unique. But a moment cannot become a whole life. She knew that. She was hungry for more.

～◦○

One of Leelamoyi's card-playing friends had become a grandmother. She would be gone to her daughter's home for a whole month. But how would they play Twenty-Nine without her? Sabitri was summoned to Leelamoyi's airy bedroom, told the rules of the game. She found them simple enough.

"Smart girl!" Leelamoyi said, smiling with her brilliant, betel-stained lips. "Can you come home right after your classes, then?"

It wasn't really a question.

Sabitri no longer had time to study in the library. She rushed home and changed into one of her good saris—she had four now, given to her for this purpose—and went to the upstairs room, where, because she was better at strategy than the other women, Leelamoyi insisted that she be her partner. In order to play, Sabitri had to sit across from Leelamoyi, on her bed. At first she was uncomfortable. The people in her village, her parents included, would have flinched at such presumption. But Leelamoyi didn't seem to mind. All she cared about was winning. Paro brought tea and crisp kachuris stuffed with spicy green peas. "Eat, eat," Leelamoyi said. She addressed Sabitri as *meye*, a word that could mean either "girl" or "daughter." Sabitri could see the rage behind the crust of politeness that was Paro's face.

> *But, Granddaughter, I found it impossible to worry. How soft the mattress was, how fine and silken the bedcover. How sweet the sandesh I had made that morning. And Leelamoyi calling me "daughter"—surely that was a sign.*

～✦○

At school she told her friends she had to help in the house. It was only a half lie, wasn't it? She felt guilty at the disappointment on their faces, for they counted on her to explain their English texts: Oliver Goldsmith, Thomas Hardy. But as soon as she stepped out of the college gates, she forgot everything: her friends, her upcoming exams, the eyes of the young Maths professor searching her out during class. It was like being bewitched.

This was what Sabitri dreamed as she rode on the tram, dozing because she didn't get enough sleep nowadays: She's in a wedding mandap, dressed in bridal red. She lifts a garland high and slips it over Rajiv's head. Under the bright Petromax lanterns, she sees her face reflected, tiny and shining and perfect, in his eyes. The auspicious sound of conches accompany them to the third floor of the Mittir home, where Rajiv has told her his room is. In the bed the years pass with swift pleasure. A baby joins them. Two. She pushes back the gold bangles on her arms to nurse them. At her waist, the cool heft of the household keys that Leelamoyi has handed over. In the kitchen the cook nods docile agreement, *Yes, Boudi-moni*, when she tells him to make jackfruit curry. Paro washes the children's soiled nappies. No. She deletes Paro from her world.

> *Perfect, a perfect dream, granddaughter. Why, then, waking with a start as the conductor jangled the bell for my stop, did I feel a constriction in my chest, a sense that I had misplaced something?*

Summer had descended upon Kolkata with epic vengeance. Sabitri came back from college bedraggled with sweat, craving a bath, cold water cascading over her body in the maids' bathroom. But a servant was waiting. Leelamoyi wanted to see her. Sabitri was surprised. There were no card games today—or had she made a mistake? Let me drink some water, she said. Change my sari. The woman scrunched up her face and shook her head. Rani Ma's waiting. Better come right now.

The first thing she saw when she entered the room was the red quilt from the terrace, crumpled on the floor like the pelt of a dead animal. The blood rushed to her head and then away; she had to hold on to the doorframe. When her vision cleared she looked around for Rajiv, who would defend her. But there was only Leelamoyi, and behind her Paro, hands on her hips, swollen with satisfaction.

From across the years, Sabitri remembers Leelamoyi's contorted mouth, spitting out invectives: *conniving slut, harlot's daughter, poisonous snake in my bosom.* Her own mouth frozen, so that when she tried to say she had done nothing wrong, the words would not obey. She learned that Rajiv had been sent away already to his uncle's home in another city. He would continue his studies there. *So don't be thinking that you can sink your witch-claws into him again.* As for Sabitri, she was to leave the house right now. No, Leelamoyi didn't care where she went, or what happened to her. *If it wasn't for the fact that your father's a priest, I would have you whipped. Now get out of my sight before I change my mind.*

Sabitri stood at the tram stop for a long while in the oppressive dusk, carrying her small painted trunk. Finally, she boarded a tram that would take her to the men's college. She could think of no other place. She opened her handbag—so light—and looked down at the frighteningly few rupee notes in there. Her trunk was light, too. Paro had followed her to her room and rummaged through it—*Let's see what you're stealing*—and taken the silk saris. She'd taken some of Sabitri's own things as well. A buffalo-horn comb that Durga had given her. A tiny bottle of rosewater Sabitri had saved up for months to buy. Sabitri had been too heartsick to protest.

The men's college loomed eerily in the gloom. She slipped through the gate, thankful that the gateman wasn't there to stop her, and ran up the stairs. On the second story, at the end of a corridor, there was a small room with a plaque on it, WOMEN'S COMMON ROOM. She had gone there once, exploring, with her friends. It was piled with dusty furniture and smelled of mice droppings. But there was a bolt on the inside, and a small toilet. She could stay there for the night. Tomorrow—ah, she couldn't handle the thought of tomorrow yet.

When she reached it, the door to the common room was padlocked.

The strength went out of her and she slid to the floor, unable to hold in her sobs any longer. Terror and rage. But foremost was the fear of what might happen to her tonight when the night watchman came by. Would he throw her out on the street? Would he do worse? Beneath it all roiled the humiliation. What would her parents, her relatives, her village, say if they knew that she had been kicked out of the Mittir home like a dog? No one would care that the love she and Rajiv had felt for each other was pure and beautiful. *Good daughters are fortunate lamps, brightening the family's name.* Could she have strayed any farther from that?

The second half of the saying, the part her mother had left unspoken, struck her like a slap:

Good daughters are fortunate lamps, brightening the family's name.
Wicked daughters are firebrands, blackening the family's fame.

She had been weeping too hard to hear the footsteps. When she felt a hand on her shoulder, she flinched and cried out, throwing up her arms to protect herself. But it wasn't the night watchman, as she had feared. It was her Maths professor.

He'd been working on his research, he said, in one of the class-rooms—something he often did, since the hostel where he stayed was very noisy. On his way out, he heard a woman weeping and came to see what the matter was. He was shocked to see her in such a state. What had happened?

She hid her face. How mortifying, that he who had always looked at her with admiration should see her like this. She made a vague ges-ture—*please go away*. But he lowered himself to the floor beside her, his lanky knees drawn up. The unexpectedness of it made her look up. His eyes were distressed. His Adam's apple bobbed up and down. Clearly, he had never been in such a situation before. She felt a hysterical laugh spiraling up and had to hide her face in her sari.

His hand—tentative, nervous—touched her shoulder. "Don't cry like that, please. Maybe I can help—"

> *Something in his voice, in those awkward, patting motions. A*
> *plan formed in my head. I held on to it like a drowning woman. I did*
> *not allow myself to think of anything, of anyone else. Tara, can you*
> *blame me? I lifted my face to him and smiled my prettiest, saddest,*
> *falsest smile.*

He took her to a cousin's house, his only family in Kolkata. "Here's a student of mine," he said, "homeless because of a rich woman's selfish whim. Please keep her until the end of the college year. I'll pay—"

"An unknown girl, Bijan?" His cousin was dubious. "Who knows why those people forced her to leave their house? Maybe she's a thief—"

"I told you—she lost an important card game where she was the rich woman's partner. The woman was furious because she had to hand over a lot of money. She threw Sabitri out into the night. If I hadn't found her, anything might have happened! I can't force you to help her, but if you don't, understand this: we will never speak again."

The inflexibility in his voice surprised me and frightened his cousin. She gave in.

He came by each evening to help with my studies, for I was dreadfully behind. When he was not around, the cousin was cold to me. Perhaps, with a woman's instinct, she saw into my crooked core. She warned him, but he would not listen. Granddaughter, he had love enough for the both of us.

Each day Sabitri checked the papers surreptitiously. One morning she saw it: "Mittirs of Shyambazar Celebrate Wedding of Their Only Son to Beautiful Coal Mine Heiress." There were photographs. The heiress was beautiful indeed. With a gritted heart Sabitri threw herself into her studies. She made herself meek and helpful in the house until she won the cousin over. Everything happened as she had planned: she passed her classes; Bijan asked her to marry him; the cousin urged her to agree. When Sabitri wept, they thought it was from grateful joy.

～❧～

The newlyweds went to the village to pay their respects. Sabitri's parents were astonished but not displeased. Her father was relieved that they had had a quiet temple wedding in Kalighat for which he did not have to pay. The relatives swung between respect for the professor son-in-law and envy at Sabitri's good luck, once again undeserved. Durga was delighted that Bijan wanted Sabitri to continue her studies.

But Tara, I didn't do that. Within a year I was expecting a child. I dropped out of college, and though Bijan encouraged me to go back

once the child was born, I no longer wanted to. Once again, I had
been seduced by a different dream.

Bijan had published his research in a journal, something very intellectual that Sabitri didn't understand. What she did understand was that several companies wanted to hire him. They were willing to pay him highly. Give him a prestigious title. Bijan would have preferred to live in their one-bedroom flat and continue teaching. Sabitri set to persuading him otherwise.

Her strategy lacked originality, but she was aided by the fact that he had never been with a woman before. Additionally, he was in love. She cooked him the dishes he most enjoyed, the comfort foods of a man who had grown up poor—rice, yellow mung dal, fried brinjal. From her own life, she knew them well. After dinner she put on a thin cotton night-chemise, which showed off her figure—she had recently taken on this Westernized habit—and laid their daughter, Bela, freshly changed and powdered, in his lap. How he loved that child! He could play toe-games with her all evening, making funny noises that set her giggling. Sabitri sat next to them, leaning her head on his shoulder. It was so peaceful that she almost forgot what she was there to do.

A sentence here, a phrase there, a small, plaintive smile, the slight press of a breast against his arm. That's all it took, because he wanted to give his wife and child the best of everything. Did he guess the game Sabitri was playing? If so, he forgave her. He joined a giant oil corporation with tentacles everywhere and found that he did not dislike it as much as he had feared. He discovered he had a special talent for solving problems. He was too honest, blunt in his answers, but the management loved him in spite of that. Or perhaps because of it. These were rare qualities in the corporate world. He was promoted, then promoted again, then sent to their headquarters in Delhi to be groomed for higher leadership.

Did I love him, Granddaughter? I'll answer by saying I was the best possible wife. Certainly I loved our life in the capital, a flat in a wealthy colony, a motorcar, respectful servants who believed that I had been born into affluence. I took classes in English conversation and comportment, and learned that I, too, had a talent. I built a reputation for hosting the best parties. I knew how to charm the most taciturn guest into chatting. I never skimped on the alcohol, even if it meant we had to eat rice and lentils for the rest of the month. I created desserts that became the talk of the town. I wonder if Bijan realized that many of his tough deals fell into place because of my dinners.

After seven years of service, Bijan was sent back to Kolkata with yet another promotion. Sabitri was both delighted and uneasy. The sooty, sprawling city of her first humiliation and heartbreak had a hold on her like no other place. The smallest triumph here meant more than the hugest victories elsewhere. They lived on the top floor of a tall building, and sometimes it seemed to her, as she stood on the balcony and looked down on the treetops, that the city had spread itself at her feet. But the past still rankled. Sometimes, after dropping Bela at school, she would ask the driver to take her past the men's college. The memory of that night when she wept outside the Women's Common Room was like a half-formed scab she could not stop picking at.

When on a visit to the village I learned from my mother that Leelamoyi was now a widow and in ill health, alone in the old mansion because her rich daughter-in-law refused to live with her, I formed a plan.
I lie, Tara. The plan had been in me for a long time, like a dormant virus, waiting.

When Sabitri told Bijan that she wanted to visit Leelamoyi, he approved. "I'm glad you've decided to forgive her. After all, if she hadn't forced you to leave her house, we wouldn't be married!"

She nodded. There was no point in telling this straightforward man that she was impelled by a darker motive. She sent a note, accompanied by an expensive basket of fruits, and received a reply in Sarkar Moshai's spidery handwriting. Leelamoyi would like to see her.

That morning, Granddaughter, I dressed with care. I wore a silk sari with a thick gold border and my best jewelry. I made your mother wear a lace dress and shiny new shoes even though she complained that they hurt her feet. (But it was only a mild complaint because she was a biddable girl. Who would have guessed that she'd give me so much grief in later years?) This I did because I knew that Leelamoyi had no grandchildren.

As the car approached the Mittir house, Sabitri found that her hands were shaking. She hid them in the folds of her sari. The house looked shrunken; paint was peeling in parts; here and there, broken shutters hung dangling. There was no darwan on duty, so the driver had to get down and push open the rusting gates. She stepped out, holding tight to her daughter's hand and carrying a platter of Leelamoyi's favorite sweets.

The driver was reversing the car, going back to the office. He needed to take Bijan from one meeting to another. "Come back as soon as you drop Bijan Babu," she instructed him. "I don't want to stay long."

She rang the bell, but no one came. When she pushed at the door, it opened with a creak. Ahead of her was the stairway. How many times had she climbed it, wearing those saris that were hers and yet not hers, her heart beating light and rapid because she believed she was moving closer to her dream. The memory of that foolish young self overwhelmed her with tenderness and shame.

There was dirt on the staircase, crumbled stucco. She held up the edge of her sari and warned Bela not to touch the banister. Familiar, familiar, the second floor, that long corridor filled with anticipation, the airy windows through which bright trees peeped, that milk-white ocean of a bed.

Today the windows were shut. Through the haphazard light that seeped in between shutters, she saw a form on the bed, widow's white melting into the sheets, so still that for a disappointed lurch of the heart she believed that death had robbed her of revenge.

But no, the form struggled to sit up. She patted the bed for Sabitri to join her, called to a maid to fetch snacks for the visitors. Leelamoyi may have dwindled, but her voice was still autocratic.

"So this is your daughter?" She frowned at Bela, who was playing quietly, as was her habit, with her dolls. She did not compliment the child, though Bela was beautiful, even more so this day, with bright ribbons in her wavy hair. But Sabitri would not allow herself to be upset. She adjusted her sari, making sure her gold bangles tinkled, and said brightly, familiarly, "But Auntie, you must have many grandchildren by now!"

Leelamoyi's face grew dark as iron. She launched into a tirade about her daughter-in-law. What a mistake they had made in choosing that spoiled, useless rich girl. Couldn't produce an heir. Refused to live with the Mittirs even though they remodeled the entire third floor for her, Western-style toilets and all. Turned Rajiv against his parents so that he moved out within six months of marriage—abandoning the home of his forefathers, can you believe that?—to live in a fancy new house in Gariahat that his wife's father bought her. That's what caused Mittir Moshai's heart attack, Leelamoyi was sure of it.

The maid did not arrive. Leelamoyi shouted invectives, wandered into other spaces. "That girl, a witch, a murderer, can you believe, she took all the wedding jewelry when she left, my own jewelry that I had gifted her! When I tried to stop her, she said, hire a lawyer if you want it back. And Rajiv—he didn't even have the guts to stand up to her and support me."

Rajiv had made a mess of the hospital, too, Leelamoyi went on to say. Oh, life had given her more than her share of trials. But at least he stopped by to see her once in a while. Where was that idiot maid, that

Khyama, who should be bringing snacks? No, she said with a scowl, Paro was no longer with her. She offered no details.

Sabitri smiled the kind, charming smile she had practiced. She assured Leelamoyi that they did not need a snack. They had had an ample breakfast. She directed Leelamoyi's attention to the platter. *Look, Auntie, your favorite sweets.* The older woman scrabbled for a sandesh, then another one. She smiled slyly and confessed that she had high blood sugar; the doctor had decreed that she must not indulge. But what other pleasure was left in an old woman's life?

"Durga," she said with a sigh, "you always did make the best sweets. You should have opened a shop of your own."

A dizziness assailed Sabitri at being called by her mother's name. Her smile fell away. Once again, Leelamoyi had forgotten who she was. How could you avenge yourself against such oblivion?

"I have to leave now," Sabitri said. She had intended to mention that her car would be waiting downstairs, but she no longer had the energy.

"Stay a little longer," Leelamoyi implored. When Sabitri apologized, she gave an angry laugh. "Yes, yes, I know. No one likes being around sick people. Even my own son is always in a hurry to leave. . . . At least help me sit up straighter before you go."

Sabitri felt a great reluctance to touch her, but out of old habit she found herself obeying. She placed her hands gingerly under Leelamoyi's armpits and pulled. It was like lifting a sack. Traces of sweat were left on her fingers. A smell of staleness, like rotten eggs. It was all she could do not to rush out to find a tap and wash it off.

"Turn on the radio," Leelamoyi ordered. A program of devotional songs came on. "Who would have thought I'd turn religious! Age does strange things to us. Ah, you'll come to it, too, soon enough. Bring the girl near me. I want to see her hair." She put out a greedy hand.

Downstairs, sitting on a bench in the dark passageway, I couldn't stop trembling. The car wasn't back yet—I knew it wouldn't be. But Granddaughter, I couldn't have stood that room, its bitter odors of disease and rage, for another second. It had been a mistake, coming here to gloat. I had wanted Leelamoyi to regret that she didn't let Rajiv marry me, to see that I would have made a far better daughter-in-law than the one she chose. But now I felt only shame. Shame, and disgust at myself for using my daughter in this game. I promised myself I would never set foot in this house again.

One good thing had come out of all this. I'd exorcised a demon. I would no longer lie awake at night, remembering Leelamoyi's twisted face as she called me a whore. I would no longer hold conversations in my head, all the things I'd been too young and afraid to say at that time. I am a good person. I did nothing wrong. He loves me. I love him. I will make him happy because I am the only one to whom he can say what's in his heart.

There was another thing, Tara. As Leelamoyi spoke of Rajiv, I began to see him differently. All these years I'd been blinded by the longing we feel for what is snatched from us. Now I realized that he had been weak and pampered, too weak to stand up for me. He must have known that his mother had thrown me out of the house. But he hadn't even inquired after me. Even if he was in a different city, it would have been easy enough to ask a friend to go to the college and find out what had happened.

~·◇

A fumbling at the door. The driver had arrived, thank God. Sabitri started gathering Bela's dolls.

But it was not the driver. It was Rajiv—as though she had conjured him up with her thinking. She recognized him at once, though he was heavier now. He wore expensive clothes, more expensive even than the fine white shirts of old, which Sabitri had sometimes unbuttoned so she could lay her head upon his chest. Once, to celebrate a promotion, she had taken Bijan to New Market to buy him a shirt like that, but he had shaken his head with a laugh. *Something that expensive would burn my skin.* He had walked out, not caring that the salesmen stared at him.

Sabitri pulled the edge of her sari over her head. She would leave now. Leave and wait on the road. That was best. But as she passed Rajiv, she glanced up. She couldn't help it. Ah, that face, those once-loved lips. How the useless past tugged at you, unsteadying the breath. Was that discontent in his heavy jowls? In the droop of his mouth, a sorrow? Surely it was disillusionment she saw in the circles under his eyes.

Nonsense. She was imagining things to suit her fancy.

"Tri!" Rajiv exclaimed, peering at her. His face, filled with incredulous hope, was young again for a moment before the years came rushing mercilessly back. "God, God, is it really you? No, don't go, please, give me just a minute." But he need not have begged. The special name he had coined for her had struck her at the core, rendering her immobile. "I can't tell you how often I've thought of you. How I've imagined—hoped—that I'd see you again—" He stammered to a stop. Were those tears on his lashes? He still had those ridiculously long lashes, like a girl's. "You must have been—must still be—furious with me—" He grasped her wrists with a suddenness that sent a wave of remembered fire up her body. He was kissing her hands, his lips on the pulse at one wrist, then the other. How long it had been. "I can see you're happily married—with a lovely child." There was hunger in his voice. "I don't want to cause trouble. Just give me another minute of your time—a chance to apologize. To explain what they did to me. Please—"

"Don't," Sabitri said. "My driver will be here any minute." But her voice shook, and she did not pull her hands away.

His words surrounded her like a dust storm. She could see Bela staring at him, openmouthed. Once in a while, she picked bits out of the roaring: *Crazy with worry locked up at my uncle's not even a phone ran away but they caught me taken straight to the wedding hated her for it hated them all—*

In the early months of her marriage, if Rajiv had come to her, she would have walked out with him. Even if he had not told her all this. She would have lived as his mistress, not caring if she blackened her family's name beyond all salvaging.

Granddaughter, here is my most terrible secret: even after I gave birth to Bela, I would have done it.

She shook her hands from his grip. It was easier than she'd expected. He was a weak man, after all. She wished to say, *You could have found me, if you had really wanted to.* But it no longer mattered. Better to say, *I love my husband.* Because that—she was surprised to discover it—was the truth. How long had it been true?

Finally she walked away in silence, Rajiv no longer worth wasting words on. Her chest was full of the new truth's brightness. Emerging into the hot yellow sunshine was like being born. Under her fingertips her daughter's shoulder bones were fragile, magical wings.

There was the car, waiting, with someone in the back seat. Bijan. Her heart flung itself around her body. How long had he been there? What had he seen?

But Bijan was exuberant with success. The morning's meeting had gone excellently. He had negotiated a better deal than anyone had hoped. A significant bonus would be forthcoming. He had decided to celebrate by taking the rest of the day off. How would they like a trip to the Grand Hotel for ice cream, and then the zoo? He sat in the middle of the car like a king, his arms around them, beaming beneficently at his beautiful girls. Bela was telling Bijan about the dirty staircase and strange old lady who kept touching her hair and how hungry she was because the lady didn't give them anything to eat, didn't share even one of Mamoni's delicious sweets. She might just starve to death before they reached the Grand. Sabitri rested her head on Bijan's shoulder, weak with relief, and smiled at Bela's theatrics. The child had widened her eyes and slumped on the seat, saying that she had to have three scoops of ice cream. Could she?

Could she, please? How blessed Sabitri was to have this family. From this moment on, she was going to be the best wife and mother to them.

"Yes, you can have three scoops," she said. "Just don't throw up afterwards."

It was the happiest moment of her life.

She wants to write all this to Tara, but she is so tired. Her fingers are cramping. They've been cramping for a while, she realizes, even the fingers of her left hand. It's almost dawn, the jackals long vanished, a couple of overeager roosters beginning to crow. She must lay her head on the table; it's grown too heavy to hold up. She places her cheek against the gouge and remembers, suddenly, its genesis. Bela had slashed the wood with her favorite Parker fountain pen, which Sabitri had saved for months to gift her with when she entered college, ruining both pen and table. This, because Sabitri had insisted that Bela stop seeing the man she was in love with, a man who would later entice her into running away to America. Who would not let her see her mother again. A man who—Sabitri had known this in every vibrating nerve of her body—was utterly wrong for her.

"Your father, Tara," she whispers. "That was him. And now he's abandoned you both, hasn't he? Is that why you're dropping out of college? Why you won't talk to him?"

Oh, this mess, it's beyond her powers to fix. She longs to close her eyes; she's finding it hard to focus. Who is that in a dark corner? Is it her granddaughter? And behind her, could that be Bela? Shadows with blank ovals for faces, waiting for her wisdom—as if she had any to give! Or was it her dead baby, the boy she had named Harsha, bringer of joy, hoping he would buy her a second chance? But no. He had left her long ago.

Sleep. She hungers for it with her entire being.

But first she must write something, because finally she knows what she needs to say. She forces her hand forward, grasps the pen.

But that moment in the car wasn't the happiest moment of my
life. Just like it hadn't been so on the starlit terrace with Rajiv. My

happiest moment would come much later. After Bijan's drinking problem, my widowhood. After baby Harsha flew away. After all my troubles with your mother. I had opened Durga Sweets by then. How Leelamoyi would have writhed in rage if she knew that she'd been the one to plant the idea in some secret chamber of my being! It had been tough going, the first few years. But with the help of Bipin Bihari— ah, what a support he had been—I'd finally managed to turn the store into a profitable concern.

One day, in the kitchen at the back of the store, I held in my hand a new recipe I had perfected, the sweet I would go on to name after my dead mother. I took a bite of the conch-shaped dessert, the palest, most elegant mango color. The smooth, creamy flavor of fruit and milk, sugar and saffron mingled and melted on my tongue. Satisfaction overwhelmed me. This was something I had achieved by myself, without having to depend on anyone. No one could take it away. That's what I want for you, my Tara, my Bela. That's what it really means to be a fortunate lamp. . . .

In the car, Bijan asked Sabitri, "Do you feel better, now that you've seen Leelamoyi?" She could feel his breath, warm on her hair. "Will it help you forget?"

The solicitousness in his voice brought her close to tears. She nodded, unable to speak.

Bela said, "There was a man, downstairs. He kept crying and kissing Mamoni's hands. Mamoni, why was he kissing your hands?"

Bijan pulled away his arm and sat up straight. In the dead silence that took over the car, Sabitri was aware of the driver's curious eyes in the rearview mirror.

"Just someone I knew long ago," she said, speaking to Bijan. "He doesn't even live in this house anymore. I hadn't expected to see him. We met by the merest chance as I was leaving. He means nothing to me." The words tumbled out of her too fast. She knew she sounded guilty, even though it was the truth she was telling.

"I understand," Bijan said. He looked coldly at her sari, her jewelry. "I understand perfectly."

"I love you, only you," she cried, though she knew it was a major faux pas to speak in this manner in front of servants.

Bijan leaned forward. "Drive me back to the office."

"Aren't we going to the zoo?" Bela asked.

"You can go wherever the hell you want," Bijan said to Sabitri. In the mirror the driver's eyes widened because Bijan-saab never spoke like this. Sabitri guessed it would not be long before the rest of the servants heard about it.

They rode in silence. Near the Maidan they passed a herd of goats crossing the street; heat rose from their coats in shimmery waves. Sabitri had never seen such a sight in the city. For a moment, with a thin spike of hope, she thought she had dreamed it all.

When they had dropped Bijan off, Bijan now transformed into someone she did not know, Sabitri told the driver to take them home. She had difficulty meeting his eyes, but she forced herself.

"I want to go to the zoo!" Bela cried. "I want my ice cream. Why can't we go to the zoo? Baba said we could. Why can't we go?" She kicked the seat-back again and again. The noise thudded inside Sabitri's head.

"It's because of you we aren't going!" she shouted. "Stupid girl—you've ruined everything." The Bengali word for "ruin," noshto, which could also mean "rotten," or, when applied to women, "unfaithful," hung in front of her, as visible as her future. Her hand arced through the air, there was a sound like something bursting, and Bela cried out in pain.

The first time you hit your child with all your strength, wanting to hurt, it changes things.

She feels that sting again now. It travels up her arm and lodges in her shoulder. The shock with which Bela had stared at Sabitri. The splotch blooming red on her cheek. The way she shrank back against the car door. Was that when the troubles between them began?

"I'm sorry, Bela," she says. "Forgive me." Words that all these years she hadn't been able to speak.

❧

The pain has taken up permanent residence in her chest. She must have dropped something with a crash, because here comes Rekha, rubbing at her eyes, then running forward with a cry. Sabitri tries to push the letter toward her. But she's on the floor. When did she fall? Rekha shouts for the milkman, who's rattling the door, to help her get Ma onto the bed.

Sabitri tries to tell her about the letter. It is the only thing that matters now. It must be put in the mail. It must. "Tell Bipin Bihari," she whispers. She thinks of his dear face, calm and steady and attentive, even in the worst of her times. "He'll know what to do."

But Rekha does not hear. She is sobbing on the phone, urging Doctor Babu to get here fast. Something terrible has happened to Ma. The milkman lifts Sabitri up. Or is she flying? The bed is very soft. The pain is very large. She lifts her eyes, and there is Death in the corner, but not like a king with his iron crown, as the epics claimed. Why, it is a giant brush loaded with white paint. It descends upon her with gentle suddenness, obliterating the shape of the world.

The Assam Incident: 1963

$\mathcal{B}$ela stands on the veranda, sweating as she watches Sabitri and Bijan—that's how she's been thinking of them lately, rather than as her parents—drive off in a cloud of orange dust into the Assam evening. It smells like thunder, but the sky is mild and pale. Nothing in this place is what she expects it to be. Why doesn't the heat seem to bother Sabitri and Bijan? she wonders angrily. In the back seat of the ancient Ambassador the National Oil Company has provided for their use, along with an equally ancient uniformed chauffeur, they lean in to each other. Their faces come together like colliding planets, and they kiss.

Bela should be happy at this effort at intimacy. It is certainly better than the fights they had before they came here, Sabitri dissolving into tears, Bijan stalking out of the flat. Still, Bela can't help feeling embarrassed—and a little worried. It's as though, in this outpost surrounded by jungles and oil fields and (according to Ayah) all manner of bloodthirsty creatures, Sabitri and Bijan have decided that the rules they used to live by in civilization (Kolkata, to be exact) no longer matter. Bela guesses that Assam, too, has its rules, but no one has taken the trouble to tell her what they are.

Just before the car disappears around the bend of the bamboo forest, Sabitri turns and raises her hand. Is she waving at Bela? Or is she ordering her to go into the house? Ayah, who stands beside Bela, carrying the baby, tugs at her arm.

"Come inside, Bela Missybaba. Mosquitoes will be biting soon, big-big like elephants."

Bela shakes her head. She can feel the prickly seeds of tears behind her eyes. They've been in Assam for three months, and still, each time her parents go somewhere, she's certain that she'll never see them again. There is no one to whom she can confess this new timidity, dizzying like the tropical fever she succumbed to during her first week here.

Bela knows that, at eleven, she's too old for this ridiculous behavior. They're only going to the club. It's part of Bijan's responsibility to attend official gatherings. They have explained this to her. Being the new manager of National Oil (Assam Branch), he needs to meet people, make the right impression, get the local big shots on his side. She knows also (though no one explained this part) that Sabitri must go along to ensure that he sticks to his tonic water so that incidents like the ones that got him transferred from Kolkata don't happen again. They are responsible parents. When they return, they will come into the children's room, no matter how late it is. Sabitri will touch their foreheads (always the baby's first) to gauge if anyone has fever. Sometimes this wakes Bela up and she cannot fall asleep again, but she minds only a little. It is a price worth paying for the feel of Sabitri's cool fingers trailing over her jawbone, so rare nowadays. For her warm, minty breath on Bela's cheek.

"Come, come, Bela Missy, getting late, darkness coming. And after sun is disappeared, worse things coming than mosquitoes."

Worse things feature prominently in Ayah's stories. To keep them at bay, when she first started working for them, she put a little dot of soot on the baby's cheek. "Bloody superstition," Bijan said when he saw it. He wiped the mark from the baby's face roughly with his handkerchief, making him cry. In the corridor, Bela saw Ayah's face, hard and sullen. The next day, she put another soot dot on the boy, but on his back so no one except the spirits would see it. She looked at Bela, eyes squinted, daring her to tell. But Bela did not. Not yet, anyway.

"You go," Bela says now. She pushes rudely at Ayah, surprising herself, because generally she is fond of the Assamese maid.

A haughty stillness takes over Ayah's entire body. She hitches the baby higher on her hip, turns on her heel, and disappears into the house without a word. Bela feels ashamed, but not enough to follow her.

That is when she hears the man.

"Namaste, Miss Bela," he says from the side of the veranda where thick hydrangea bushes give way to wild honeysuckle, where snakes may be hiding.

Bela spins around and there he is, a little blurred by her tears: tall, thin, dark as a burnt chapati. His cheekbones are craggy and crooked, as though they might have been broken and then put back together. The band tied pirate-style around his forehead shimmers in the last of the sun. His cloak—or maybe it is a large shawl—shimmers as well, and when he smiles, there's gold in his teeth.

Her breath is a solid thing, stuck like a bone in her throat. "How do you know my name?" she manages to say.

"I know." His eyes crinkle in amusement. "Your father is Bijan Das Babu, and the company has brought him here to help them put in better pipes to take our oil away."

He bends forward slightly and Bela can see, for a moment, the oil rushing through steel tunnels, swirling black flecked with gold, rushing with a great roar that dies away, and then the tunnels are empty and then they, too, are gone.

The man steps out from behind the bushes and begins to walk toward Bela. The fear she had forgotten rises in her again, because only yesterday Ayah had warned her about the children-snatchers. "Always looking-looking," Ayah said, "most of all for girl-children to sell. Fair-skinned like you, lot of money. Better watch out."

Bela gathers her breath to push a scream out from the clogged tunnel of her throat, but the man shakes his head in such a knowing, indulgent way that she feels foolish. Besides, he isn't carrying a giant-sized sack to put children in, as snatchers are supposed to. His hands, which he holds out in front, are empty and elegant and curiously smooth. Even his palms are unlined. As she watches, his fingers do an intricate dance like the leaves in the breezy pipal tree above, weaving a pattern of light and shadow.

"Who are you?" Bela asks.

The man bows, his long hair swinging around his glistening chocolate face, and Bela knows what he is going to say before he speaks. Then he reaches out and pulls something from under her chin. She gasps and he puts the coin on her palm, the silver dull and cold as though it hasn't been touched by human hands in a long time. She sees the profile of Queen Victoria staring haughtily into the horizon, like in her history book. "How—?" she begins, but Cook is at the door, swatting at mosquitoes with his dish towel, yelling for her to come to dinner right now, food's getting cold, and why is she standing outside at this time of evening, does she want to catch a fever again?

By the time she turns back to the magician, her palm is empty and he is gone.

～✺～

"Do you believe in magicians?" Bela asks Bijan on the way to school. Immediately she regrets the question. She treasures this time, her only chance to be alone with her father. It is so peaceful in the back of the Ambassador, so silent. Also, he might respond with his own question: *Have you made any friends at school?* And then what would she say?

The morning breeze, still cool, sifts through Bijan's hair so that for a moment he looks glamorous, one of those fathers who appear in advertisements for Cinthol soap, or Horlicks steaming in oversized glasses. Bela scoots closer until she can lay her head against the sleeve of his starched blue shirt. He smells of English Leather, wholesome and clean and reassuring, and as she breathes in the scent, she can almost believe that this is how he has always smelled.

Bijan smiles. "You mean the kind that draws rabbits out of hats? Like the one that came to Leena's birthday last year? There's nothing to believe. It's all tricks, sleight of hand. But it was fun to watch, wasn't it?"

Leena used to be Bela's best friend in Kolkata; they had known each other since class one. After Bela left for Assam, Leena had written twice to her. Bela tried to write back, but she was struck by a strange paralysis. How to describe the riot around her: the night-blooming flowers with their intoxicating odor, the safeda tree with its hairy brown fruit, the oleanders with their poisonous red hearts? She wanted to tell Leena how much she missed her. At times her heart felt like one of the towels Ayah wrung out before she hung it up to dry. She wanted Leena to be here, to run hand in hand with her across a lawn so large it was like a green ocean. But what was the point of wanting the impossible? She never answered the letters.

Some days now, Bela can barely recall what Leena was like. Did she have one braid, or two? What was her favorite game? Her favorite movie? Did she like ice cream better, or sandesh? She doesn't reveal this slippage to Bijan. She senses that it would distress him almost as much as it distresses her. But she knows this much: Leena's magician (whom she cannot remember at all) could not have been anything like hers.

～✦～

Bela has decided that she hates school. She has kept this fact carefully to herself, because she doesn't want to add to her parents' troubles. It has been a difficult move for them all. They had to give up their charming high-rise flat near Deshapriya Park, with a courtyard filled with tamarind trees in whose shade Bela played hopscotch with her friends after school; Sabitri's elegant dinners, where Bela was allowed to stay up and watch guests whispering in their glittery saris and imported suits; Bijan's air-conditioned office on the top floor of the company headquarters, from which Bela could see the Victoria Memorial, tiny as a toy palace.

But inside loss there can be gain, too, like the small silver spider Bela had discovered one dewy morning, curled asleep at the center of a rose. Their evenings, on the nights when Sabitri and Bijan stay home, are wondrously uneventful. Bijan leafs through the local newspaper, reading aloud tidbits that amuse or exasperate him. Sabitri labors over a gray sweater that Bela cannot imagine it will ever get cold enough here to wear. Deposited on a quilt on the floor, the baby contemplates his plump, kicking legs. All of a sudden he turns over and looks astonished. At such times, Bela feels for him a piercing love, though she continues with her homework, saying nothing. Once in a while—but less each day—she finds herself holding her breath. She is waiting for the old noises: the crash of items hitting the floor, glasses or furniture or bodies; the sour smell of vomit next morning in the upholstery. And that lightning glance from her mother's eyes, as though somehow it was Bela's fault.

How, into this precarious peace, can she inject her petty problems? She is friendless among the local schoolgirls, children of oil-field employees who look upon her with nervous suspicion as the daughter of the man who controls their fathers' destinies. Heads bent together, they whisper in Assamese when she approaches. If she happens to answer a question in class (but nowadays she has stopped doing this), they snicker at what they term her fancy city accent. Even the teachers, with their heavy Assamese-tinged English, narrow their eyes at her. Her handwriting, hampered by the fountain pen they insist she use instead of the smooth ballpoints she is used to, has been judged woefully inadequate. And tomorrow she will have to recite Tennyson's "The Lady of Shalott," in its entirety in elocution class for Miss Dhekial, who is known to rap knuckles with her ruler. Bela's knuckles ache already in anticipation, for though she has been practicing the poem all week, under the critical gaze of the class she continues to blank out, sometimes as early as stanza two.

Bela is sitting in the Sunday garden under the mango tree, thinking all this instead of doing her homework, when the magician suddenly appears. Startled, she drops her fountain pen, which makes a spidery black splotch in the middle of her arithmetic assignment. Then it rolls down her lap onto the lawn, leaving a dark, accusing trail on her uniform.

"So sorry," the magician says, bending his long, elegant back. "Please allow me." He removes his hands from the folds of his shawl and a glowing falls from them onto the notebook, on the smudge, which disappears. Lightly, lightly, he runs his fingertips over the stains on Bela's uniform, and that, too, is clean again. Then he seats himself, cross-legged, at her feet. Bela looks around wildly for someone who can confirm that this is really happening, but they are alone in the garden. Under her uniform, her knee tingles where the magician had placed his fingers.

The magician's eyes flit from side to side as though he were reading something very rapidly. Their whites are a pale yellow, the color of drowned sand at the bottom of a river.

"It's called learning by heart, you know," he says. "You can remember anything if you use your heart." He taps his chest as he says this. Something seems to shift in her chest—her own heart, perhaps, sluggish, muscle-bound, finally coming to life. She feels the same tingle there as she did on her leg.

"Anything?" she whispers, thinking of entire worlds lost within her.

"I can help," he says. He opens his fist and shows her a small globule the size of a pea, the color of his tamarind face.

This is exactly the kind of thing that Sabitri and Bijan have warned her of. She begins to shake her head. Then the magician says, "It will teach you not to care what people think about you."

The tingling starts on her tongue but then travels all over: fingers, face, the curved backs of her calves. Her throat is a tunnel lined with red silk. Words pour out from it. "Good girl," says the magician. He is small now and hazy; his face shimmers like dragonfly wings on a lake. She tries to tell him this, but she can't get through that waterfall of words. Sorrow rakes her as she watches him become tiny, then tinier, until he spins away like a spore on the wind.

The tingly sensation is leaving her now. She feels drained and disoriented and a little sick, like the time when she rode too long on the Ferris wheel at the Kolkata Maidan with Leena. Leena had thrown up afterward. Bela remembers how red her nose had been, and her eyes, embarrassed behind her glasses. She remembers how she had rubbed Leena's back and said it was okay. She remembers!

"That's wonderful, baby."

Bela whirls to find Sabitri standing behind her chair, wearing a flowery salwar kameez that makes her look too pretty. She's suddenly angry, because Sabitri seems untouched by this move which has torn Bela into pieces and then reassembled her haphazardly, and Sabitri doesn't even realize it. She's angry, too, because Sabitri has had something to do with her father's drinking, though if anyone asked Bela what, she wouldn't be able to explain. A memory stirs inside her, something that happened in a car and changed everything, something terrifying that ended with a slap that flung Bela against the car door—that's all Bela can recall. Perhaps if her magician comes back, he will help her salvage more.

Thinking of him makes her angry all over again because Sabitri might have seen him. Bela's magician. Bela's secret.

"How long have you been standing here?" she asks with a hard scowl.

Sabitri's mouth falls open like a scolded child's. "Only a few minutes," she says, apologetic. "I came to ask if you want fresh sugarcane. Ayah brought some from her village. I remembered how much you liked it last time. I didn't want to disturb you, though. It sounded so lovely."

"What did?"

Through the pounding of her newborn heart she hears Sabitri say, "The poem you were reciting. Is it something for one of your classes? *There she weaves by night and day / A magic web with colors gay. / She has heard a whisper say, / A curse is on her if she stray.*"

"It's *stay*, not *stray*," she whispers, but Sabitri continues, oblivious.

"I loved the way your voice rose and fell in all the right places. Better than anything I've heard you recite before. And the emotion—almost made me cry. It was as though someone had trained you—"

Chewing on the hard sweet sticks of sugarcane that leave fibers between her teeth, Bela asks Sabitri, "Do you believe in magicians?"

"Like in *Sleeping Beauty*?" Sabitri says as she spoons mashed banana into the baby's mouth. "But no, that was a wicked fairy—and a good one, wasn't it, that kept the princess safe? I want to believe. It would be lovely if a good fairy was watching over us here. We could do with some extra protection." She looks into the distance, where a tiny train puffs soundlessly across the rice fields. She watches it for such a long time that Bela thinks that she has been forgotten.

Then Sabitri swivels toward Bela with a mother-glint in her eyes. "Why do you ask?"

Bela wishes she could press her head into her mother's chest, the way she did when she was little, and tell her everything. But she no longer trusts her mother that way anymore. Besides, if she talks about him, the magician will never return. She is certain of this. It's a calamity she can't bear on top of all her other losses.

"Just a book I read," she says, nonchalant. As Sabitri busies herself with the baby again, Bela presses her tongue against the ridges of her palate, trying to find the exact spot where the globe melted into her, trying to recapture the taste.

"I did well in school today," Bela tells Ayah, who carries into her room a tray with her afternoon snack of milk and biscuits. "In elocution, I recited my poem without a single mistake. Miss Dhekial was surprised."

"Why surprised? You smart missy."

"Not here in Assam. Here I feel stupid. I was terrified that I'd forget my lines and everyone would laugh. But it was perfect—like magic." She isn't sure Ayah, who has never attended school, can gauge the height of her achievement, but the woman nods solemnly.

"Like magic," she says.

"Do you believe in magicians?" Bela asks, her breath quickening.

Ayah looks at Bela speculatively. Then she settles herself on Bela's bed, on the peacock-colored bedspread, though as a servant she's only supposed to sit on the floor. She picks up one of Bela's biscuits and bites into it. Bela knows she should chastise her, but she doesn't.

"In my village," Ayah says in a hushed tone as she munches, "is big magician. Very strong. Very danger." She proceeds to describe to Bela how he once battled an evil lake-spirit by burning mustard seeds and chanting a powerful spell until the spirit was forced to flee, bleeding from its eyes and mouth and anus. Now it wanders around looking for unwary individuals that it can drag to a watery death. Bela listens in horrified fascination even though she knows she will wake at night with the worst nightmare.

≈•◦

Bela is on the old swing at the far edge of the lawn, urging it higher than the branch it hangs from—something she has been expressly instructed not to do. She has been out here under the hot sun for a while. That, too, she has been told not to do, but no one at home seems to have noticed. She is waiting for her magician, but with each moment her hopes wilt further. When he does appear, perched on a nearby branch, she is so startled that she forgets to push into the arc of the swing, which plummets downward. The rope makes a terrible snapping sound. She feels herself sliding off the seat. But the magician catches her before she hits the ground. Then he cocks his head, birdlike, and looks at her sadly.

"I have come to say goodbye."

"No!" Bela cries. "Don't go." There is so much she wants to tell. The admiration on the faces of her classmates in elocution, and how in the afternoon they let her join their games. The bitter sweetness of remembering Leena. The nightmare that terrified her and the way she handled it. The gauzy, stippled dragonflies she keeps seeing everywhere, which remind her of him. There's so much she wants to ask him, too. What happened in the car. What happened to her father afterward.

"You can come with me," the magician says, spreading his arms like wings. His robe falls open and his body gleams like polished metal. Something dark and tidal rises inside Bela. But then she remembers Sabitri and Bijan, their faces bending to kiss her good night. She begins to back up toward the house, its solid, square predictability. The magician makes no move to stop her.

"Is that what you really want?" he asks in his kind, reasonable voice. "They have the baby. They will not miss you much. They might even be happier with you gone. After all, you ruined everything for them."

His voice echoes in her head, and her eyes fill with blinding spots as though she has gazed too long at something bright and burning. "No," she whispers, but she is not sure which part of his statement she is refuting. When his fingers part her lips, she holds her mouth open for the globules he is placing on her tongue. One, two, three . . . A tingling opens up the top of her skull.

The magician shakes out his headband and brings it to her face. "It is forbidden to see the way," he tells her. Obediently she begins to close her eyes. Then she remembers. Last night, when she woke from the nightmare with her heart smashing against her ribs, she went to the baby's crib and lifted him out, grabbing him awkwardly around the middle like a package. He didn't even awaken. She brought him to her bed and lay down and held him. His head fit perfectly under her chin. Harsha, she whispered, saying his name for the first time. Harsha. She fell asleep listening to his breath—he snored a little, he had a cold—and the dream did not return.

"No," she cries, but already the ground is tilting up to meet her.

The room is full of papery whispers, and there are more floating around outside the door. Snippets of moments flash by Bela. She was in an ambulance, strapped onto a stretcher, escorted by sirens. They carried her to this room, this bed. Fingers examined her, pulling back the lids of her closed eyes. Heatstroke, someone said. Dehydration. IV. Someone else pushed a needle into the hollow of her elbow, not caring that it hurt.

"I think she's waking up!" Bela hears Sabitri exclaim. Her mother's face looms large over the bed, alarming as an out-of-orbit moon, fading in and out of focus. In a hushed, sickroom voice, she adds, "Bela, sweetie? Can you see me? Do you know who I am?"

Beyond Sabitri, servants crowd the room, muttering among themselves. At the foot of the bed, a white-coated man stands, garlanded by a stethoscope. It takes Bela a few moments to recognize him as the company doctor who treated her when she had the fever. Beyond him, by the hospital window, stands her father, tieless and crumpled, gesturing at a man in a police uniform.

"Talk to me, baby!" Sabitri's voice cracks. "Can you talk?"

Bela wants to reassure her, but her head hurts. It's too much of an effort to speak, and even to keep her eyes open. The light from the window burns them. On the other side of her closed lids, she hears her mother begin to weep.

"Madam, please calm down," the doctor says in his slow country voice. "Your daughter is conscious, and that is a good sign. We should clear the room. I need to check her again to make sure she does not have a concussion." He holds Bela's wrist between cool fingers. "Her pulse has normalized, though I suspect her reflexes are still slow. Clearly, she needs to rest."

"But what about the man she was rambling about? Do you think he could have given her drugs? She said something— Do you think he harmed—?" Sabitri's cut-off words waver in the air.

The doctor gives an embarrassed cough. "No, madam, there are no signs of . . . *that*. In fact, I am not sure there was a man at all. Your daughter may have just fallen from the swing and hit her head—she does have a bump. Also, she may have been out in the sun too long. Such things can disorient anyone."

No, Bela wants to cry. *There was a man. There was.* A special man, sparkly as a gold tooth, opening up locked doors inside her mind. Making meaning out of the Morse code of fluttering dragonfly wings. She couldn't have mistaken something so important.

"I don't think she's disoriented," Bijan interjects, suddenly, hoarsely. Bela hears him striding to the bed, her champion. She waits for him to throw his arms around her, but he isn't paying attention. "There definitely was someone. Someone who intended to harm Bela. I want you to test her blood for drugs. Last week, I had a big argument with the workers' union about overtime pay—I bet they had something to do with this."

Are his words slurred? Is an old odor rising from him, raw and pungent? Bela's eyes fly open in alarm.

"The bastard—and anyone else who was involved—they're going to be sorry they messed with my daughter." Bijan leans over the bed. Like cracks in porcelain, lines run from his nose to the corners of his mouth. He grabs the doctor by his white sleeve. Bela can taste his anger. It's bitter and desperate, like the dregs left at the bottoms of whiskey glasses, the ones she sometimes sipped from in the morning in Kolkata before her parents awoke.

"Sir, please don't jump to conclusions," the policeman says. He is a burly man, and Bela notices dark blotches of sweat under the armpits of his khaki uniform. "We will definitely be on the lookout for a stranger— in case there was one. As soon as the doctor allows, I will get a detailed description from your daughter. I would like to question the maidservant, too, since she was the one who found the girl at the edge of your property."

Bela's eyes skid across the watching faces until she finds Ayah's. She tries to read what Ayah might have seen. A dragonfly that hovered for a moment before the wind snatched it away? The wooden seat of the swing thwacking the back of a head? A man with a polished metal body wrapped in a robe of fire? But Ayah's eyes are black stones. She stares at the IV machine with its endless silver dripping as though it were a holy mystery.

"Question the union leaders," her father says. "Find out what kinds of alibis their henchmen have."

"The union is very strong—better not to accuse them unless we have proof," the policeman says. Bela hears the warning in his voice.

And where is Harsha? Why is he not in this room with Ayah? Who is watching him? Is he alone at home? Someone needs to go and get Harsha right now. Bela tries to tell Sabitri that it isn't safe to leave Harsha alone, nothing is safe here, doesn't she know that? But her mouth is gummy and her lips will not open.

Hands fisted, Bijan rises to face the policeman. "I'm going to get to the bottom of this, if it's the last thing I do. I'm not afraid of any damned union."

"Bijan, please." Sabitri puts a hand on his arm.

"Don't touch me! None of this would be happening if it wasn't for you!" He pushes her away so hard that Sabitri's shoulder hits the wall. The doctor has to grab her to keep her from falling.

"And if I don't get the necessary cooperation from you," Bijan says to the policeman, his voice rising, "I won't hesitate to complain to your superiors."

The policeman's eyes narrow. He lowers his forehead like a bull about to charge. And Bijan faces him, standing tall, glowing with exhilaration, because isn't this what he's been missing ever since he got here, an opportunity for battle? For destruction?

But Bela does not see any more because she has squeezed shut her eyes. She is crying so hard that her body shudders and her indrawn breath rasps her throat, until finally the doctor has to give her a shot. Even then sobs burst out of her, intermittent, effortful, as though through viscous mud. Her heart is changing from iridescence back to a flesh-bound lump that thuds uncertainly in her chest. She has lost something, but what? An opportunity to remember? To understand a mystery? To make amends? She knows this much, though: More losses are on their way. She feels a shift in the air, an imminent storm. And no one in this room knows how to stop it.

American Life: 1998

*B*lanca bursts into the utility area in the back of Nearly New Necessities as I'm dumping the latest batch of donated clothing in the washer.

"Hola, girlfriend!" She sets her grocery bag on top of the dryer and frowns. "How come you're banished back here? Aren't you supposed to be working the cash register? What did you do to piss off Mr. Lawry?"

I execute an elegant shrug. "Do I have to do anything?"

"Well, there was that time when you told a customer that the pants she tried on made her look like a fuchsia hippo."

"She asked me. I was trying to be truthful and expressive."

"There are times when it's good to be that. This wasn't one." She narrows her eyes. "Tell me, Tara!"

"This man—he was about to buy a stereo system. I pointed out that the speakers didn't work."

"I bet Mr. Lawry didn't take kindly to that. Let me guess: he said, *We never told him that the speakers were working. If he didn't check them out, whose fault is it?*"

"Something like that."

"You're going to get yourself fired one of these days, Tara."

"It isn't right to cheat people."

Blanca sighs, then changes the subject. "Look what I got us from Jehangir's Take Out."

She rummages in the bag and holds up a greasy brown-paper package.

"Can't eat pakoras. I'm on a diet."

"Why? Did El Roberto say you're too fat?"

"I don't need a man to tell me what I am."

Blanca cocks her head. "Had your first fight, did you? I was wondering how long it would take—"

She sees my expression and stops, then brightens again. "Picked this up, too." She hands me a crumpled copy of the *Indo-Houston Mirror*. "You need to be in touch with your people."

It's a sore point between us, what Blanca sees as my abandonment of the Indian community and I consider self-preservation.

Mr. Lawry's voice, mournful as a turtledove's, floats into the utility room. "Girls, girls, why is it I get the feeling that someone back there is wasting their time and my money?" His tone turns snap-crackly. "Get your butts up here. Now."

～✺◯

Blanca and I work at Nearly New Necessities on Mondays, Wednesdays, and Fridays. Just a pinch short of thirty hours, she says, so Mr. Lawry doesn't have to give us benefits. But she doesn't care because she's almost done with her beauty school courses, and the manager at the Hair Cuttery, who's sweet on her, said she can start working for him as soon as she gets her diploma.

I'm happy and sorry, both. Ever since I wandered into Nearly—soon after I took a semester off from college, a semester which stretched into a year and then another and some more—Blanca has been a good friend. No. In the interests of truth, I must modify this statement: at this point, Blanca is my only friend.

Sometimes when Mr. Lawry is particularly contentious, I think of quitting. My boyfriend Robert could get me a waitressing job at Pappasitos, where he has connections. With tips I'd be earning twice as much. We could move to a bigger place. This is important because lately our one-bedroom seems to be shrinking.

I feel guilty thinking this. Just last week, after I told Robert I'd had a rough day, he sat me down on the couch, put my feet in his lap, and rubbed them with peppermint oil until they tingled. I could see why he's the most popular massage therapist at Bodywork. But what touched me the most, pun fully intended, is that he was willing to do this for me at the end of a long day spent wrestling with flesh.

In the mental conversations I can't seem to stop having with my mother (which are the only conversations we have anymore), I ask, *Can you imagine Dad ever doing this for you, even before he decided to leave?*

My mother responds with one of her sayings: *He who laughs last laughs longest.*

No. She turns her face so I won't see her tears, and I feel rotten.

I don't think I'll quit Nearly anytime soon. I love navigating its cavernous interior, replacing on hangers pants that have fallen to the floor, folding curtains into a compact squareness, rummaging with missionary zeal to reunite a lost sandal with its mate. I sweep the ancient feather duster over escritoires, andirons, a Jesus statue with an index finger chopped off. Sometimes I stay on even after my shift is over, running my hand over stains and rust-tattoos, imagining the adventures these objects had before they ended up here, their tribulations when they leave. Once in a while I take something small, a saltshaker that's lost its pepper partner, a talking doll that makes a strangled sound when you pull on the cord attached to the back of its neck. I carry it around in my car for a few days, and then I leave it in a freeway underpass so a homeless person can have it.

So far I've only taken things that no one else wants, but I can feel something growing in me, restless and cresting like a storm wave. I find myself watching the Jesus statue. One of these days, I'm going to snag it.

When people bathe in the Ganges, I once read somewhere, or maybe my mother told me, their sins are forced to leave them and wait on the banks because the river is so holy that nothing impure can enter it. The sins will repossess the bathers when they climb out, but as long as they're immersed, they're free of sorrow.

Nearly is as close to a holy river as my life can get.

～✦○

After our first fight, I made a list to remind myself why Robert is special:

4. He's a great cook. (I'm not.)
3. I love his hands. I've loved them ever since he ran them over my naked back at our very first meeting. (This is not as risqué as it sounds. I was at Bodywork for the Weekday Half-Hour Special, which Blanca had bought me as a birthday gift.) He gave me a full hour and then invited me to dinner. Over souvlaki and ouzo, we discovered that we shared a passion for sci-fi movies. A month later, he asked if I'd move in with him.

     I knew it was too soon. Plus I'd never lived with a man. Yes, I said. Oh, yes.
2. He's an intriguing mix of contradictions. He loves literature. (On our first date, we discussed Paul Auster.) Yet every Friday night he gets together with his high school buddies to play pool. Sometimes it bothers me, how he has these different compartments in his life. (He hasn't introduced me to the Friday buddies. Not that I want to meet them. But still.) I wonder which compartment he's placed me in.

Are these frivolous reasons? How about this one, then:

1. Robert is nothing like my father.

At three p.m. Mr. Lawry perches his hat, a startling spinach-green, atop gray corkscrews of hair and informs us—as he does every afternoon—that he has errands to run. He leaves Keysha, his favorite, in charge and exhorts Blanca and me to use our time gainfully by price-tagging a box of kitchen supplies. We know he's going down to La Cariba, where he will get happily intoxicated, but we're careful to pretend ignorance. We understand the rituals of subterfuge.

Keysha pops her purple bubblegum and says, "Don't you worry, Mr. Lawry. We be just fine."

With Mr. Lawry's departure, an air of truant hilarity settles on Nearly. Blanca and I eat pakoras and read the classified ads from the *Indo-Houston Mirror* out loud to each other. Keysha, who's getting married soon, uses the store phone to call her mother in Amarillo to discuss bridesmaid gowns. ("Ecru? Mama, you serious? We going for hot pink." She punctuates her sentences with a flurry of jingles from the bells woven into her braids. "Uh-uh. No bows. Definitely no bows.")

"*Sister Shireen, god-gifted problem solver,*" Blanca reads. "*Will remove curses, reunite loved ones, heal marriage and business.*"

I read, "*Parents looking for match for fair-skinned homely Punjabi lady doctor. Must have green card. Prefer 5'8" but 5'4" ok.*"

Then Blanca says, "Dios, Tara, look at this one. *Family requires respectable Indian woman with car to take care of Mother over long weekend.* That's what you and Robert need, a bit of distance-makes-the-heart-grow-fonder."

"You want me to babysit an old woman all weekend?"

"Not just any old woman. An old *Indian* woman. It'll be like staying with your abuela." Blanca knows that my grandmother died about three years ago, right around when I left school. I never met her. When I was younger, I used to ask my mother about her all the time, but she'd mostly change the subject, until finally I gave up. I don't think about her much nowadays. I have other problems. But Blanca's obsessed with my lack of family and always trying to remedy the situation. "Maybe she'll teach you how to cook some proper Indian food. El Roberto might fancy that."

This reminds me of my discussion with Robert this morning, the one that ended in me walking out of the apartment. I didn't slam the door, but only because I am not that kind of person.

"Oh, very well," I say.

⚮

I'm late for my interview, having been lost twice since I got off the freeway. The geometric houses, the look-alike pruned bushes, the subdivision names—Austin Colony, Austin Glen, Austin Crossing—make me feel like I'm in some kind of suburban funhouse. Really, I should feel right at home, having grown up in the suburbs myself, but I am no longer that girl.

Finally I park my beat-up VW next to a Camry that stands, docile and squeaky-clean, in the Mehta driveway. I am attired in clothes that Blanca culled with care from Nearly's stock: shapelessly loose slacks ("You don't want to show no legs, trust me, legs get employers all worked up") and a deep pink top with puffy sleeves to cover my scorpion tattoo. I hear the disembodied laughter of the gods: *Who's the fuchsia hippo now?*

Mr. Mehta opens the door: neat side part, navy blue pants, shirt buttoned to his neck, brown leather sandals, kind of Stepford-husband-meets-Walmart. He's about five-foot-four. I feel like I've stepped into the wrong ad.

"It's six twenty-five." He jabs at his watch. "Your interview was at six." His eye falls on the silver ring inserted into my left eyebrow, which I refused to let Blanca remove, and his mouth puckers.

"For heaven's sake!" a female voice clangs from the room beyond. "It's not like you have ten other candidates lined up."

Heartened by my invisible champion, I lie my way through the interview conducted by Mr. Mehta and his wife, a surprisingly glamorous woman several inches taller than him, her hourglass figure draped in a chiffon salwar kameez. No, I don't drink. No, I don't do drugs. I've never had an encounter with the law. Only when they ask if I have a boyfriend do I stumble. I know the right response. But if I deny Robert, something will go wrong between us, I just know it.

"Yes," I say.

Mr. Mehta's Adam's apple bobs in agitation, but his wife touches his arm. "We can't be picky. We only have two days left before the Masala Cruise."

From the back room: "Yes, yes, no need to be picky. Just dump the old woman with whoever shows up, so what if they suffocate her with a pillow and steal her jewelry. Why don't you kill me off yourselves? Then you can go on all the Masala Cruises you want."

Perhaps I've been overly optimistic about my champion.

"You're hired," Mrs. Mehta says. I wait for them to introduce me to my charge, but they hurry me to the door. I tell them I need half the money up front, as Blanca advised. When Mr. Mehta hesitates, the voice snaps, "You mean you're ready to leave me at the mercy of someone you can't trust with a few measly dollars?"

❦

The reason for my fight with Robert is a stuffed raccoon. He won it from Victor, his best buddy, the result of a pool-playing bet involving something called a bank shot with throw (the intricacies of which I fail to grasp), and installed it on our chest of drawers two weeks ago. Apparently, the raccoon is valuable. More important: Victor had shot and stuffed it himself, and he was terribly cut up at having to part with it. He offered to buy it back from Robert for two hundred dollars.

"And you refused?" I eyed the creature with disbelief. Its upper lip was lifted in a snarl, and one front leg was shorter than the other (though that could have been the result of Victor's taxidermy). It appeared ready to spring off the chest of drawers and launch itself upon us.

"Naturally," said the love of my life. "You should have seen Victor's face." He ran his hand over the raccoon's back. "Feel the fur—it's incredible, soft and bristly at the same time."

I declined. The only thing I found incredible was that he expected me to sleep in the same room with this monstrosity.

"Want a shower?" Robert offered as a peace gift.

I considered sulking, but I love showering with Robert, his fingers unbuttoning my clothes, letting them drop where they will, the way he holds me as he soaps my back, as though I were a child who might slip and fall.

But afterward, I couldn't sleep. I stared at the sliver of moonlight that had edged through our window, illuminating our belongings: secondhand waterbed, two gooseneck lamps that didn't match, chest of drawers, a teetering stack of books. Coming from my parents' overcrowded home, I'd felt proud of our minimalism. But tonight it frightened me, how either one of us could walk out the door and not feel we'd left behind anything we cared for.

Except, now, the raccoon.

I became aware of a musky odor. The raccoon? Surely it couldn't smell, except of whatever embalmment Victor had used. Was it the scent of another woman? I couldn't stop myself from imagining Robert at work, his hands caressing female curves. What did he say to them? What made him the most popular massage therapist at Bodywork?

The raccoon's glass eyes glinted. Its tiny teeth shone, so white they could have been in a toothpaste ad. I pushed myself closer to Robert and held him tightly until he gave a drowsy grunt and twitched away.

In the morning I wanted to confess my fears, exorcise them with laughter. But I couldn't. In her twenty-one years of marriage, my mother had never suspected my father. When one morning at breakfast, as she was serving him a crisp dosa, he told her that he loved someone else, she smiled, thinking it was one of his jokes. Here, she said. Have some coconut chutney.

So instead I asked Robert to move the raccoon to the living room. He refused. I claimed he was inconsiderate. He accused me of not caring about what was important to him. I took to covering the raccoon with a pillowcase when Robert was out of the house. He took to checking on it, first thing, when he returned. Without a word, he'd ball up the pil-

lowcase and throw it with vicious accuracy into our dirty-laundry basket. I'd rescue it surreptitiously so I could use it again. It was like a
vaudeville show, except not funny.

But today I don't want to fight. I'm going to be at the Mehtas' start-
ing tomorrow, Thursday evening until Sunday night, and I want to re-
pair matters before leaving. I pick up a bottle of ouzo and rent a DVD of
Total Recall, the original one with Schwarzenegger. It must be telepathy,
because when I enter the apartment, Robert has made moussaka. We eat
sitting cross-legged on the couch, replaying favorite scenes, refilling
glasses. Robert laughs when I describe the Mehtas. But when I tell him
that I got the job, he frowns.

"Victor's throwing a barbecue party Saturday," he says. "I wanted to
introduce you to the guys."

I'm flattered—and surprised. It looks like our relationship has just
been bumped up several notches.

"I can't believe you're abandoning me the entire long weekend for
some old woman."

"Not just any old woman. An Indian woman. She could be my
grandma. Maybe she'll teach me some great Indian dishes that I can
cook for you—"

Robert looks skeptical, so I offer to make it up to him the only way I
know, in bed.

❧

When I arrive, the Mehtas are standing at the door attired for adventure: he in a Hawaiian shirt, she in a sundress. Of the mother there is no
sign. He hands me the house key and a sheet with phone numbers: the
family doctor, the hospital, and Mr. Mehta's brother, who lives in Pough-
keepsie. In case of an emergency, they are to be contacted in that order.
At the bottom, in tiny digits, is Mr. Mehta's cell number. It won't work
once they set sail, Mrs. Mehta informs me happily. She leans toward me.

"Be careful," she whispers. "She can be tricky."

Watching them hurry to their car, I think they make an unlikely pair. Then she reaches out and puts her arm around his waist, even though she has to bend a little. He opens the car door for her and tenderly tucks in her dress.

What do I know about love, anyway?

~∽∘

I discover Mrs. Mehta, a tiny woman in a widow's white sari, crumpled in a heap on the kitchen floor, her glasses askew. My stomach cramps. I'm halfway to the phone to call the Mehtas when I remember the warning and swing around. Sure enough, I catch a glint under her closed lids. She's watching me. I'd love to empty a pitcher of ice water over her and watch her gasp and sputter and not be able to complain. But I am not that kind of person, so I say, "I'm not going to call your son and force him to cancel his vacation, if that's what you're aiming at. However, I'll be happy to call an ambulance. You can spend the weekend in the hospital, getting poked and prodded and having your blood drawn."

For a long moment, she lies there. Then, just as I'm thinking maybe she did have a stroke, she sits up and announces that she would like dinner.

I assemble the feast that the younger Mrs. Mehta left for us: garbanzo beans glistening in a dark gravy, green pepper curry, rice, yogurt, mango pickle, sliced cucumbers, burfi for dessert.

She casts a jaundiced eye over the offerings. "Where are my chapatis?"

"Chapatis?" I look in the refrigerator, but there's only a ball of dough inside a Tupperware container.

She speaks slowly, as though to an imbecile. "She makes them hot-hot, when I sit to eat."

"That's not going to happen. Unless you want to make them yourself."

"You're the maid. You should be making them."

I take a deep breath. "I am. Not. The maid." She's waiting, so I try to figure out what I am. "I'm your—caretaker, here to make sure you don't fall down and break your hip."

Her lips tremble. "But I can't eat without chapatis."

I consider telling her that I'm no good at making chapatis, but I'm afraid that revealing this vulnerability would place me at a strategic disadvantage. I dish out portions onto two plates. When she makes no move to join me, I eat, although it's not exactly a happy meal, with her watching. After I'm done, I wash up, put her plate in the fridge, and say good night. She doesn't reply. When I leave, she's still standing at the counter.

I've been looking forward to a relaxed, raccoon-free slumber in a bedroom all my own. But when I snuggle under the satin comforter that smells like lavender, I find myself thinking of the old woman: the razor-sharp curve her collarbones made under her skin, the way her arms hung at her side, as though they'd given up.

❦

Confession: I have been disingenuous. I did not inform my employers that on Friday—in a couple of hours—I must go to work. It is true, as Mr. Lawry would say, that they did not ask me about this. However, I feel guilty, and a little worried at having to break the news to Mrs. Mehta.

She's in the kitchen pulling out pots, making a great and unnecessary din. Of the uneaten dinner there's no sign.

"I brewed tea," she tells me, "since you probably don't know how. This morning we'll have aloo parathas. You can boil the potatoes, then peel and mash them. I'll mix in the spices."

"Can't. I have to go to work."

I steel myself for histrionics, but she just looks at me, mouth slightly open. Her lower lip is ragged, like she's been chewing on it.

"Only for a few hours," I say. "You'll be fine—"

She sets down the pan. "I'll come, too."

Visions of her sweeping through Nearly, her nose turned up, run through my head. (You work *here?* she'll say, ruining the place for me.)

"No."

She grabs my sleeve. "It's so quiet. Not one live person, not even on the street, to look at or wave hello. I feel like I'm being buried alive."

When my mother first moved from India to Northern California, she felt dreadfully alone. One winter day when my father was at work, she walked to a park and sat on a bench, just to get away from the dark, empty apartment. A storm started, but she didn't move. She sat there in the freezing rain until my father came looking for her. He had to carry her home, her feet were that numb. He made her take a hot shower, rubbed Vicks on her chest, and forced her to drink her first glass of whiskey. In spite of that, she fell ill with pneumonia.

She told me this after he moved out of the house. She said, "He showed me so much love. I wish I'd died then."

Mrs. Mehta senses me weakening. "I'll take my knitting bag and sit in a corner. You won't even know I'm there." She scuttles upstairs to change her sari before I can forbid her.

It's only when we're halfway to Nearly that I notice she isn't carrying anything.

"Where's your knitting bag?"

She turns toward me a face as innocent as applesauce. "Oh, my goodness! All this excitement made me forget it."

"This is not a crèche," says Mr. Lawry. "This is not a senior center. This is a business." His voice rises operatically. The entire population of the store—Blanca, Keysha, and two teenage girls who should have been in school—congregate around us. "People come here to buy." He glares at the bagless Mrs. Mehta.

I consider pointing out that fully three-quarters of our customers never buy anything, and that another 20 percent demonstrate a proclivity toward wandering out with purchases before they've paid for them. But before I can jump to her defense, Mrs. Mehta says, "What makes you think I haven't come to buy?" Houdini-like, she pulls out of her sari-blouse a small cloth purse and extracts from it several twenty-dollar bills, which she waves at Mr. Lawry. "Not that it looks like you have anything I want." She strides haughtily toward the bed linens. Mr. Lawry glares after her and sentences me to scrubbing the floor.

Mrs. Mehta reappears after a couple of hours. She has sifted through mountains of chaff to discover a fine pair of black pants, a sporty aqua knit top, and a barely used leather tote that I wouldn't have minded finding myself. When she goes inside the fitting room, everyone gives up the pretense of working and waits.

The Western clothes suit Mrs. Mehta surprisingly well. Along with the frumpy cotton sari, she seems to have shed several years. She takes small, self-conscious steps. I realize that she has never worn pants be-fore. She sees me watching and flashes me a terribly guilty look. I can tell she's on the verge of retreating to the fitting room and changing back into her old clothes.

I clap loudly and whistle. Blanca joins me. Keysha cheers. A shy, girlish smile breaks out on Mrs. Mehta's face.

After that, there's no stopping her. She finds a leopard-print skirt, jeans, a sweater, an embroidered peasant blouse, and a pair of capris, all of which she throws down with an air of triumph on the checkout counter. Mr. Lawry is so taken aback that he charges her the yellow tag price even though none of the articles are on sale.

By now a surprisingly large number of customers crowd the store. Has someone been spreading the news? Mrs. Mehta points them to the corners where she discovered her treasures. "There's a gorgeous bed-spread on the left, by the wedding dresses," she calls after a bearded man who looks as though he hasn't been acquainted with a shower in the recent past. When he shuffles back with the bedspread and two pairs of shoes, Mr. Lawry promotes me to cashier. Mrs. Mehta has taken off her glasses. "They were for reading only," she confides with a grin as she slings the tote over an insouciant shoulder.

I pull her into a corner and warn her not to use up all her money.

"But I haven't had so much fun since I came to America," she says. "Everyone here is so *real*. Even that Mr. Lawry—he is all bark, no bite. I told him he can call me Sonu. It's my pet name, what my parents used.

"Besides," she adds, "what should I be saving for?"

She looks at me inquiringly, and I see it's a genuine question, one to which I have no answer.

❧✦◯

During my break, I phone Robert to inform him of the developments.

He laughs, a sound that's like a sliver of ice on a parched tongue. "A hip Indian grandma! Maybe you should bring her to Victor's." He adds, quietly, "I miss you."

My heart balloons in my chest. I miss him, too, more than I expected.

When I invite her to Victor's party, Mrs. Mehta's face scrunches in apology. "Oh, dear. Mr. Lawry just hired me for tomorrow. And you, too, because I said I wouldn't come otherwise. He says he hasn't had such good sales since Christmas. Plus, tomorrow Blanca is giving me a haircut."

"A haircut! What—"

I'm interrupted by Mr. Lawry, who waves as we leave. "Bye, Miz So-noo. Don't forget our lunch date."

Things are spiraling out of control. "A lunch date?" I say, once we're in the car. "Are you crazy? I can't let you go off alone with him. He's— he's—" I rummage my mind for details that will shock her into canceling. "He's an alcoholic. He cheats his customers. He—"

In reply Mrs. Mehta touches my eyebrow ring, the one I bought after my father left, a shivery, bird's-wing caress. It silences me.

❧✦◯

Nighttime. Mrs. Mehta and I are making chapatis. My efforts—as always—look like cutouts of various U.S states. But Mrs. Mehta says they are delicious. She eats three of them—mostly to encourage me, I think.

I'd called Robert from Nearly to tell him we couldn't make it to the barbecue.

"Leave her at the store and come," he said. "The guys want to meet you."

"I don't feel comfortable leaving her alone. She's like . . . a newborn."

"You're going overboard with this. She isn't a newborn. She isn't anything to you except a few extra dollars. And here I am, your boyfriend, asking you. Doesn't that count?"

Words jostled in my mouth. It counted. I loved him. I couldn't abandon Mrs. Mehta, who was counting on me. She wasn't just a few extra dollars. I tried to formulate these thoughts into coherence, but all I managed was, "Sorry."

"Fine," Robert said.

I called him twice before I left the store; both times I got his voice mail.

Over dinner, Mrs. Mehta tells me of her India days, growing up in a joint family with eleven cousins. They lived in an old house that had so many wings added on that it resembled a warren. They didn't bother to make friends with outsiders because they had each other.

I've never been to India. Never felt the desire to go. But now, as I listen to Mrs. Mehta's stories, I feel a jab of regret.

Her husband, she tells me, saw her at a Diwali party when she was seventeen and sent his uncle to her parents with a proposal. She didn't want to get married so soon; she'd been accepted into one of the better women's colleges. But she gave in—that's what girls did those days. They were married for forty-five years, mostly good ones. Then one night while they were watching TV, Mr. Mehta slumped to one side. He was gone before she could call the ambulance. Soon after that, it was decided that she should come and live with her son.

Mrs. Mehta pauses. I expect sorrow, or complaints, or, worse, a request for similar confidences, but she says, "Tell me about American life."

I want to offer her something deep and true—but what? So much that I was sure of has proved undependable.

I tell her I'll have to think about it.

Mrs. Mehta nods. "We need to sleep, anyway. I have a big day tomorrow."

In my ocean of a bed, without Robert to protect me, I'm invaded by memories. One of the last times I saw my father was the day he moved out of our house. I remember him walking toward the door, lifting his feet with fastidious decisiveness over whatever was in the way.

Toward my father, whom I'd loved more than anyone ever, my feelings are as unambiguous as a knife. My mother is a more troublesome case. She's probably still living in the Houston suburb where I grew up, though not in our house, which was a casualty of the divorce. The last time I saw her—just before I dropped out of college—her face had been puffy, the beautiful bones of her face blurred by grief. She hadn't made the bed or taken out the trash. She poured wine into two paper cups for us. "Chin-chin," she said, with a gaiety that was worse than tears.

～✒✦◯

Dressed in her leopard-print skirt, Mrs. Mehta moves regally through the store, wielding the feather duster like a wand. Sales are brisk; she has a talent for saying just the right things to customers. Late morning, she and Blanca go off to the utility area with an armload of fashion magazines. She emerges with a perky bob and a defiant smile.

"Come here," says Keysha. She outlines Mrs. Mehta's mouth with her favorite lipstick, Raisin Hell, and stands back to appraise. "Awesome!"

She's right, but I make a mental note: collect rest of money before letting Mrs. Mehta's son set eyes on her.

Then it's lunchtime. Mr. Lawry is wearing, in Mrs. Mehta's honor, a checkered suit and a matching brown hat. "After you, Miz So-noo," he intones, opening the door with a flourish.

"Relax, girlfriend," Blanca says. "They're just going down the street. How much trouble can they get into?"

To distract myself, I ask Blanca's advice about what Mrs. Mehta wants to know.

"You can't *tell* people about American life," she says. "You got to show them. Take her a couple places—maybe a club in the Montrose, or the Art Car Museum. Maybe she'd like a massage. You could ask El Roberto for a friends-n-family rate!"

I glare at that suggestion. Then I give in to the longing gnawing at me. This time when I call, Robert picks up, but my efforts at meaningful conversation are hampered by ear-endangering music, raucous shouts, and the fact that he's had a fair bit to drink.

"You should have come," he says, his voice truculent. "I was all ready to show you off. You let me down."

"Next time. Promise!"

He doesn't respond.

"Tell the guys that I'm dying to meet them." Not exactly, but this isn't the time to be truthful and expressive.

He sounds a tiny bit placated. "What time are you coming home Sunday?"

I inform him that it'll be night by the time the Mehtas return. I fear resistance, but he merely says he'll stay over at Victor's tonight, then.

Voices in the background, male and female, are yelling his name.

"Gotta go. Love you, babe." To his credit, he waits until I say I love him, too, before he hangs up.

～✦◌

Mrs. Mehta and I have spread a map of Houston on the dining table. I point out various attractions: NASA, the Art Car Museum, the gator reserve, but she zeroes in on the blue expanse to the south.

"Is that the ocean? My son didn't tell me we were so close! I've never seen the ocean."

"Would you like to go for a beach picnic to Galveston?"

Mrs. Mehta informs me that there's nothing she would like better. She has had some experience with picnics, girlhood excursions with carloads of provisions: potato curry, puris, jalebis for dessert, countless thermos flasks full of tea, a goat for the grandmother, who had to have fresh milk.

"We're only getting bread and cheese and maybe a salad," I warn.

She accedes magnanimously. "But of course. I understand. I am in America now."

Before we sleep, she lays out plans for our future. She will encourage the younger Mehtas—through bad behavior, if necessary—to take several vacations in the coming year. Each time, she will insist on me being her caretaker. We'll work at Nearly and go on forays into American Life.

I nod, trying not to imagine the fireworks this would cause between Robert and myself.

❦

Our first stop is a department store because Mrs. Mehta insists on swimming in the ocean. Tales of the jellyfish that infest the Gulf have failed to shake her resolve. She hovers dangerously over the bikinis but finally, to my relief, picks a decorous emerald-green skirted swimsuit. She assures me she is a good swimmer; all the cousins learned in the pond behind the family house. But her eyes skitter away, and I make another mental note: keep Mrs. M within grabbing distance. This means I, too, must get in the water.

"We'll have to stop at my apartment to pick up my suit," I say.

"Cool. I want to see where you live."

I warn her that it's nothing like the Mehta home.

"I should hope not. Will that nice man of yours be around?"

"Robert's staying over at Victor's. He probably won't get back until evening." But I wish hard for him to have returned home. I want Mrs. M to meet him.

On the way we pick up a feast: French bread, Brie, fruit, a chocolate tart, two bottles of Chardonnay. Mrs. Mehta insists on paying.

"I have plenty of money," she says. "From my son. He tries to be a good boy, to make me happy." I think I hear her sigh.

The music hits me as soon as I open our apartment door. Led Zeppelin. Robert's back! I'm about to call his name when I notice the high heels. The frilly blue blouse, abandoned in a heap halfway to the bedroom door. I glance at Mrs. Mehta, but she's examining her palm as though a crucial secret is etched there. On our beat-up sofa, slumped over as though someone tossed it there in a hurry, the raccoon regards me mournfully through its sideways eyes.

We lie on the deserted beach in the dark. We reached Galveston late—it took a while for my hands to stop shaking after I got back to the car. I'd been afraid Robert might come looking for me—or had I been hoping? Either way, he did not appear.

I am sorry that Mrs. Mehta didn't get to swim or have her picnic. We left the hamper in the trunk. Neither of us was in an eating mood. We did bring the bottles of wine, which now lie toppled between us, mostly empty, next to the raccoon.

Yes. It was the one thing I snatched up before I fled. A shock had gone through me when I grabbed it by the leg, like it was charged with electricity. A furious thrill. My nerves still ring from it.

Mrs. Mehta and I are telling each other stories about the stars. "There's Kalpurush," she says. "See his sword. See his crown. He guards the gate to heaven. In exchange for his power, he had to take the vow of celibacy."

"That's Hercules," I say, though perhaps I'm pointing at Ursa Major. I tell Mrs. Mehta of his death at the hands of his wife, who suspected him of loving another woman.

"Should I have confronted him?" I ask. "Should I have been that kind of person?"

"I can't stay with them," she says. "They fight because of me. The other day, I heard them mention divorce." She adds, "Maybe it wasn't your Robert in the bedroom. Maybe he loaned the apartment to friends for the day."

I understand. She's offering me a way out. The stars hang over my head, a blurry, jeweled net. My cell phone rings, and rings again. I reach for the last of the wine and encounter the raccoon. Robert was right. Its fur is soft and bristly at the same time. The tide is coming in; waves break at my feet. The shock I'd felt, standing in the doorway, was a terrible thing. But what was worse was that in a moment it was gone, as though all along a part of me had known that this was where I was headed. That I, too, hadn't been worth a man's faithful loving.

"My dad cheated on my mother," I say. "Still, the day he was leaving, she fell at his feet and begged him not to go."

"Don't be too hard on her."

"She asked me to beg him, too. But I wouldn't. Later she said, If only you'd done what I told you, he might have stayed."

Mrs. Mehta sighs. "People get addicted to love. Or just to having someone around. So many times Mr. Mehta gave me grief. I had to get his permission for every little thing: read a book, go to the cinema, even phone my parents. A lot of times he'd say no just because he could. Yet when he died, I wept and wept. I didn't know what to do with myself."

"Will you come with me tomorrow to pick up my things?" I ask.

"Yes. But where will you go?"

"Don't know. Maybe Blanca will let me crash at her place for a while."

"You could come with me," she says, "when I return to India. I still have a flat there."

India! The word surges inside me like a wave.

I hug the raccoon. In the salt breeze, it smells damp and raw, the way it was meant to. Soon it'll be bobbing on the ocean with its small, fierce smile. The phone has fallen silent. Ebb and flow, ebb and flow, our lives. Is that why we're fascinated by the steadfastness of stars?

The water reaches my calves. I begin the story of the Pleiades, women transformed into birds so swift and bright that no man could snare them.

Durga Sweets

*T*he phone call about Sabitri came very early in the morning, but that was not a problem because Bipin Bihari Ghatak was up already. In fact, he had been up for some time. In recent years, after he had turned fifty-five, sleep had become a fickle mistress. And he was not the kind of man to lie in bed wishing for its return once it had abandoned him. He had finished brushing his teeth with a neem stick, chewing on its fibrous end, relishing the cleanly bitter taste it left in his mouth. Not many people used the sticks nowadays. He had to go all the way to Taltola Bazaar to get his week's supply, but he didn't mind. Ever since he had quit his job as manager of Durga Sweets, he didn't have much to do.

Bipin Bihari had finished his bath, too, shivering a little because, being by necessity frugal and by nature spartan, he preferred not to heat his bathwater. Besides, the ancient heater in his one-room flat was moody. When it refused to cooperate, he had to heat water in the rice pot and ferry it from stove top to bathroom. He didn't want to become dependent on such a troublesome habit.

On the small table where he both ate and worked, he had moved aside a stack of forms (intermittently, he took on auditing jobs) and set out his cup and saucer. He had measured from a monogrammed wood box a spoonful of the premium Darjeeling tea that was his one indulgence, and poured boiling water over it. But this morning the tea would go to waste, because on the other end of the line was Sabitri's maid Rekha, calling from the village, and crying so hard that twice he had to ask her to calm down and repeat herself.

Once he grasped what had occurred, Bipin Bihari only took the time to pull a worn kurta over his undershirt and to grab, from its hiding place under his mattress, the plastic bag in which he kept his emergency money. He thrust it into his satchel, hurried down the narrow, ill-lit stairs to the street, and hailed (for the first time in years) a taxi, though he knew it was going to be dreadfully expensive because Howrah Station was at the other end of Kolkata. He leaned forward and grasped the resin seat-back and asked the driver to kindly hurry, it was a matter of life and death. The man raised an eyebrow at that, but Bipin Bihari, who was not prone to exaggeration, was merely telling the truth.

At Howrah, he bought a ticket to Porabazar, the nearest station to Sabitri's village, ran to the platform, and managed to wrestle his way onto the crowded train as it was pulling out. He must have looked quite ill, because a young man got up from his seat, which young people never did nowadays, and said, "Here, Dadu, you had better sit down." At any other time, being addressed as a grandfather would have stung, for Bipin Bihari took pride in keeping himself fit, walking for an hour each evening around the park near his flat. But today he lowered himself with heavy thankfulness onto the wood bench and wiped the sweat from his face with the edge of his dhoti because in his rush he had forgotten his handkerchief. His heart was beating too fast, an erratic, dismayed drumroll. How could this have happened? Only last week he had phoned Sabitri to check up on her, and she had laughed and called him a worrywart and said she was doing fine.

On the train, a vendor was selling tea and biscuits. Bipin Bihari bought a cup, along with two small packets of Parle biscuits. He made himself drink the tea, even though it tasted appalling (*what* had the man used to sweeten the brew?), and eat the biscuits, which were stale and crumbly. If his blood sugar dropped, he would be of no use to Sabitri. He focused on the rhythm of the train, which was at once jerky and soothing, to keep from imagining what he might find when he reached the other end. It was a long journey; in between, he dozed and thought he was back at Durga Sweets, sitting at his desk in that windowless back room lit by a bulb hanging from its wire, sweating because it was always too hot there. Sabitri leaned over his desk, looking at the slogan he had just come up with: *We Make the World a Sweeter Place.* Her hair, its silky hibiscus smell, fell tangled onto his neck. "It's perfect!" she exclaimed, clapping her hands. That was when he knew it was a dream. Sabitri would never have come to work without her hair tied back in a bun; she would never have clapped with such teenagerish abandon.

Awake, he felt bereft. Then something Rekha had mentioned on the phone swam back into his mind. *Ma said that if anything happened to her, I was to call you first, no one else.*

But of course, Bipin Bihari thought as he waited for station after station to pass, for the sooty factories of suburban towns to give way to young paddy fields so brilliantly green they hurt the eye. For as long back as he could remember, wasn't he the one Sabitri had turned to, in good times and bad? In the midst of his anxiety, the thought made him smile.

～◆◇

Walking into the small house that Sabitri had built after retirement on the plot where her parents' mud hut had once stood, Bipin Bihari knew he was too late. Not because the front doors were carelessly ajar on their hinges. (He closed them behind him; Sabitri would not have wanted flies in her home.) Not because there was a gaggle of servant women, Rekha in their center, gathered in the inner courtyard, rocking back and forth, keening. (He instructed them to control themselves; Sabitri detested histrionics.) Not even because of the body (it was not Sabitri; it would never be her), laid out on a mattress on the floor, covered with a white sheet. He knew it because his heart had not stuttered and stumbled the way it always did when he was about to see her. His heart, now reduced to a mere muscle, resigned for the rest of Bipin Bihari's life to the task of stolid pumping.

Fortunately, there was no time to dwell on such things. He sent for the doctor, ascertained the cause of death (failure of the heart), and set in motion the process for getting a death certificate. He phoned the village cremation grounds and asked them to make the necessary arrangements. He told Rekha to inform Sabitri's friends of the funeral (but Sabitri had kept mostly to herself, so there were not many). Searching guiltily through drawers, he managed to locate Sabitri's address book and phoned her daughter in America. He made several calls, each time leaving a detailed message, trying not to think of the bill, and who would take care of it. But Bela did not pick up. In this heat, the body could not be kept in the house any longer. Already the room was filling with a sickly sweet stench. Finally, Bipin Bihari had to tell the cremation society folks to load the body into the back of their lorry and take it away.

~⚬~

Sabitri's village was small and old-fashioned, and so were the cremation grounds. Unlike in the electric crematoriums in Kolkata, here the body would be burned on a funeral pyre in the open air; then Sabitri's ashes would be scattered in the sluggish brown river that ran by the cremation grounds. A deep tiredness overtook Bipin Bihari as he climbed down from the back of the lorry where he had accompanied the body. His bones ached, and the fillings in his teeth seemed to vibrate, giving him a headache. Still, he stood next to the pyre to make sure that the workers placed on it the right amount of sandalwood (for which he had paid extra) and that the corpse, draped in Sabitri's best sari and covered with garlands, its face now uncovered so that the spirit might leave more easily, was handled gently.

When the priest asked who would light the funeral fire, since Sabitri had no blood kin in the village, he stepped forward. He had thought he could do it, touch the flaming brand to the body, but when he looked into that face, rigid and bereft of its humanness, his hands shook so much that the priest had to help him. He was an old man; it had been a long day; the few neighbors gathered around the pyre thought nothing of it.

By the time he got back to the house, it was dark. He would have to stay over and return to Kolkata in the morning. There was only one bed in the house. Sabitri's. Rekha had made it up for him to sleep in, but he told her it would be disrespectful to the dead.

"Ma would not have minded," Rekha said, cocking her head stubbornly. But he could be just as stubborn, so finally Rekha laid out a mat and bedsheets for him on the floor of the sitting room. He bathed and ate the food that she forced upon him: overcooked rice and dal that, in her distraction, she had salted twice. Before he retired for the night, he reassured her that Ma had made certain she would be taken care of. He knew this to be true because Sabitri—a planner, like him—had years ago shown him a copy of her will, of which he was to be the executor. Finally, he asked Rekha if she knew what had brought on the heart attack. Had Sabitri had been ill?

"Ma was just fine," Rekha said, "and happy, too, until Bela Didi called." Her face twisted and Bipin Bihari could see that she (like him) had never forgiven Sabitri's daughter for the grief she had caused Sabitri when she eloped all those years ago. For a moment he gave in to his resentment of Bela, remembering with dull anger how he had tried several times to befriend the girl as she was growing up. But she had been suspicious and thorny, treating him as though he had an ulterior motive.

"Bela Didi was crying loudly—even I could hear it. That one, it was problem after problem with her. She never cared how much she upset Ma with her news. After she hung up, Ma got real quiet. So many times I asked, but she refused to eat dinner. In the night, she started writing something. A letter, I think. She wouldn't go to bed. I told her she must lie down, her pressure would go high otherwise. She shouted at me to leave her alone. To go to sleep. But I shouldn't have listened to her." She dissolved into tears again.

Bipin Bihari waited until Rekha was done sobbing. Then he asked where the letter was. She led him to the table where Sabitri had been sitting. He picked up one of the sheets of notepaper that lay on it. It struck him that this was the last thing Sabitri's hands had touched. He wanted to raise it to his lips, but Rekha was watching. The desire to know Sabitri's final thoughts swept through him like fire. *Dearest Granddaughter Tara*, he read.

But no, he could not invade her privacy this way, now that she was powerless to stop him. He gathered all the sheets, even the ones thrown on the floor. He smoothed them out and put them carefully in his bag. Here was an envelope, addressed in Sabitri's handwriting, which he knew so well, to Bela's daughter at her university. He took that, too.

Upon his return to Kolkata, Bipin Bihari would mail the entire packet to Sabitri's granddaughter. He would put in his own address and a phone number, in case someone called him from America, wanting details. He would wait a long time, hoping for that phone call. He wanted Sabitri's family to know that she had spent her last hours thinking of them, trying to communicate something so crucial and difficult that it had caused her death. With a fierceness that was rare for him, he wanted them—especially Bela, who had so summarily abandoned her mother—to feel guilty. But no one ever contacted him. Had the letter even reached Tara? There wasn't any way for him to find out.

After the cremation, the pyre workers had scooped up Sabitri's ashes in an earthenware pot and handed them to Bipin Bihari. There was an old motorboat waiting at a makeshift dock. It would take him to the middle of the river so that he could scatter the ashes. Three other men with the same mission were in the boat already. This annoyed Bipin Bihari, who had hoped to perform his task privately, but there was nothing to be done. The boat chugged ahead in jerky spurts; something was wrong with the engine. From the water, looking back at the cremation grounds, he noticed for the first time vultures, circling, swooping down once in a while like black arrows, more graceful than he would have ever believed birds of prey could be.

The boatman slowed the launch and told them it was time. One of the men—a young fellow with a shaved head, which indicated the death of a parent—began to weep, not caring who watched. There was something infectious about his unselfconscious grief; Bipin Bihari found himself close to tears. But Sabitri had hated displays of emotion, so he gazed into the distance with a stern expression.

They emptied the ashes overboard and set the containers afloat. The boat began its journey back to the shore. Bipin Bihari kept his eyes on the pot that he had been holding. It seemed important, somehow, to be able to distinguish it from the others. But his eyes were no longer as sharp as they had been; soon he could not see any pots at all.

"Was it your wife?" one of the men in the boat asked.

Bipin Bihari wanted to say yes, to claim Sabitri in death the way he had never been able to in life. But he was not a liar. It would have been accurate to have replied that she was his employer, but that, too, was far from the truth between them. Finally he said, "She was my friend."

1991: Aerogram

"You can't do this!" Bipin Bihari exclaimed, leaning over Sabitri's desk. They were in the back office at Durga Sweets, which over the years seemed more of a home to him than his one-room flat. It was late evening. The cooks had left, and the salespeople, too, so he allowed himself to raise his voice. He held up the typed sheets Sabitri had given him and shook them. "It would be the worst mistake. I won't let you do it."

"And how do you propose to stop me?" Sabitri asked, her tone expressing a mild interest.

He could feel the rage pressing into his brain like an aneurysm. She was the only person who could make him feel this way. He wanted to shake the stubbornness out of her. "Very well. I can't stop you. But don't you see what a terrible mistake it would be? To sell the business now, when it's the most profitable it has ever been? After we got that excellent write-up in the *Telegraph* that's bound to bring us a new, younger crowd?"

She had on her obstinate face, the lower lip jutting out slightly. He tried a different tack.

"What's going to happen to all your faithful employees, who stood by you through the hard times? Are you willing to turn them out on the street? People like Balaram and Shirish Kaka, who are too old to look for other jobs——" And what he couldn't say: *What will happen to me, without you?*

"Clearly you were too impatient to read through the contract, Bipin Babu," she said, addressing him in the formal manner, employer to employee, the way she did when he had managed to get beneath her skin. "Page four: *The first term of sale is that everyone will be kept on.*"

How well she knew him. It was true. He hadn't read past the first page of the document. He'd been too upset. But concern for the workers—or even for himself—had been only a small part of it. Mostly, he had been afraid for her. "What about you? What will you do if you sell this place?"

"I'll retire to my parents' village."

"But you hate the village. How many times have you told me about those petty-minded people, their gossip, their backbiting. . . . And Durga Sweets is your life——"

"There's no longer a reason for me to hold on to it," she said flatly.

Her words were like a punch to his chest. What did she mean by *it*? Durga Sweets, or her life?

"Why do you say that?" His voice was small and damp.

In response she slid an aerogram toward him. From the red and blue border he knew it was from America, from Bela. He had tried hard to be fond of Bela, had ferried her back and forth from school when she was young, had even cleared his manager's desk for her so she could do her homework at Durga Sweets, close to her mother. But the girl had been sullen and thankless.

Looking at the aerogram now, he felt a constriction in his gut. A letter from Bela—at least the ones that Sabitri showed him—meant trouble. He didn't want to read it. But Sabitri was waiting, and he knew that he was the only person with whom she could share these letters.

> Dear Mother, I'm very sorry to tell you that I'm canceling my trip to India. I know you were really looking forward to it, and to seeing Tara for the first time, and so was I. But Sanjay absolutely refuses to let us go. Yesterday we had a huge fight over it. He claims that it's not safe. He's afraid that since he and I both left India with documents that weren't exactly legal, I might be detained, and Tara along with me. He's also afraid that certain parties might find out that we're coming and harm us, since he'd been on their hit list before he escaped. I'm not sure if any of this is true, but since he feels so strongly, I've decided not to argue any more about it, at least for now. It's the only thing he asks of me, and he's such a good husband, always watching out for whatever I need. Most of all, he's the best father to Tara. Helps her with schoolwork. Coaches her basketball team though he really doesn't have the time. She adores him. And you know how sensitive she is—fights between him and me always make her sick. After our argument yesterday, she started throwing up. . . .

"She's never going to come and see me, is she?" Sabitri asked.

Bipin Bihari could tell by her tone that she knew the answer to that question already. Anger coiled through him. He wished he could force Bela to see her mother—how the letter had shrunk her, making her look suddenly aged. But he remained silent. An expression of sympathy now might make Sabitri break down, and that would mortify her.

"That husband of hers—from our very first meeting he hated me. He'll continue finding ways to keep us apart. All this time, I've been holding on to Durga Sweets for Bela's sake—in case something happened to her and she needed to come back and start over. I don't trust that Sanjay. I don't. But it's no use. He's got his claws deep into her. And now he's got a new weapon—Tara. That poor, softhearted child. He'll use Tara to get Bela to do whatever he wants . . ."

She was working herself up, her voice getting high and wobbly. She was usually such a strong woman, but her daughter was her Achilles' heel. He had to stop her before she said things she would hate herself for divulging, and him for having heard them.

"I don't think Sanjay's as bad as you make him out to be," he said. "I think he loves Bela and his daughter."

Sabitri glared at him. He could feel her brain whirring, trying to find something suitably spiteful to say to him. He folded his arms and held her gaze. What he really wanted was to pull her close. She was a tall woman. Would her forehead be at the level of his lips, like he imagined? But he had to satisfy himself by being the rock against which she could dash her anger until it broke into harmless pieces.

～✢◯

Years ago—Bela was still in college then—in the middle of a rainy day, there had been another letter. A young man, a stranger, had delivered it to Durga Sweets. Bipin Bihari had brought it to Sabitri at this desk, and Sabitri, recognizing Bela's handwriting, had smiled. "She probably wants some sweets," she said. "I'm guessing it's chocolate sandesh. That's her favorite. I'm surprised she didn't call. The phone line must be down again. Tell Rekha to wait and I'll send them back with her."

"Rekha isn't here," Bipin Bihari said, but softly, so that no one except him heard the words. They weren't necessary, in any case. By then, Sabitri had read the letter, which was just a few lines, and pushed it toward him. The handwriting was rounded and innocent as a child's.

Durga Sweets

*By the time you read this, I will be on my way to America to
marry Sanjay. His life was in danger here. That is why he had to
leave Kolkata. And I can't live without him. Please forgive me for not
telling you earlier, but you would have stopped me.*

Sabitri's face was sickly pale. She swayed when she rose to her feet. "I
have to go home," she said, her voice so unsteady that he had to lean forward to decipher her words. "I don't feel well. Will you take care of
things?"

He put out his hand to support her, but she had stepped back already.
"Yes," he said. "I'll take care of everything."

And he had. He opened the store each day at six a.m. so the cooks
could light the big stoves and boil the milk that would then be curdled
into the chhana from which many of their specialty sweets were made.
All day he manned the phone, taking orders for engagements and
baby-naming ceremonies, and even though he didn't have Sabitri's facility
for polite talk, he did well enough. In the late afternoon, when the shop
got really busy—commuters coming in for fresh-fried singaras and jalebis, along with a cup of sweet tea, before they headed home—he helped
out at the counter. In between, he tried to get his own work done, checking accounts, calling customers whose bills were overdue, adding up ex-
penditures, and making the required payments. If anyone asked, he said
that Sabitri had come down with a bad case of the flu. By the time the
store closed at nine p.m. (Sabitri liked Durga Sweets to stay open longer
than the other shops, so she could catch those individuals with a late-
night craving for crunchy gawja or silky-sweet yogurt), he was exhausted.

After he locked up Durga Sweets at night, Bipin Bihari caught the
bus to Sabitri's flat to see how she was doing. Seeing her—it was all he
thought about through the day. But he did not get to actually see her; the
bedroom door would be shut tight, and she would not open it even when
he knocked and called her name. He had to be satisfied with whatever
specks of information he could glean from Rekha, the minute progresses
they indicated. *I got Ma to drink a glass of milk today; she was crying all day*

in Bela Didi's room, but in the evening she took a shower and sat on the balcony; tonight she ate some rice. Sometimes he was so tired that he would fall asleep in the middle of a sentence, sitting on the floor, leaning against Sabitri's bedroom door. Rekha would have to shake him awake regretfully, because it was not proper for a man to spend the night in a household of women.

Two weeks passed. One morning he came to the store and found the doors already unlocked. Sabitri was at her desk, looking through the calendar, making notes. She was thinner, and when she smiled she did so guardedly, as though a sudden movement might split her face open. But she was as energetic and sharp-eyed as ever, and soon everyone except Bipin Bihari forgot that she had been away at all.

～⋆◯

Now Sabitri was folding and refolding the aerogram into a tiny rectangle. "I can't do it anymore," she said without looking at him. "I should have listened to you years back. Do you remember—that time when you asked me to sell the place?"

He should have felt happy, or at least vindicated. She rarely admitted that she was wrong, and even more rarely that he was right. He wanted to say, *Forget that night? How can you ask? Can one forget the moment when one's life fell to pieces?* He wanted to say, *Don't leave me here.* But it was too late for words. In her mind she was gone already, billow of dust on a dry riverbed, the long wind blowing.

1980: Ice

It was late, only Bipin Bihari and Sabitri at Durga Sweets, the last salesman having gone home a while back, pulling down the collapsible gate in the front of the store with a clang, clicking shut the lock. Bipin Bihari had finished his day's work and put away the account books. But Sabitri wasn't ready to leave, so he waited. He didn't want her to be alone in the store this late at night.

She had received, this afternoon, her largest catering order yet: she was to supply lunch for three hundred people for Mahendra Biswas's grandson's first birthday. Mahendra Babu had come to the store himself to hand her the advance—an old-time businessman, he dealt only in cash. It was a very large amount, 50 percent of the total. Most importantly, Mahendra Babu had left the menu to her: *I trust your judgment, Mrs. Dasgupta. And remember, no expense to be spared.* Now she sat at her desk, biting the end of her pen, creating list after list, writing down extravagant items she never got the chance to cook, and then crossing them out as too impractical, while Bipin Bihari tried to stifle his yawns.

Just as she was asking him which would be better as the main dessert, rasogollar payesh or kheer, they heard the whirr of the collapsible gate being lifted up. Before he could wonder how that was possible, three men were in the room. Their faces were covered by monkey caps made of dark brown wool. They carried pistols. Bipin Bihari had never seen a pistol. He couldn't stop staring at the black metal, gleaming like something alive. The monkey caps obscured everything except the men's glittering eyes and their mouths. Their lips were cracked and thirsty-looking. The leader, a thin fellow with bad teeth and a leaping, jittery glance, asked Sabitri to hand over the money in the safe. Sabitri pushed a fat bundle of notes at him, but the leader gestured with his pistol. *Playing games with us, lady?* Clearly they knew about Mahendra Babu's advance. Bipin Bihari tried to figure out which of their employees might have been the informant, but his brain was jammed. When Sabitri begged the leader to let her keep half the money, she would be ruined otherwise, he raised his pistol in one swift motion so it pointed at her chest. Bipin Bihari thought he heard the click of a safety catch. Terror crashed over him, an ice-wave freezing him in his corner. Then—he wasn't sure how—he was between Sabitri and the gun, hands extended in front of him, babbling. The leader made a disgusted sound and gestured to one of his men. Something came crashing down on his skull; a brief, hard light flared behind his eyes; everything disappeared. *Death*, he thought, and then, *Useless*, for he hadn't been able to protect her after all.

❧

He awoke to a pain worse than he had imagined pain could be. It took him a moment to realize that he was lying on the floor of the back room, his head resting on a pile of towels. Sabitri knelt next to him. She had wrapped some ice chips in a straining cloth and was pressing it against his temple, which throbbed with a bottomless dullness.

"The money?" he asked. The words came out sounding wrong, but she understood.

"I should have given it to them right up front. How stupid I was to think they'd listen to anything I said." She laughed angrily. "They took it all." He must have winced, because she added, "Hush, don't worry about it. Thank God they didn't shoot you—just knocked you out with a pistol butt. They tore out the phone line, so I couldn't call an ambulance, and I didn't want to leave you alone while I went in search of a phone. We'll have to wait until morning. Fortunately you're not bleeding anymore, though it must hurt terribly. Shall I give you a couple of my Cozin tablets?" She held up his head so he could swallow and repositioned the towels to make him more comfortable.

Then she said, awkwardly, "What you did for me—that was very heroic."

The sleepless night had left pouches under her eyes; the harsh overhead light tinged her skin with yellow. How beautiful she was. He put out his hand.

She pressed it against her cheek. He could feel, against his knuckles, the dried salt-tracks of tears. "And very foolish," she added.

He said out loud the word that had been waiting in his mind for a long time. "Love."

"Oh, Bipin," she whispered, closing her eyes. Her lashes were newly wet, spiky against his knuckle.

"Sell the store," he mumbled. "Let's get married. Go away. Far. Forget everything." A poster he had seen, passing by a travel agency, came to his eyes. Hills upon shadowed hills. "Nilgiris."

She was whispering now. He had to strain to listen. "Every day of my life, I'm thankful for you. Without you, Durga Sweets would have gone out of business a long time ago. But more than that, you're my friend, the only one to whom I can really talk." This time he heard the sadness in her voice. "I love you, too. But not like that."

Humiliation forced his eyes shut. How could he have been so blind, all these years? The room was quiet except for the coughing of the old refrigerator. Against his back the concrete floor was cold and sticky, melted ice or blood.

"Is this going to ruin things between us?" she asked finally. Her voice was small and gravelly with fear.

He shook his head, though it hurt like damnation to do so. *Never*, he thought, but perhaps it was a different question he was answering. He focused on the feel of her cheek against his fingers, the soft give of her aging flesh, imprinting it on his memory against the years to come.

1970: Saffron

Sabitri had become obsessed with a new idea, a signature dessert she was going to name Durga Mohan, in honor of her mother. She had been working on it for weeks in the cooking area of the store. She had taken over one of the stoves, slowing down production, disrupting schedules, terrorizing her employees. She insisted that the staff taste each version, made with different proportions of pureed mango and sugar, chhana and cardamom. When they pronounced the sweet to be delicious, she scowled at them, unsatisfied. She was a martinet, that woman. The only thing that made her zeal bearable, thought Bipin Bihari, was that she was harder on herself than on any of them. She rejected batch after delicious batch, wrinkling her nose, claiming that something was off. Twice last week Bela had phoned (she was in her final year of school, and her exams were just a month away) asking her to come home; she wanted some help with homework. Sabitri said yes both times, but within a few minutes she forgot all about it. When Bipin Bihari brought it up, suggesting that her daughter needed her more than Kolkata needed a new dessert, Sabitri requested him, in an icy voice, to kindly keep his opinions to himself.

It was late afternoon now, a slow time. The staff had gone for their lunch break. Bipin Bihari, whose habit it was to bring a tiffin carrier to work, ate by the cash register: whole-wheat rutis with potato and pumpkin curry, which he had made last night. There was more food in the carrier than he needed. Some days, Sabitri would ask what he had brought, and he would persuade her to eat with him. You're a good cook, she would say to him, always sounding surprised. But today she was in one of her moods. He could hear her banging pots and pans in the back, exclaiming in annoyance. Then the sounds died down and the smell of boiled sugar filled the air.

"Bipin," she called in a little while. "Come quickly!" Her mood had changed, and her voice sounded joyful and wild, like that of a mynah bird that hadn't yet been snared. Even as he thought this, he knew the analogy was wrong. She had known plenty of darkness. The loss of her infant son to illness in Assam. The death of her husband in a refinery fire which, some people whispered, had been started by the union workers. Afterward she had to fight the company lawyers, a bitter, lengthy court battle, for compensation. Not that she had told him any of this. But in Kolkata it's always possible to learn someone's history if you want it badly enough.

When Bipin Bihari hurried to the stove, Sabitri was holding a plate with a sweet on it.

"Isn't it beautiful?" she asked.

It was, indeed, an elegant-looking dessert, the palest orange-red against the white china, and shaped like a tiny mango. "Yes," he said, but he was distracted by her flushed, glistening face, the damp curls clinging to her forehead. It took him back to the day they met—had it been only five years?

"I tried something different," Sabitri said. "Tell me what you think. Be honest, now!" She broke off part of the sweet and put it in his mouth, then ate the rest herself.

That swift touch of her finger against his tongue. The smell of her sweat, like no one else's. He couldn't speak. The sweet melted in his mouth, the flavors perfectly proportioned.

"Well?" She looked at him anxiously.

"You've got it," he said.

"I think so, too!" she cried, clasping her hands. "It must be the saffron I put in. Oh, Bipin, I'm so happy, I don't think I've ever been happier."

"Me, too," he said. But that was not completely true.

1965: Umbrella

She wore a white widow-sari, unrelieved even by the thinnest border. She had pulled her hair back in a tight bun for this interview, attempting to look professional and severe, but a host of unruly tendrils had escaped. They danced about in the breeze from the fan. By the pulse beating in her neck, he saw that she was new at this and trying very hard not to do it wrong. The knowledge formed a small wound inside him.

Sabitri (though he did not think of her in that way yet) pushed his application back at him, across the stained table of the teahouse where they had met for the interview. "You're overqualified. Surely you know that. Someone like you, with an accounting degree from Scottish Church College—you're bound to get an offer from a big firm."

Guilt pricked him. Only this morning he had received a letter from Philips International, where he had interviewed last week. They were ready to hire him as assistant manager of purchases, Kolkata head office. The salary had made him blink in delighted disbelief. He was planning to call them tomorrow morning and accept.

"Why did you even apply for this job—business manager for a small sweet shop that hasn't even opened yet?"

Among his friends, Bipin Bihari was known as quick-witted. But in front of this woman he grew tongue-tied, though he couldn't have said why. She was not pretty like he had expected her to be; her chin was too sharp, and there was a slight gap between her front teeth.

She narrowed her eyes at him. "Did you come to gawk at me? The young widow who fought an oil company and won? That's it, isn't it? You men, you're all the same."

It was not untrue. News of her case had rippled through the city, and her name had been in the paper a few weeks ago, along with a photo where she held tightly to the shoulders of a thin, unsmiling girl. The photographer had caught her at a flattering angle. A group of his friends, laughing in the manner of young men, remarked on her curvaceous waist, her intense, passionate eyes. A few lewd jokes were made. He was not one of the jokers, but he'd been intrigued. When, searching for a job, he saw her advertisement in the paper, he recognized her name and circled it. Now here he was.

She flung some rupees on the table for the tea they'd drunk and stood up, incandescent with outrage. She was at the door of the tea shop before he could react. He had to run to catch up.

"Please," he said, desperate to stop her. "I want the job." The words startled him because he had not intended to say them.

"Why?" She stared at him distrustfully.

He didn't have an answer—he who was usually so pragmatic. A part of him was already berating himself. *Impulsive stupid idiot.* To appease it, he thought, *Just for a month. I'll quit after a month.* A group of his friends were going for a holiday in the mountains to celebrate their graduation. That's what this would be. His adventure. Afterward, he would pick up his real life again.

This was what he believed, ignorant of the perilous mutation that had already begun inside him.

She gave a small, bitter laugh. "You probably think I'm going to pay a lot. But I won't. I can't. The lawyers took most of the money."

"That's fine," he said. Craftily, so that she wouldn't guess his plan, he added, "I'll expect a raise, though, if I make the business grow."

"It's a deal," she said, holding out her hand. He put his own in it and was startled by her firm, urbane grip.

"Although you probably won't stay with me long enough for that," she added.

He smiled, continuing his charade. "You might be surprised." But the handshake distracted him. Where did a Bengali woman dressed in widow-white learn to shake hands like that? It was a mystery worth deciphering.

They walked together to the bus stop. She had dropped her stiff manner and was telling him her hopes about the store. She was going to name it after her mother, who had died two years ago.

"She was the most talented sweet-maker I've known, and the hardest worker. She never had a day's rest in her life. Never received the appreciation she deserved."

With a pang he thought of his own mother. She had scrimped for years so that he could have a decent education. "Baba," she told him sometimes, "you are my jewel."

"Just wait, Ma," he would reply. "Once I get a job, I'll take care of everything you need."

"She died when I was in Assam," Sabitri was saying. "I couldn't even be at her deathbed, I was so tangled in my own troubles then. But through Durga Sweets I'll make her into a household name in Kolkata.

You'll help me, won't you? Oh, here comes number seventy-five. That's my bus."

The bus approached them, wobbly and belching exhaust, bloated with passengers. Bipin Bihari hailed it. He positioned himself behind Sabitri, blocking off the others who were trying to board, ignoring their angry comments so she could climb on without being shoved around.

He had not noticed that the sky had grown black. It began to rain, fat drops darkening his blue shirt.

"Take my umbrella," Sabitri shouted from the bus window, and though he said no, she lobbed it at him. "I'll see you tomorrow!"

He unfurled it, gripping the curved handle which she must have touched a hundred times. It was a lady's umbrella, too small for him. The rain fell earnestly. His new leather interview shoes, which had cost more than he could afford, grew waterlogged. He tried to feel concern but was unsuccessful. *Tomorrow.* What an amazing word. He could smell, on the rain, the odor of kadam flowers, a little like molasses, a little (in his imagination) like the recesses of a woman's body. He maneuvered past puddles toward the little flat he shared with his parents and two sisters, whistling a tune from a recent movie. "Gaata Rahe Mera Dil, Tu Hi Meri Manzil." You, My Destination. Magnanimously, he imagined befriending the stiff little girl in the photo, taking her, perhaps, to the zoo. Sabitri would like that.

He had no idea of the troubles waiting for him on the other side of tomorrow, the acrid clashes with his parents, who were bewildered by his refusal to accept the better job offer, who grew convinced that the widow had cast a black magic spell on him. At the end of a particularly vicious argument, he moved to a hostel. They would not take his phone calls after that. His letters, with checks folded inside, were returned unopened. But how could he abandon Sabitri? Oh, the jagged tear when love pulls you in opposite directions. He would not be invited to his sisters' modest weddings. He would find out about his mother's death from a distant relative.

But for now he whistled jauntily through the downpour. Soaked through, his pants flapped muddily around his shins. His heart arced up in the dark chamber of his chest like some wild sea creature. This, this was happiness: the lightning carving its signature into the belly of a cloud; the little birds in the kadam tree, scattering yellow pollen as they fluffed their feathers; the tender curve of Sabitri's arm as she tossed him the umbrella. When he reached home, he decided, he would ask his mother to fry him a plate of crisp onion pakoras.

Beggars Can't be Choosers: 1973

When Bela arrived in the United States at the age of nineteen, carrying papers that falsely claimed she was a tourist, Sanjay was the only person she knew in the whole country. He wasn't her husband yet; the plan was for them to marry as soon as she got here. She was crazy about him—how else to account for this desperate thing she had done? But perhaps she didn't trust him all the way, because when the airplane landed in San Francisco, her palms were slick with sweat. Where would she turn if he wasn't out in the lobby waiting for her? But there he stood, on the other side of the frosted double doors, thinner than she remembered, his scruffy student beard replaced by a trim, responsible-looking mustache—grown, he later told her, so that Americans would take him seriously. He looked as worried as she felt. It struck her that he, too, had had his doubts. Would she really give up, for his sake, everything she was familiar with? Drop out of college? Cut herself off from her mother—a wound never to be totally healed, because that's the kind of woman her mother was?

Bela had thought she knew what love felt like, but when she saw Sanjay at the airport after six long months, her heart gave a great, hurtful lurch, as though it were trying to leap out of her body to meet him. *This*, she thought. *This is it.* But it was only part of the truth. She would learn over the next years that love can feel a lot of different ways, and sometimes it can hurt a lot more. But on that day the lurching made her forget the cart with her suitcase on it and run through the crowd to Sanjay. She threw her arms around him the way she never could have done in Kolkata and kissed him on the mouth. No one catcalled. No one harassed them or took umbrage or even noticed, except for an old man who offered them a pensive smile.

When she had enough breath to speak again, Bela said to Sanjay, "I think I'm going to be happy in America."

And he, smiling, said, "I know you will."

But Bela had been wrong. Someone else had noticed them kissing, and once she surfaced, she noticed him, too. He was taller than Sanjay and more muscular; his mustache, though similar to Sanjay's (so similar that later she would wonder if Sanjay had copied him), was aggressively luxurious. Next to him, Sanjay appeared young and inexperienced, not much more than a boy. Bela had never thought of Sanjay in that way. In Kolkata, he'd been the student leader of an important political party, someone people respected and even feared. His new American avatar made her uncomfortable.

The man had been watching their reunion with a mildly sardonic expression. Now he said, "Shonu, go get the cart before someone steals that suitcase."

Sanjay's smile grew embarrassed and he nodded sheepishly. "Yes, Bishu-da."

And suddenly Bela knew who he was: Bishwanath Bhaduri, Sanjay's childhood friend in Kolkata, his next-door neighbor and mentor; his—and thus, her—savior. Her face burned because the first thing he had seen her do was behave in such a wild way.

Bishu loaded the bag into the trunk of his car.

"This is really light," he said. Bela flushed, not sure if the comment was compliment or reproof. She'd had to pack in a rush; it had been hard to find a time when both her mother and Rekha the maid were out of the house. She had thrown in a few salwar kameezes and saris, a couple of sweaters, and her dance costume, though she would probably never get a chance to wear it. At the last moment, with the taxi already honking for her downstairs, she'd snatched up—guiltily, because it wasn't really hers—the family photo album from the almirah in the living room. Now she wished she had thought to pick up gifts—a couple of packets, at the very least, of the hot dalmoot mix that Sanjay loved.

Bela climbed into the back. The men had offered her the front passenger seat, but she was still mortified. She wrapped the end of her sari around her shoulders. She hadn't thought it would be this cold in California. At the airport, she had been too flustered to take note of her surroundings; now she longed to see what America looked like. But they were speeding along a dark freeway and there wasn't much to observe except arched light-posts that loomed up suddenly, looking like they belonged on the set of a science fiction movie, and disappeared just as fast. The men spoke about work, Bishu telling Sanjay that he tended to trust people too easily. Bela tried hard to stay awake, but jet lag had her in its leaden grasp. The conversation up front had turned to Bengal politics, something about police encounters. The men's tones grew truculent. She tried to shut them out and thought she heard, far away, her mother calling.

By now Sabitri would have received the goodbye note Bela had entrusted to Bishu's friend in Kolkata, the one who helped her get her passport and ticket. Sabitri would be very angry. Bela had been afraid of what she might do—to herself as much as to Bishu's friend. She had instructed the friend to deliver the note to Durga Sweets so that her mother would be forced to control herself in front of her employees. Give it to Bipin Babu, the manager, Bela had said, and then leave right away. Bipin Bihari, who had been at Durga Sweets ever since it opened, was her mother's confidant, the closest thing she had to a friend. In her youth, Bela had been jealous of how much more time Sabitri spent with Bipin Babu than with her, and had curtly refused his tentative overtures of friendship—an outing to Magnolia's for ice cream, a visit to the circus. But now she was thankful for his presence. A stable sort, he would know how to defuse the situation.

Bela pictured Sabitri's face as she opened the note. She would have drawn herself up to her full height—Sabitri was a tall woman—and pursed her lips to keep them from trembling. She would have resisted the impulse to crush the note and throw it on the rubbish heap outside the store. She would have put it away inside the scuffed brown purse she had carried ever since Bela could remember and gone back to work, discussing catering orders with Bipin Babu in her calm voice, or giving suggestions to her customers. *Cauliflower singaras go well with rasogollahs.* Or, *With malpua you should order dal puris and potato curry, they taste excellent together.*

But what would she have done once she reached home? Would she cry? Bela didn't think so. In all her life, she had never seen Sabitri in tears, not even when her brother Harsha had died of dengue fever at the age of two. After the cremation, when Bela and Sabitri had returned to the house—her father had died a few months earlier, gone all of a sudden in that horrible fire accident—Sabitri had gone into the children's bedroom and lain on Harsha's bed, which was too small, so that her legs dangled down, and stared at the ceiling. When Bela tried to comfort her, she did not seem to hear, and finally Ayah had come in and taken Bela away. But tonight in America as sleep pulled her under, an image came to Bela, she didn't know from where. It would return over the next few years even though she told herself that she made it up: Sabitri slumped on the floor of the cramped living room of their Kolkata flat, her head pressed against the armrest of the fawn velvet chair that had been Bela's favorite (Bela had curled up in it just two days ago), weeping until the fabric turned dark with her sorrow.

~•~

Three years of married life, but even now when she heard Sanjay's key rattling at their apartment door, a shiver of pleasure went through Bela, no matter how tired she was. Usually that was very tired, because of the long hours she put in at Tiny Treasures Child Care. She hated the job—the endless diaper-changing and vomit-cleaning, the colicky babies that screamed like banshees as soon as you put them down in their cribs—but it was the only place that would hire a woman like herself, untrained, inexperienced, at the bottom of the food chain. Then came the household chores. Cart the groceries back from Lucky's, three blocks away. Lug the laundry down to the washing machine on the ground floor. Lug it up again. Sweep and mop the pocked linoleum floor that refused to look clean no matter what she did. And finally the cooking, which always took too much time because Bela was a perfectionist—like her mother, though she hated to admit it. She disdained American food and took pride in preparing, from scratch, spicy fish curry or potatoes seasoned with panch phoron and whole red chilies.

Sanjay was tired, too, when he got home. After he came to America, he worked a minimum-wage job all day and went to school at night. Since he didn't have a degree from India, he had to start over. This time he studied computers. Only recently had he found a job as a programmer. At first Bela had been elated by this coup, but she soon realized that it was a less-than-ideal situation. The economy was shaky; the company was threatening to downsize. Sanjay had to work whichever shift they gave him; also, he worked overtime whenever he could because they needed to save money. Sometimes it seemed to Bela that they hardly saw each other. Still, he had a little routine for when he came home. He would set down his bag at the door, drop his jacket, and launch into one of his favorite movie songs, something from his college days like "Yeh Shaam Mastani" or "Pal Bhar Ke Liye." He'd open his arms wide and Bela would sashay into them. Even as she laughed at the silliness of it, she silently thanked whichever unlikely power had brought—and kept—them together.

They had met in college. She was brand-new; it was his final year. She was a shy arts student; he was studying chemistry. More importantly, he was the charismatic leader of the student branch of the powerful Communist Party, CPI (M). She fell in love with him as she stood in the back of a crowd the first week of classes listening to him speak, overcome by his incendiary rhetoric, the fluent way he quoted revolutionary poetry. *Priyo ful khelibar din noi adya. / Dhangsher mukhomukhi amra.* She repeated the words to herself with reverent delight. *Dear one, today there is no time for flower-play. / Together, today, we face catastrophe.* She stood there after everyone else had left, still mesmerized by the words, until he came down from the platform and asked her what her name was.

"But what made you fall in love with *me?*" she would ask later. "I was so ordinary."

"It was the wonder in your eyes. It made me believe I was capable of great things. And in any case, you weren't ordinary. Don't you remember, you'd just danced in the college's annual talent show and won first prize?"

When she told her mother about Sanjay, they fought more bitterly over him than they ever had—and they'd had their share of fights. Still, Bela brought Sanjay over, hoping Sabitri would be won over by his confident charm. She wasn't.

"For you, this romance with Bela is just a college fling—like your fling with politics," she told Sanjay. "Pretty soon you'll settle down in what you now deride as a 'bourgeois' job—with a nice little wife chosen by your parents. And my Bela will be left with a broken heart and a ruined reputation."

Sanjay had walked out of their flat, slamming the door. It had taken Bela an entire day of apologizing and pleading before he would speak to her again. But he never forgave Sabitri for the things she had said, especially her comment about his parents. After Bela learned more about his childhood, she would understand why.

When Bela told her mother that she loved Sanjay, Sabitri insisted that she was too young to know her mind. "You'll regret it all your life if you tie yourself down to someone so quickly," she said. When Bela informed her that Sanjay had asked her to marry him as soon as he graduated and got a job—which wouldn't be too difficult because chemists were in demand—Sabitri pleaded with her, "First finish your studies. That's the only thing you should be thinking of now. Do you want to be dependent on someone else for every expense? Every decision? Believe me, I know how that feels." When Bela proved stubborn, Sabitri pointed out that the CPI (M) had many enemies. Sanjay was playing with fire. One misstep and he would get in trouble, maybe even get killed. Did she want to get embroiled with someone like that?

Bela retorted that Sabitri was being paranoid. And as for being dependent on Sanjay, it didn't matter, because she loved him.

"Love!" Sabitri gave a short, mirthless laugh. And then, "Since you refuse to listen to reason, I'm going to insist that you stop seeing him."

"You've bullied me all my life, but this time I won't let you."

"We'll see about that," Sabitri said. She paid the night watchman of their building extra to accompany Bela to college and back.

"Wait outside her classroom," she told him. "Make sure Didimoni doesn't speak to any men."

"I'll hate you forever," Bela said.

"Only until you have your own teenage daughter," Sabitri said.

She did not know that love had made Bela ingenious, that during lunch break she would slip away to the library stacks, where Sanjay waited for her.

Overnight, as though the universe were in collusion with Sabitri, the political climate in Kolkata darkened. A little-known militant group, the Naxals, rocketed to prominence. There were escalations, bombs, clashes with the police, slashed-up bodies of young men. The CPI (M) was blamed for much of the violence. The United Front coalition government collapsed. Colleges were shut down, exams postponed indefinitely. In the midst of all this, Sanjay disappeared. Was he injured? Was he dead? He did not contact Bela, who grew frantic.

One must give Sabitri credit: she did her best to console her daughter, and she did not say that she had been right. She sent people to the police station and to Sanjay's neighborhood to try and find out what had happened. For a while, she even hired a private detective. But nothing came of it.

One afternoon, Bela sat desultorily on the fawn chair in their living room. She hadn't been out of the house in a week. Where would she go, even if she could have summoned the requisite energy, now that the college had been closed up? She was alone at home, Sabitri having gone to Durga Sweets because, no matter how tense the situation, Bengalis had to have their desserts. She had invited Bela to accompany her. But though Bela liked visiting the shop, which always smelled of chocolate sandesh, on this day she'd shaken her head, too depressed to speak. She hadn't bathed since yesterday; she hadn't changed her sari; she had picked at her breakfast without eating anything. When the phone rang, she almost didn't pick it up.

But thank God that, at the last moment, she had changed her mind. Because it was Sanjay on the line. As she sobbed with relief and resentment, he whispered apologies for his long silence. His life was in danger. He'd had to go underground. The police were looking for him, as were certain members of the Naxal party. They were watching his house—probably hers, too. Her phone might be tapped. That's why he hadn't dared to get in touch until now. He was leaving for America—he was at the airport gate already, and thus out of reach of his enemies. He would board the plane in a few minutes. Yes, he was leaving without a degree. What choice did he have? He was just thankful that he could escape with his life!

When Bela wept, certain she would never see him again, his own voice grew rough with tears. "Don't cry. I love you. I'll send for you as soon as I can, God-promise. I've written everything down for you, what I want you to do meanwhile. Go to your mother's sweet shop tomorrow morning at ten. On the way, someone will give you a letter."

Sure enough, the next day, as she was getting down from the bus near Durga Sweets, a scruffy young man pressed a crumpled note into her hand. Bela learned that Sanjay's friend Bishu, who was now working in America and possessed connections, had somehow managed to arrange fake documents for him. He would do the same for her. When her papers were ready, and her ticket, the same young man who had given her the note—a friend of Bishu's—would call her. Meanwhile, she was to act as though she had given up on Sanjay and do whatever her mother wanted.

Bela believed Sanjay because the alternative was unthinkable. Following his instructions, she dressed neatly each day in an ironed sari and placed a matching bindi on her forehead. When college started back up, she no longer complained about the doorman. Sabitri suggested, gently, that she needed to forget the missing Sanjay and move on with her life; she didn't argue. She let Sabitri take her out to Flury's on her birthday (a special treat; Flury's was generally beyond their budget), where they ate meringues with cream. A few months later, Sabitri asked if she would be willing to have an arranged marriage—to someone who would let her complete college, of course. Bela protested mildly but then acquiesced. She sat meekly through the bride viewings, smiling as she recited a fierce litany inside her head: *Don't choose me, don't choose me.* Perhaps it worked, for the matches fell through. At night, she massaged Sabitri's legs with glycerin water—she tended to get cramps from being on her feet at work all day. This last act was not a pretense. It was Bela's apology to her mother, whom she loved more than anyone except Sanjay, for her upcoming betrayal.

Tonight when Sanjay came into their little apartment, there was no song and dance because Bishu was with him, huffing from climbing the stairs. (The elevator was out of order again.) The years had gifted Bishu with a prosperous paunch, though actual prosperity had proved more elusive. He worked at odd jobs ever since he was laid off from his engineering firm a year ago. Recently Sanjay had told her that Bishu's wife, a white woman he had met at his office some years back, was filing for divorce. She had asked him to move out of their house, Sanjay said angrily. He did not volunteer further information, and Bela, though curious, thought it best not to ask.

From the first, Bishu was a thorn between them. Sanjay often chided Bela for not being as friendly as she should be to him. "Like I told you, I was an orphan, brought up in my uncle's home, where nobody cared for me. All through my childhood, Bishu-da was more than a brother to me. He helped me with studies, made sure I was included in the neighborhood football games, got me a doctor, even, once when I was very sick. If Bishu-da hadn't called in favors when I got in trouble, if he hadn't taken out a huge loan so that people in India could be bribed into providing me—and later, you—with false papers, neither of us would be in America now. In fact, I'd be dead."

Bela realized the truth of this. She was grateful to Bishu, she really was. But she couldn't help being annoyed that Bishu felt entitled to drop in unannounced for dinner whenever he wanted.

"Ah, good, solid Bengali food, Bela," he would say with an appreciative belch once he had finished eating. "That fried fish was quite fine. But the cauliflower curry could have done with a little more coriander." She resented him, too, for continuing to advise Sanjay about his career, though Sanjay now made more money than he did. She hated how, at such times, Sanjay, though otherwise masterful (just last week he had fought with a neighbor who had parked in their spot, making him remove his car), regressed into a teenagerish deference. *Yes, Bishu-da, you're right, Bishu-da, I should be careful about what I say to my supervisor.*

This night, once he had caught his breath, Bishu said, "We have some great news for you, Bela!"

Bela looked at her husband. *Why*, she asked in wordless husband-wife code, *didn't you tell me this great news? Why do I have to hear it from a stranger?*

Bishu-da isn't a stranger, he coded back with a frown.

"You tell her, Shonu," Bishu offered regally.

A boyish grin split open Sanjay's face. "We're buying a house!"

The words swooshed around in Bela's head like wild birds. That was her secret dream: a house of her own. She had lived in a house only once, in her childhood, a magical sprawling place in Assam with giant hydrangea bushes that leaned up against the walls. Her father was still alive then; she remembered walking with him in the mango grove, gathering golden fruit from the ground. Was that why she wanted a house so badly? She hadn't told Sanjay because it was an unreasonable longing, with her earning only minimum wage, and loans, so many of them still: his student loan, their ticket money, payments to various middlemen who had arranged their visas.

"Bishu-da found us an excellent deal," Sanjay said, handing her a blurry photo. "Look!"

She thought the shingle-roofed tract home was the most beautiful house she had seen. She traced, with a shaky finger, the narrow front window, the line of the roof, the wood fence. She imagined herself cooking in a kitchen with new flooring and enough shelves so her spices and dals didn't have to be piled in untidy heaps on the counter. She would sit with Sanjay at the dining table drinking tea on a Sunday morning, and look out at the backyard where she had planted gardenias. In bed they wouldn't have to worry that the neighbors heard their cries.

"We can't afford it," she said flatly, though she couldn't bear to hand the photo back to him.

"It isn't to live in, silly." Bishu was avuncular in his kindness. "It's an investment. We're pooling our savings for the down payment. We'll rent it out. The rent will cover the monthly mortgage. Property values increase fast in the Bay Area. In a few years we can sell it, or take out a second mortgage and buy another home."

All through dinner, the men discussed the things they'd have to do: negotiate with the realtor, who was known to Bishu, and bring down the price; get the loan—thank God Bishu knew an agent, because otherwise they wouldn't qualify; advertise for a tenant. The house needed new carpets; the rooms had to be painted so they could charge more rent. They could do the painting themselves, couldn't they, and save money? Their voices were excited and self-assured and conspiratorial, the way they used to be in India, when they were political leaders. As she watched them it struck her that America might have saved their lives, but it had also diminished them.

Immersed in her own plans, Bela heard only snippets. As she carried dishes back and forth from the kitchen, she glanced at the photo, which she had propped up on the counter, and which she would paste, afterward, into the album where she was accumulating—slowly, because film was expensive—Polaroids of their American life. She had seen an announcement at Lucky's a couple days back. They needed shelf stockers. She could get on a late shift, after her stint at Tiny Treasures. Save the entire amount. When she had enough, she would hand it triumphantly to Sanjay and insist that he buy out Bishu. Finally, then, she would have a house of her own.

❧✦❧

Sooner than she had believed possible, they were the proud co-owners of a small house in Fremont, just a few miles from the apartment. Over the weekend the three of them went there, armed with rollers and brushes. Bela carried a bucket filled with mops, sponges, Comet. How big the house was, at least three times the size of their seven-hundred-square-foot apartment. It had a separate living room, and an upstairs master bedroom with its own bathroom. From the window you could see all the way across the freeway to a grove of eucalyptus. She polished mirrors, wiped down kitchen shelves, scoured the wide boat of a sink, and cleaned up paint spills from the bright faux-marble hallway. (The men were enthusiastic but clumsy.) Every so often, she had to stop, close her eyes, and breathe deep, so overcome was she with jealousy of the woman who would live here. Foolishness, but she couldn't stop herself. Her apartment, when she returned to it, seemed newly dingy, unbearable. Each cracked shower tile, each discolored patch of linoleum, each stain in the shag carpet that smelled of ancient pets made her want to throw up.

But no. The nausea was because she was pregnant. The discovery terrified her. How could it be? Hadn't they taken precautions, buying all those expensive condoms they couldn't afford? At Tiny Treasures, she moved like a sleepwalker, wiping noses, separating fighting children, vainly trying to soothe the two-year-olds who routinely threw themselves on the floor, screaming. On weekends, instead of conversing with Sanjay she turned on the TV, feigning a manic cheerfulness as she watched one comedy show after another. It was the only way she knew to keep herself from dissolving into tears. She missed Sabitri more than she had in a long time. She was constantly tired. Weeknights, she fell asleep on the sofa before Sanjay returned, and woke grudgingly when he shook her shoulder, calling her name. Taking up a second job was out of the question. *Goodbye, dream house.*

Dangerous fantasies flitted through her mind. If she had allowed Sabitri to arrange her marriage, she would have been living in India. She would have gone to her mother's home for the birthing, as was the tradition, to be cared for and pampered. Sabitri knew what she liked in a way that Sanjay never would. Her favorite desserts from Durga Sweets, sandesh stuffed with chocolate, or dark, glistening balls of pantuas in rosewater syrup. Her tea made with so much milk that it turned a pale pink. Sabitri would have made sure she got a mustard-oil massage each day, fresh-fried rui fish for protein.

She couldn't bring herself to tell Sanjay about her body's betrayal, but he suspected it after he caught her throwing up in the bathroom. She was afraid he would blame her. However, once he got over the shock, he was mostly happy. She would have preferred them to keep the news to themselves for a while, but Sanjay insisted on telling Bishu.

She steeled herself for Bishu's response—an overabundance of parental advice (though he had no children himself), or perhaps chastisement about their inopportune timing, their lack of planning. *Didn't you realize that you don't have enough money to bring up a child, which in America, let me tell you, is horribly expensive?* But he only said, "I'm going to be an uncle! How about that!" For the rest of the evening he sat on the sofa, unusually quiet, a bemused smile on his face. She watched him from the kitchen alcove as she washed the dishes, a little bemused herself. Why, you could be acquainted with a person for years, thinking you knew them. Then suddenly they'd do something that showed you there were layers to them you hadn't ever suspected.

Before he left, Bishu said, "This baby will bring us luck, I'm sure of it."

Maybe Bishu was right, because that same week, just as Bela was beginning to worry about how they would pay the mortgage, they found a tenant. He worked at an auto dealership. A solid family man, with a wife and a three-year-old boy. Sanjay and Bishu took Bela with them to the house to hand him the key.

The tenant had a frank guffaw of a laugh and clapped the men on the shoulder, promising to take care of the place like it was his own. His son peeked curiously at them from behind his mother. His wife gave Bela a smile and said hello and what a pretty house this is and how clean you've kept it. Bela tried not to hate her, but she didn't try very hard. Why should this cabbage-faced woman get to live in spread-out luxury in Bela's house, while Bela and her baby were crammed into a tiny, mildewed apartment?

The tenant also had a Pekingese about whom he had not told them, a small, grizzled, pesky animal that yapped around their ankles. Bela could see that Bishu was annoyed by this omission. But he controlled himself. What was the point of a fight now, with the rental papers signed already? Plus they couldn't afford to have the house sit empty any longer. He told the tenant that he'd have to pay an additional pet deposit, and the man agreed to send it in.

On the way back, Sanjay grumbled that dogs peed on carpets and chewed up the edges of cabinets.

Bishu shrugged, surprisingly philosophical. "Beggars can't be choosers."

The phrase startled Bela with its unexpected familiarity. She had learned it in class three, filling out a blue handwriting sampler where students copied sentences over and over in order to learn penmanship. How could she have forgotten those thrifty proverbs? *A stitch in time saves nine. Waste not, want not. A friend in need is a friend indeed. Beggars can't be choosers.* What else out of her past, she wondered, had she pushed into oblivion?

~⋅✦⋅◦

One Tuesday evening a few weeks later, Bela saw the woman at Lucky's with her son. She followed them at a distance, a kind of recon mission. The little boy sat cross-legged in the grocery cart and pointed to the things he wanted, and his mother picked them up and handed them to him so he could arrange them in neat piles. Bela memorized their shapes and colors so that later she could examine them. What exotic items they chose, a window into an America she didn't know. Betty Crocker Supermoist Rainbow Chip Cake Mix. Chef Boyardee Mini Ravioli in Hearty Tomato and Meat Sauce. Beef was forbidden, but Bela bought a can of cheese ravioli, though later she was disappointed at its blandness.

Bela changed her shopping schedule to Tuesday evenings. As she had hoped, she saw the mother-and-child pair several times. She observed them carefully. Sometimes the woman shook her head in refusal, and the boy agreed with good grace. He was a docile child, not like the monsters Bela had to deal with in Tiny Treasures, who sometimes kicked her on the shin when they were in a bad mood. She had even been bitten a couple of times. Bela had to admit that the woman was a good mother, though this did not lessen her resentment of her. Once, the woman turned around and noticed Bela and waved to her in a friendly way. She said something to the boy, and he waved, too. Bela almost waved back, but then she turned her cart and hurried into the next aisle.

~⋅✦⋅◦

She did not know much about being pregnant, what to expect from it. Her mind felt as bloated as her body. Was that natural? The advice in the books she borrowed from the library seemed confusing and contradictory; the world grew newly dangerous. Exercise more. Too much exercise can cause a miscarriage. Rest. Don't be sedentary. Drink fruit juices. Cut out sugars. Avoid runny eggs, caffeine, paint, nonstick frying pans, insect spray, household cleaners. How was a woman to manage, then? And had she damaged the baby by breathing in Comet fumes when she cleaned the house that was and was not hers? She thought longingly of calling her mother, asking her opinion. But Sanjay hated Sabitri. Though reasonable about most things, he still fumed about the humiliation of Sabitri sending that doorman-guard to college with Bela, to protect her from him. And he always checked the phone bill because Bishu had told him that phone companies had a habit of charging you for calls you hadn't made. He would see the call to India, Bela would have to explain, there would be an argument—oh, she didn't have the energy for it. So she wrote instead.

The reply came so quickly that Sabitri must have sat down and penned it as soon as she received Bela's letter.

> *Don't worry about all those newfangled notions. You and your*
> *baby come of sturdy village stock. You'll do fine. I want to go to*
> *America to take care of you—and the baby when it arrives. When*
> *should I plan my trip? Bipin Babu will be quite capable of running*
> *Durga Sweets once I go over a few things with him. I can cook for*
> *you, give oil-massages to the baby. You won't have to buy my*
> *ticket—I have enough in my bank account—*

When she read that part, Bela began to cry. She knew her mother didn't have much in her savings. She'd put everything into Durga Sweets, but because she took pride in using the best ingredients and serving only what was made fresh each day, the shop wasn't as profitable as it might have been. Growing up, Bela had both loved the shop and been jealous of it because Durga Sweets was Sabitri's life. Even on her days off, Sabitri would stop in there—just to breathe that sweet air, she said. How much she must love Bela—and even more, the little one who was coming—to be willing to hand it over. But Sanjay would never agree to having her here.

Great, racking sobs erupted from Bela. She hadn't wept like this since she was a child. She couldn't stop even though she knew that getting worked up was bad for the baby: all the books had agreed on that. But everything she had tamped down, all her disappointments since—yes, for the first time she admitted it—her marriage, swirled in her like a dust storm. She was stuck in this dingy apartment, stuck in a dead-end job she hated, stuck under a load of unpaid loans so heavy that she'd probably never be able to squirm out from under them and go back to college.

"Oh, baby," she whispered. "What am I going to do?"

Then she felt it, a movement, for the first time. It was like a tickle inside her. *As though you were trying to cheer me up*, she would tell Tara later, *to stop me from all that crying.*

Shocked into silent wonder, she walked to the bed and lay down, holding her belly, waiting for it to happen again, for her baby to talk to her with its body. Warmth pulsated from her stomach through her hand to the rest of her body. All the things she had been so upset about a few minutes ago faded in its glow.

She ran to Sanjay when he came in the door, pressed his palm against her. *Move, Baby,* she whispered, and as though it heard her, there was a flutter. Once, twice. She laughed at the disbelief on Sanjay's face. *It's really real*, he kept saying through dinner—tomato soup and grilled cheese sandwiches, which he ate uncomplainingly night after night because everything else made her nauseous. What a good husband he was. Lying in bed with his arm around her, his lips nuzzling the back of her neck, she thought, *Tomorrow I'll ask him about having Ma come and visit. Maybe, for the baby's sake, he'll agree.*

Waking in the middle of the night, she found herself alone. He was at the dining table, scrunched over their checkbook, his forehead furrowed.

"What is it?" she whispered, afraid.

"Nothing, nothing."

She massaged his tense shoulders and waited.

"It's the tenant," he finally said. "He's lost his job. We called him when he didn't send in his check. He's asked for a month to get the money together. I was looking to see if we have enough to pay our half of the mortgage."

Her heart raced with anxiety. It tended to do that easily these days. "Do we?"

"Yes."

She let out her breath.

"But only just," he added. "We'll have to tighten our belts. . . ."

"That might be tough right now," she joked, patting her stomach. Inside her, the worry pulsed like a live creature. Determinedly, she pushed it into the locked part of her mind where she kept all the things she did not wish to think about. They laughed together, and the baby gave a small, responding leap. Back in bed, she held Sanjay's hand until his breath steadied and deepened. But sleep would not come to her. Disappointment pressed on her chest like a slab of concrete. She'd have to wait until the situation improved before she could ask Sanjay if Sabitri might visit them.

～•◦

The situation was worse next month. The tenant did not pay. Now he wasn't answering their phone calls. One day, Bela saw the woman in the grocery. She wondered if she should say something. When the woman caught sight of her, however, she turned and moved quickly away, her small heels skittering on the Dur-A-Flex. Finally, one evening, Sanjay and Bishu went to the house in an attempt to talk to the tenant. When they rang the bell, no one opened the door, although Bishu was sure he caught a movement at an upstairs window. Sanjay tried their extra key, but the lock had been changed. Bishu shouted and banged on the door.

It was no use. After a while a burly man came out of a neighboring house and told them to quit making such a racket and leave. Otherwise he would call the police.

Sanjay told Bela all this, pacing up and down the dining area, while Bishu sat at the table, holding his head in his hands. Bela had never seen him this way, and it frightened her.

"Can't we go to the police ourselves?" she whispered. "Surely there's some procedure to evict people for not paying rent?"

Bishu stared down at the table. He'd been ebullient the last time he came to the house, bringing expensive, out-of-season mangoes because Bela loved them. "You need to eat special things at this time," he had said. "If there's anything else you want, tell me and I'll get it. That's the uncle's job." Now his lips moved soundlessly and he dug at the tabletop with a fingernail.

Sanjay said, "Eviction is a messy process. I looked into it. First we'll have to serve a notice, then go to court to get a judgment. Just that much would take another month. Then we'll have to serve the judgment to the tenant, then go to the police for . . ."

Bishu shook his head. When he spoke, Bela had to lean in to hear him. "No police," he rasped. Was it just his natural distrust of American institutions? Or had he been in some kind of trouble in the past? Did he have a record he couldn't afford to have scrutinized?

"But Bishu-da," Sanjay said, "I don't have enough money in the bank for my share of next month's mortgage. Neither do you."

When Bela turned eighteen, Sabitri had given her a gold chain, fastening it around her neck with her cool, skillful fingers. It was a thin chain, nothing special, and Bela hadn't cared for it much in India. But here she wore it every day because it bore her mother's touch. Apart from her wedding ring, it was her only piece of jewelry. Now, hiding the pang she felt, she took it off and slid it along the table toward the men.

"No!" Sanjay whispered. There was a broken look in his eyes. But it was Bishu who pushed the chain back toward her.

"What kind of men would we be if we sold our women's jewelry?" he said roughly. "I'll borrow the money from a friend for this month." He stretched his lips in an attempted smile. "Bela, you must not worry. Tension is bad for the baby. I'll think of something. We'll get that bastard out of there soon, I promise."

～✦◦

It used to annoy Bela in the early days of their marriage when Sanjay exclaimed, "That Bishu-da, he's a magician. He can get anything done!" Once she told Sanjay that, though Bishu was efficient, he was nothing like a magician. She had come across a real magician in her childhood in Assam, so she knew.

"Oh, really?" Sanjay said in an annoyed tone. "Tell me, what's a real magician like?" But she didn't answer. Already she was sorry that she'd brought up that distant time. Bad things had happened to her family in Assam, and she was afraid that Sanjay might ask her about matters she was not ready to discuss.

This time, though, it seemed that Sanjay was right. Within three weeks, amazingly, the tenant was gone. When Bela asked Sanjay how, he said that Bishu had waited in his car for the wife to come out of the house. He had followed her to a shopping mall and threatened her when she stepped out of her car.

"Scared her shitless, he did!" he said triumphantly. Bela winced at the unexpected coarseness of his words, but Sanjay didn't notice. "She must have gone running back to her husband and nagged him until he agreed to move. It's too bad we had to threaten her like that. But if you think of it, it's really her husband's fault. If he hadn't been such a son of a bitch, we wouldn't have been forced to resort to these tactics."

Sanjay was right. Still, Bela felt a heavy unease, like the indigestion she had begun to experience nowadays and which, her doctor warned, would probably get worse. She remembered the child waving to her in the grocery. "Was her little boy with her? That would be scary for him—to see someone shouting at his mom."

When Sanjay didn't answer her, she repeated the question. He often seemed preoccupied nowadays. He had told her that he was working on a difficult project at the office. Now he frowned, trying to remember. Finally he said no, the woman was alone. The boy must have been in nursery school.

~ * ~

Her mother's letter waited, unanswered, on the countertop. Bela felt guilty each time she passed it, but she couldn't decide on the right words with which to soften her refusal. After some time, it was covered over by flyers and bills and passed out of her conscious mind.

Then she came down with a bad case of the flu.

As Bela tossed and turned, delirious with fever, Sabitri appeared in front of her, looking as she had on the day of her husband's funeral. It was the first time Bela had seen her mother dressed in a coarse white widow-sari, her forehead wiped clean of the vermilion mark that was the privilege of married women. A well-meaning neighbor-woman said, "You've got to cry and let it out, or you'll go mad." Sabitri had looked at her, her face expressionless. "I won't go mad. I have a daughter to bring up."

That was what Sabitri dedicated her life to, from then on. Durga Sweets, Bela saw now, had been important to her mother only because it was a means of providing Bela with all she needed. And then Bela had abandoned her.

"I'm sorry," Bela cried, thrashing about under the blanket, which felt like a sheet of iron. She was speaking to her mother, but also to her father. Her fever-mind had dredged up another half-remembered conversation, two women at the funeral, whispering about how that unfortunate incident with Bela had set him to drinking again, and then one thing had led to another. But what was the incident? What had Bela done? She couldn't quite remember, except that it had involved a hospital. And, somehow, the magician, whom she remembered, oddly, as a dragonfly. They had never talked about his death, Sabitri and she. They never

talked about the really painful things. "I'm sorry." Now she was thinking of her brother, how he had gone into convulsions, his hot little body
rigid and shaking in turns, his face splotched red and white, and then
Ayah had pulled her from the room. What was his name? She couldn't
remember. In her mind he became one with the fetus inside her and she
called out to them both, "Baby, baby, don't die."

Sanjay's worried face suddenly loomed overhead; he was laying wet
rags on her forehead, across her arms. He spooned ice water into her
mouth. *Hush, shona, don't stress yourself, the baby's fine.* How cool his fingers
were. Bishu was there, too—or was this another day? He had brought a
man with him—a friend who used to be a doctor in India, she would
learn later. *Give her the flu medication. If her temperature goes up any further
she might have a seizure and that would be worse for the baby.* Bishu held her
head over a basin while Sanjay poured cold water. *Hush, don't struggle so,
we'll get through this.* Water dribbled into her ears, pooled in the corners
of her mouth, tasting brackish. When the fever finally broke, Sanjay
helped her drink some broth, lifting the cup to her lips, running a soft
hand over her hair, turning his face so she wouldn't see his tears. All
night he sat up, rubbing her back, giving her medication at the right in-
tervals. Even her mother could not have done more. Later, when things
started going bad, she would remember this. It would make her give
him another chance, and then another, until the chances ran out.

After she was better, Bishu came to see her, bearing gifts. Little
soaps and shampoos. Tea bags. Red-and-white-striped peppermints. He
had found a job as the manager of a motel. The motel served dinner to
its guests, so some nights he brought coleslaw and chicken wings. Lasa-
gna. She ate the unfamiliar American dishes with ravenous pleasure,
crunching through the thin bones. She was over the nausea now and
always hungry. Sometimes she caught the men watching her approv-
ingly. She didn't care. She no longer resented Bishu's intrusions. The
crucible of illness had melded them, finally, into a family.

The men found a new tenant for the house. An Indian this time,
thank God. Sanjay's project turned out better than expected, and he got

a promotion. With his first month's salary, Bishu bought a secondhand crib, ignoring Sanjay and Bela's protests. The baby was big now. Each time he moved (Bela had decided it was going to be a boy), they could see a ripple go across Bela's stomach. When that happened, everyone stopped what they were doing and smiled.

Bela was seven months along now and hardly able to fit behind the steering wheel of the secondhand Chevy Sanjay had recently bought. He himself wasn't comfortable with American roads yet and preferred taking BART to work. She had been scared, too, but determined. Knowing how to drive would allow her to look for a better-paying job once the baby was born, to reclaim her house-dream. She splurged and took a driver's ed course and drove every chance she got. *House, house, house,* she chanted to herself when she found herself in challenging traffic situations.

Today she had used the freeway for the first time to drive to the clinic, which was some distance from their apartment, for her checkup. The doctor was pleased. Everything was progressing normally. There was a grocery near the doctor's office, and on the way back, she decided to stop there for ice cream. She deserved a treat.

As she was sifting through the magazine rack (she did a lot of her reading at the grocery because she couldn't afford to buy the glossy food publications she loved), she felt that someone was staring at her. She didn't think much of it. People stared at her routinely, especially when she wore her Indian clothes. Though this annoyed Bela, she had accepted it as one of the costs of living in America. But the sensation of being watched didn't go away, and when she turned around, she discovered that it was the tenant-wife. Scrunched up in the shopping cart she was pushing sat her son, sucking his thumb, though surely he was too old for it. There was something unkempt about them both, like birds that have had their feathers ruffled the wrong way. Bela decided it was best not to acknowledge them. She stuffed the unread magazine into the rack with regret and moved to get her treat.

But the woman followed her. Usually Bela liked to take her time in front of the ice-cream freezer, gazing at the cornucopia of choices, imagining all those fantastical tastes before she made her decision. It was one of the things she liked best about being in America. This time, though, feeling uncomfortable, she just grabbed a carton of vanilla and made her way toward the cash registers.

She had paid and was almost out the door when she heard the woman say, "Are you happy now that you have your house back, you murdering bitch?"

Bela whirled around, startled. The woman was right behind her, her grocery cart empty except for the child, who was hugging his knees and staring at her with wide eyes. Had she gone crazy? Her eyes did, indeed, hold a strange glitter. Bela's stomach began to hurt. She found herself laboring for breath. She considered shouting for help. Instead, she found herself saying, "What do you mean?"

"Don't act all innocent," the woman said, glaring at Bela. But after a moment she laughed an acid laugh. "They didn't tell you what they did, did they?"

⚬✦⚬

Bela sat at the kitchen table, staring at the wall. Her hands were still shaky, though it had been some hours since she reached home. She had driven badly on her way back. Several motorists had honked at her, and one man had leaned out from the car window and shouted, making a rude gesture.

She had let the woman accompany her to the parking lot, although every instinct told her that she shouldn't. She had stood in the glaring sun, sweating, as the woman described to her how Bishu had followed her one day to a similar parking lot and approached her when she stepped out of the car. He had shaken his fist in her face and threatened her: bad things would happen if they didn't move out in a week's time; worse things would happen after that. She pleaded with him, told him they didn't have a place to go, or enough money to move to an apartment. They needed more time.

"But he didn't care," the woman said. "He said he wasn't running a charity."

Bela was torn, but finally she said, "He was right. We didn't have enough money to keep paying the mortgage while you lived for free in our house—"

"I went home and told my husband," the woman rushed on, as though she didn't hear Bela. "But he wouldn't listen to me. He never does. He said that if that man bothered me again, I should threaten him back, tell him I'd call the police."

Bela's feet hurt. The ice cream she had bought was melting, she was sure of it. "I have to get home," she said. "I know all this already."

She tried to reach her car door, but the woman blocked her way. And then she told her.

About a week after the woman's encounter with Bishu, her son had gone into the backyard to play. She heard him scream and came running. She found him crouched over their dog, Hank, who was lying near the fence. He'd been poisoned.

The ground seemed to tilt and rush at Bela. She reached out and held tight to the nearest car, even though it was not hers.

"Maybe he just . . . died of old age," she said. Even to her own ears, her voice sounded unconvincing.

The woman looked at her with contempt. "Hank had foam all over his mouth. And some brown caked stuff. When I checked the yard, I found that someone had thrown an open packet of baking chocolate— that's the kind that's most dangerous for dogs—over the side gate."

~⚬~

It was evening, but the lights were not turned on in the apartment. Dinner was not cooked. Bela couldn't focus on anything but the woman's voice.

"Jimmy went crazy after finding Hank," she had said. "I went pretty crazy, too. We've had that dog for ten years. He was family. Jimmy hasn't talked since that day. I took him to the clinic, but they couldn't help him. Look, just look at him! We don't have proof, so we can't go to the police or anything. But I want you to tell your friend I hope he rots in hell. . . ."

What was she going to do with this information, this thing that Bishu had done? If she revealed it to Sanjay, it would destroy their little world of three. Worse, because Bishu was the person Sanjay had trusted most of all, ever since he'd been an unwanted boy in his uncle's house. He loved Bela, yes, but he depended on Bishu. How could she take that away from him? And she—she had grown close to Bishu, too, these last months. She remembered his hands steadying her fevered head and felt, simultaneously, nausea and a sense of loss.

Bela forced herself to get up, dragging her feet like an old woman. The baby hadn't stirred since the woman had accosted her in the store. Was he in shock, like her? What a world she was bringing him into. What if someday someone did to him what Bishu had done to Jimmy?

A frozen pizza in the oven, a carton of juice on the table. She had to save the rest of her energy so that when Sanjay came home, she could smile and kiss him as though nothing had happened. She loved him, this man who rubbed her aching back night after night, this man for whose sake she had made herself write to her mother, *The apartment is too small, maybe you can visit later*, knowing that Sabitri would never ask again.

But when they were in bed in the dark, Bela lying on her side and Sanjay behind her, their bodies fitted together, his hand caressing her stomach, she couldn't hold it in. She couldn't imagine spending the rest of her nights with this secret wedged like a shard between them.

She felt his body stiffen as the words rushed from her. But she couldn't control her shrill outrage. "It was criminal. You should have seen that child, curled up in the shopping cart, sucking his thumb. You'll have to tell Bishu that we found out what he did. You'll have to tell him that he can't come here anymore because I don't think I can stand to look in his face. And all this while, he pretended to us that he got rid of the tenants just by talking to the wife! Please, let's sell the house so we don't have to be partners with him anymore. . . ."

Sanjay was saying something. It took a moment for Bela to register his unsurprised tone. "We didn't have the money for any more mortgage payments. Bishu was afraid the house would go into foreclosure. We'd lose it, lose all our savings. Our credit would be ruined. We'd never be able to buy a house again. We had to come up with a plan that would work for sure—"

"You *knew* what he was going to do?"

"Yes. The week before he did it, I went over to the motel and we talked about it. We decided not to tell you because you'd be upset. And we were right—look at you now."

She ignored the comment and jerked upright. "You didn't try to stop him?"

"No. In fact, I told him to go ahead and do it."

She could hear the hardness in his voice, the lack of apology. A part of her raged against him for that. But another part grudgingly respected his refusal to lie.

"How could you encourage such a terrible thing?" she whispered.

"Because I have a family to support. And they're more important to me than some dog belonging to a bastard who was taking advantage of us. Bishu felt the same way. He told me, No one's going to cheat our baby out of his birthright. No one's going to take away the house Bela loves so much. Oh, yes, he knew how you felt. And you—look at you, acting like you're so much better than him. Than us. You know nothing of what it takes to survive in the world, the values you have to sacrifice, the choices you have to make. You never had to learn, because he and I were taking care of you all along."

The dark swayed around her like seaweed, choking. For the first time, she hated Sanjay with a deep and committed hatred for the way he had unhesitatingly taken Bishu's side against her. But that other thing he accused her of, could it be true? She pushed herself to the edge of the bed and got unsteadily to her feet. In the dark she grabbed a pair of pants, a top. She went to the family room and pulled them on. She picked up her purse and car keys. She slid open the corner drawer in the kitchen carefully, so it would not squeak, and took her passport. She ignored Sanjay's voice: *Come back to bed, it's the middle of the night, what on earth are you doing?* Soundlessly, she closed the apartment door behind her. It would take her five minutes to reach the ATM, another five to withdraw enough money for an air ticket to India. She could be at the airport in an hour.

But no. She was still sitting on the bed, motionless, because there was an anchor inside her belly, heavier than anything she had known. It held her down. Sanjay was wrong. She did understand about sacrificing values for the sake of love. She'd learned it just now—as Sabitri, too, must have, during those long widow years, bringing Bela up on her own. It was a lesson all mothers had to memorize.

Bela slid down in bed and pressed her hand against her stomach until the baby, who must have been sleeping, gave a displeased kick. All of a sudden, she was certain it was a girl. The knowledge filled her with tenderness and sorrow. She needed to pass on something wise to her daughter, something that would help her with the choices the relentless world would force her to make. But the darkness fell upon her, blotting out all eloquence, so that all she could think to whisper was, *Baby. Baby. Baby.*

Before We Visit the Goddess: 2002

I'm in a foul mood. Driving down 288 will do that to me anyway because of the memories, and it doesn't help that last night's vodka makes my skull feel like someone's going at it with a baseball bat. But today I have another reason to be pissed, and he's sitting in the back seat, scowling. Though what *he* has to scowl about I don't know, being chauffeured as he is in air-conditioned luxury all the way out to Pearland for sightseeing. He's about five-foot-one, bald, very dark skin, thick-framed glasses, and Indian like me.

That's what my supervisor Yvonne said when she called me at home at the crack of dawn asking if I could come in early, they needed me for a job. I pulled the ratty blanket over my head, hoping she'd give up, but Yvonne knows me well. I've been working for her part-time in University Transportation since I dropped out of school, six years now. She kept calling back until I rolled over swearing and groped for the phone. I knocked over a bottle of Hawkeye, but it didn't matter because it was empty already, and in any case the carpet has so many stains that one more wouldn't have made a difference.

Yvonne's voice boomed through my head, "He's Indian, Tara. Just like you. He's visiting the university, and he wants to go to the temple in Pearland. I figured you'd be the perfect person to take him."

I wanted to tell her, no, I wouldn't. I was certain this person—whoever he might be—was nothing like me. I'd never been to India, I didn't hang with Indians, I didn't even think of myself as Indian. And even if I had, no two Indians were *just like* each other. But it was too early, and my mouth was dry and my tongue was large and floppy like a beached fish.

My silence didn't deter Yvonne. She told me that the Indian was some kind of genius economist from India. Last night he'd given a lecture to a packed hall about a small-business model he's come up with to improve the lot of poor women in third-world economies. Got a standing ovation.

I wasn't surprised. People love hearing about other people's misery. Keeps their mind off of their own shitty lives.

"Were you there?" she asked, though not with much hope.

"Please, Yvonne," I groaned, "can't you find someone else? I don't know where the damn temple is. Hell, I don't even know where Pearland is."

"I'll get you a map," Yvonne said. Her voice went hard and supervisorial. "Don't be late. You'll have to drive him to the airport right after, to catch his flight." She hung up.

I lay there wondering if I could dial her back and say I felt sick. Except I'd already called in sick twice this month. I threw the phone down, picked out a pair of jeans and a semi-clean T-shirt from the tangled heap on the floor, and stumbled into the bathroom.

That was when it hit me, what I'd almost managed to forget with the help of the vodka: what today was. I walked out of the shower, dripping and soapy, to tell Yvonne I just couldn't do it. But finally I didn't call her, because it struck me that staying at home alone today would be the worst thing of all.

⁓•○

When Dr. Venkatachalapathi had caught sight of the young Indian woman in the hotel lobby that morning, he experienced a cramping in his abdomen and sent up a belated prayer. *May she not be my driver. Please send me instead someone of a different race, white or black, I do not care which.* This was not because he was at ease with people of other races. (He was not.) But being forced to consort with an Indian woman with spiky dyed hair and a ring through her eyebrow (and a stud, he would discover, all too soon, pinned to the center of her tongue) was far worse. The fact that she appeared to be about the same age as Meena somehow complicated matters. For this reason, when she opened the front passenger door for him with a half smile, he told her in a stern tone that he would prefer to sit in the back.

"Suit yourself." Her smile vanished. She popped her gum loudly, conveying, at once, annoyance and disdain, and banged the door shut with undue force, causing him to jump.

<hr />

This same month, two years back, I'd been traveling on 288. I was in the passenger seat of a souped-up secondhand Mustang, the darling—the car, not me—of my boyfriend. I was doubled up and in the process of vomiting; Justin was in the process of instructing me to do so inside the barf bag he had handed me, thus solidifying my suspicion that he cared more for the car than his girlfriend's condition—for which condition he was responsible. When I got out, I skillfully tipped the bag so that the vomit fell into the impossible-to-clean-out area between our seats. Sorry, I said in my most contrite voice, so that Justin would never really be sure whether or not it was an accident.

I thought I'd won that one, but I hadn't won shit. A few weeks later, when I drove back down 288 to Planned Parenthood, I had to drive alone because soon after the barf bag incident, Justin had exited my life.

<hr />

Dr. Venkatachalapathi could see that the young woman had a less-than-perfect knowledge of their destination. From time to time she consulted a sheaf of directions, causing the car to veer in an alarming fashion on the narrow lane. The single frown line between her brows was uncannily like Meena's. They had left the towers of the medical center behind them long ago; even the garish strip malls that seemed ubiquitous to this city were gone. Recently, they had passed a field of cattle with enormous, unfriendly horns. It seemed that they were heading for deep country. Would the girl be able to get him to the temple and back to the airport in time?

He shook out from his pocket a white handkerchief that Mrs. Venkatachalapathi had ironed and placed in his suitcase before he left India, and patted his perspiring neck. He wished he had not mentioned to her that there was a Meenakshi temple in one of the American cities to which he had been invited. Her face had paled for a moment and then flushed. She had delicate, fair skin, which he loved and which their daughter had inherited.

"It's a sign," she cried, her eyes hot and shiny. "An opportunity. Promise me you'll visit the temple and offer a puja for our Meena." It was the first request she had made in a long time. He did not have the heart to say no.

⚓

For a while I've had a suspicion; now it's a reality. The road, which had narrowed as we continued along it, had just ended at a gate bearing a sign: PINEY CREEK RIDING STABLES TRESPASSERS WILL BE SHOT. In Texas when they say that, they might not be kidding. I try to turn the car around, but there isn't enough space. We tilt alarmingly. It feels like one of the back wheels is dangling over the ditch. Shit! I glance in the rearview mirror. My passenger appears apoplectic, so I look away quickly. I'm not feeling that great myself. I can feel my heart doing its crazy-prisoner thing, throwing itself against my breastbone like it wants out right now.

I try what Dr. Menaghan in the counseling center has told me to do when I get one of my bouts of panic. "Calm down, girl," I mutter. "You've

been through worse and you've survived. You can survive this, too."
Sometimes it works, and sometimes it backfires. Today's one of the bad
days. I can feel the memories pushing and shoving each other behind my
eyeballs. I'm not sure which one will win. Dad coming up to campus my
very first semester and taking me out for dinner to my favorite restaurant and telling me that he and Mom were getting a divorce. Or Robert,
my first real boyfriend, and the day I came home unexpectedly and
found him in bed with another woman. Today the medal goes to the
clinic with its blinding white ceiling lights. Two years ago. What I remember: lying in the recovery room by myself for a lifetime. What I
feel: the freeze cold stirrups into which you have to put your feet before
the doctor inserts the dilators.

～✦～

At first Dr. Venkatachalapathi was not sure what was happening. Had
the girl suddenly taken ill? She had yanked up the hand brake and was
now holding on to the steering wheel as though it might spin away. She
had broken out in a sweat and was breathing unevenly. In the rearview
mirror, her eyes were unfocused. The car swayed in a most unpleasant
fashion. It was distinctly possible that they would topple into the ditch,
making him miss his flight to India. He might even end up in the hospital. He could feel tension building inside him like steam in a pressure
cooker.

He closed his eyes and focused on the way the breath moved through
his nostrils. As it steadied, his mind cleared and he knew what to do.
Hadn't he handled worse crises in the past? When they brought him the
news about Meena, he had taken his hysterical wife into the kitchen and
splashed cold water on her face. She clawed at him but he held her hands
firmly in his and said, *We've got to help each other get through this.* It had
quietened her enough to climb into the back of the police car that was to
take them to the hospital.

Now he said to the girl, "I shall step out and guide you."

She scrunched her eyebrows at him and muttered something that sounded like, *I can handle it.*

"I insist," he said, and, climbing out into the pulsating heat, he called out instructions. Back and forth, back and forth, minuscule amounts each time. But finally they managed to reverse the car.

Pleased with this small victory, he allowed himself to observe the girl as she drove back the way they had come, hunkered and sullen, without a word of gratitude. She intrigued the scientific part of his mind. She was a puzzle, with her Indian features and Texan boots, her defiant piercings, the skin stretched thin across her cheekbones and crumpled under the eyes. And that spiky hair, now fallen limp as a child's over her forehead. He had read somewhere that it was a style that lesbians affected. What kind of Indian family, even in America, would produce such a hybrid?

But first, practical matters: they needed to find the temple. He offered to read her the directions. She fiddled with the radio, from which cacophonous sounds began to spurt, as though she hadn't heard him. But having lived through a daughter's teenage years, he knew what it meant: she was embarrassed to accept help. He reached over the seat-back and grabbed the sheets before she could pull them away.

Here was the problem: the county roads they were on were numbered, but on the directions sheet, the roads only had names. He made the girl retrace their route to a main thoroughfare. From there, he counted the miles indicated in the directions sheet—another puzzle— and managed to point her to the correct turns until the sculpted white tower of the temple was visible in the distance.

When they finally pulled into the parking lot, she said, "Thanks." The small, grudging pellet of a word made him oddly happy.

He consulted his watch. "I will be here only for twenty minutes. There is not enough time for you to get lunch. I am afraid you will have to wait until you drop me off at the airport."

She nodded. Then, with an effort, "Sorry I got lost and made you late."

"It does not matter," he said, and realized suddenly that truly it did not, because time (like so many other elements that had shaped his life) was a man-made thing. "The goddess doesn't care how many minutes you spend in front of her," he said. "Only how much you want to be here."

The girl stared at him, weighing the verity of his statement. Under that glance he felt like a fraud. Had it not been for his reluctant promise to his wife, he would not have wanted to be at the temple at all. He rushed awkwardly into speech. "Would you like to come inside?"

Even before he finished the sentence, he regretted his impulsiveness. What if she was Christian or Muslim? An atheist? Young people nowadays, one never knew what they might turn out to be.

He was ready for a brusque refusal, but she pointed to her jeans, to the tight black T-shirt stretched over the bony torso. "Is it okay to come in like this?"

He quelled his own doubts. "It will be fine. The goddess does not care about what we are wearing, only what is in our hearts."

"I'm not sure I'd qualify on that count, either," she said.

❧✦❀

Far as I know, I've never been inside a temple. My father, who was a Communist in his youth, was dead against it. My mother had to fight him just to set up an altar in the kitchen, where a tiny ten-armed goddess statue shared shelf space with her spices. Because he was the fulcrum of my existence, I grew up convinced that religion was the opium of the people. When my mother gave me a holy picture to take to college, I tossed it in the bottom of my suitcase and didn't bother to take it out when I unpacked.

Stepping into the temple, I'm assailed by a scent. A mix of crushed flowers, incense, and a woodsy odor which I'll discover is holy ash—it's strangely familiar. Had my mother secretly taken me to a temple when I was a baby, incapable of giving her away to Dad? She'd have been right to be cautious; as soon as I learned to communicate, I told him every-thing. Until he destroyed our family, at which point I stopped talking to him.

I didn't talk to my mother much, either, after the divorce. The last time had been two years ago, the night before the abortion. I'd called her cell from the pay phone outside Walmart because I didn't want to use my own phone, didn't want her to call me, weeping and drunk, late at night, as she had gotten into the habit of doing before I'd changed my number.

I'd called because I was scared. Because suddenly I wasn't sure if I was doing the right thing. I said to myself, *If she says, Don't, I'll cancel the appointment. If she says, Come, I'll drive up to wherever she's living now.*

But I never got to talk to her. A man picked up at the other end. At first I thought it was a wrong number because it was so late at night, but he told me it wasn't. Hold on, he said. He put the phone down and shouted something, his tone familiar and intimate. I heard her shouting something back. I didn't catch the words, but I heard the laughter in her voice. I'd never felt so alone.

I hung up then. Clearly, my mother had moved on with her life. I needed to do the same.

We make our way through a pillared hall toward the deities, each glistening within his or her enclosure. Dr. V—he said I could call him that, it'd be easier—gives me a quick introduction to the divine family. Here's the goddess, with her husband to her right and her brother to her left. Here are the brother's consorts. Here are the animals the deities ride. Fascinating, these intricate heavenly relationships. Their multisyl-labic names are too complicated to remember. In any case, I don't put much stock in remembering things. Being able to forget is a superior skill.

A sleepy old priest in a white dhoti sits on a metal folding chair outside the goddess's enclosure. He stares at me suspiciously though—for Dr. V's sake—I removed my eyebrow ring before entering the temple. I've even swaddled myself in a shawl that Dr. V pulled out of his suitcase. Still, the priest's eyes say, *You can't fool me. You don't belong here.*

～･○

The temple was an architectural disappointment, thought Dr. Venkatachalapathi, another valiant but doomed attempt by the immigrant community to re-create the Indian experience. This could never compare to the original Meenakshi Amman Kovil of Madurai, fourteen sculpted gates rising twenty stories tall. The energy inside that sanctum, born of centuries of chanted prayers—how could you hope to re-create that in this flat landscape dotted with strange trees, on the wrong side of the black waters? Even he, who wasn't a temple-going man, had felt that power. Twenty years ago, at his wife's insistence, they had journeyed there to offer thanks because the goddess had finally given them a child that had lived. It had taken an entire day by train. Himself, his wife, and the ten-month-old Meena. She had clapped her hands in delight when they came upon a procession of temple elephants. Jewel of his old age, gift of the goddess, now gone. . . .

No. He had wandered in that dark forest long enough. He called to the priest in Tamil and briskly requested that an archana be performed for Meenakshi Venkatachalapathi. He provided the necessary information and the priest limped off toward the goddess, carrying his bell and his bowl of vermilion powder.

For a moment, thinking of Meena, he had forgotten the girl. But now she came up to him, glowing in his white shawl, whispering questions with an avidity that surprised him. What was the priest going to do? What was an archana? Did the prayer have a special significance? Her eyes, full of wonder, made her seem suddenly younger.

"It's for good luck," he said. "For blessing, in this life and the next. Wait, I will offer one for you, too. But I will need your name."

"Oh, no! You don't have to do that." But her face was bright with pleasure as she gave him the information.

"Why," he said in surprise, "you're named after the goddess, too."

When Venkatachalapathi asked the priest to add Tara's name to the archana, the old man scowled.

"What is her clan? Her birth sign? Her star?" he demanded. They both knew the system. Without this crucial information, a prayer offered in the temple would not be fully effective.

Venkatachalapathi glanced at Tara. She was looking at him inquiringly; she had caught the disapproval in the old man's tone. He feared that she would not know the answers to any of the priest's queries, that she came from a family that did not keep track of such things. She probably did not even possess a birth chart. He hoped he was wrong. Without a birth chart, how would you know who you really were? Adrift in the universe, how would you navigate your life?

"What's he saying?"

"Nothing important." He turned to the waiting priest. "She is from the same family," he said firmly. "Same gotram."

"But—" the priest began.

He cut him off, giving the name of his own birth star as hers.

It was clear that the priest didn't believe him. But ultimately he was only a hired man. All he wanted, Venkatachalapathi correctly surmised, was to finish his shift and get back to his apartment so he could take a proper nap. He shrugged and, in surprisingly resonant tones, began to chant the holy names.

~·✦·~

Something had happened in the temple. I'd read the lines of the priest's body, the tenor of his voice. Distrust isn't hard to decipher, no matter what the language. I was ready to leave, but Dr. V stopped me. He spoke to the priest, glowing with authority, until the man muttered and looked away. A prayer was offered in my name—probably for the first time in my life. Now I'm jubilantly carrying back a handful of squished flowers, an apple, a paper cone of ash, and a Styrofoam container filled with mushy porridge. And the magical smell. I wonder how long it'll last. But I know that answer already: nothing good lasts long enough.

Outside, I fold the white shawl and hold it out to Dr. V. I will him to tell me to keep it, but he takes it from me with an absent nod and lays it on the back seat. I'm surprised by my disappointment, and, yes, a surge of anger. Stupid, I know. What would I do with a shawl like that, anyway? I'll never have an occasion to wear it again, and the last thing I need is more stuff in my tiny hole of a studio.

We get in the car, crank up the air conditioner, and eat. I hadn't realized how hungry I was. The upma—that's the name of the porridge—tastes a lot better than its gooey texture led me to expect. When I step out to throw away the garbage, I open the back door and pretend to fix something. But what I do is stuff the shawl under a seat in one quick, surreptitious motion. This way, Dr. V won't remember it when he gets down at the airport, and I'll get to keep it.

I slide back into the driver's seat, heart pounding. I know I shouldn't have done that, but I can't help it. It's the way I feel sometimes, like a fever I can't stop from spiraling up. And then I have to take whatever's in front of me, even though I know it'll get me in big trouble someday.

Inside the temple I hadn't understood what the priest was chanting, but the rise and fall of the syllables was hypnotic. Dr. V had told me that the mantras were thousands of years old. For a long time they had been considered too sacred to write down. I thought about how they'd wandered through the centuries until they found their way here, to America, to be recited for me. There was something breath-stopping about it.

"What was the priest chanting at the end?" I ask Dr. V. "When he went over to the black Shiva stone and made circles with the lamp?"

"That was the forgiveness prayer," he says. I'm hoping he'll tell me the meaning, but he's busy crushing his Styrofoam container in his fist, and then he says, "It's time to start for the airport."

I drive while Dr. V navigates; he's in the front passenger seat now, and we've got it down to a science. Pretty soon we're on Broadway, which leads us to 288. In less than an hour we'll be at the airport, and he'll be gone. I'm surprised to realize I don't want that to happen. But why? Ever since Dad went on his merry way, I've avoided Indians, males in particular. Why should this bald old man mean anything to me?

Dr. V's staring out the window, clearly somewhere else. I want to follow him there. I ask, "The woman you offered the prayer for—is she related to you?"

"My daughter." He's silent for so long, I think he's done speaking. Then he says, "She died last year."

Shit.

"I'm sorry—" I begin, but he turns further into the window, ending my attempt at apology.

We pass the exit that leads to the Planned Parenthood clinic. We're close to downtown now. Lanes split and merge. Traffic's getting heavy, folks driving with Friday frenzy, like the world's going to end if they don't make it on time to wherever they're rushing. I maneuver around a flotilla of trucks, searching for something to say. I don't want this to be our final exchange.

Maybe he feels the same way. With an effort, he says, "What are you studying?"

It's that favorite fallback Indian question, one my parents' friends annoyed me with routinely as I was growing up. I'd toss off flippant, outrageous answers to them, but today I'm not sure what to say. If I tell Dr. V I've dropped out of school and am working at a dead-end job, he'll look down on me. On the other hand, he told me a truth and deserves the same. I opt for something in-between. "I'm taking some time off from college."

I glance over to gauge his response. He flinches and flings up his arms. I hadn't expected such a dramatic reaction to my disclosure. Then I see it: an eighteen-wheeler moving into our lane, blithely oblivious to the fact that its tail end is inches from the side of our car. In panic I wrench the steering wheel sharply to the right, but I'm too late. The truck's rear wallops our front. There's a huge bang, sparks from metal tearing metal. But maybe the sparks are inside my eyes. The impact sends us flying across the next lane. We crash into the guardrail. More sparks. Someone's screaming. I think it's me. An airbag rushes out from nowhere. It punches me back into my seat. Everything goes white and silent, like when someone dies in a movie and wakes up in heaven.

But then the bag deflates and the world takes over. Cacophony of honks, brakes screeching all around, stench of burning rubber. My mouth fills with salt. Bile or blood, not sure which. The front of our car has accordioned up so I can barely see over it. Pellets of broken glass are scattered across the dashboard. I can feel some of them inside my T-shirt. Steam pours from under the hood. Are we going to blow up? It feels like every bone in my body is jarred loose. I glance over at Dr. V, who has an ugly gash on his forehead. He's trying to unbuckle his seat belt, but his hands are trembling too much. I yank it off him, and somehow we're on the asphalt, crawling away from the car. Then we're sitting on the shoulder of the freeway, scrunched up against the bent guardrail, and it hits me, what just happened. I start shaking. The sensation is oddly familiar. Then I remember. After the abortion, I'd been this way, chilled and shivering, unable to stop.

"Sorry," I mumble. "Sorry, sorry, sorry." The traffic shrieks around me. I'm not sure whom I'm addressing.

❧

When Dr. Venkatachalapathi saw the monstrous rear end of the truck swinging toward him, he was surprised at how indifferent he felt about the imminent ending of his life. He feared the pain, of course, and he was filled with sorrow for his wife, who would now be alone in the world, and for the girl in the car, who would be gravely injured, if not worse. But the actual shucking off of his own life—he almost looked forward to it. In the video games that Meena used to play obsessively, when the odds were against her, she would just let her character die and start again, clean and new, without scars. Would this be similar? As his head struck the dashboard, he wondered if he would meet Meena in the afterworld, as the scriptures suggested, and what he would say to her. Would she respond? Would she turn away?

But he was not dead, after all. Somehow he was out of the ruined car and sitting on the hot asphalt, gulping smoggy air, vehicles swooshing past perilously close. In the distance he could see that the truck that had hit them had pulled over, a rear light blinking like a Cyclops eye. The driver had climbed down and was hurrying toward them. Other cars had pulled over. How kind strangers were in America. Someone was talking on a cell phone, gesturing toward the smoking car. A face hung over him, lips moving. He did not respond, and after some time the face went away.

Next to him, the girl rocked back and forth, crying. *Sorry, sorry, sorry.* Now she was talking in a garbled rush. She had done something terrible. He couldn't pluck the words out of the weeping, to make sense of them. Nausea climbed, burning, up his gullet. *Please, goddess, not the added indignity of throwing up in public.* The girl's face twisted, shiny with snot. Pity and disgust fought inside him until he was overcome by a great exhaustion and rested his forehead on the guardrail.

But she would not let him go. She was clutching his shoulder, digging in with her nails. "I had an abortion. Do you hear me? An abortion. I never told anyone this. Two years ago, this exact day, I killed my baby."

The words echoed inside him as though his body were a huge, empty room. He wanted to leave them behind, leave her, but he had no right.

"I thought you might understand," she said, "but you don't. How can you? Nothing you ever did could be this terrible."

So easy to agree. To end this conversation. Pat her back and tell her he was sorry. The moment would pass. The police would arrive, the medics, the fire engine with its familiar, consoling redness.

Instead, he made himself touch her hand. It took all his willpower not to jerk away when she clasped it. He started to talk about Meena. Haltingly, then faster, because he only had these minutes. Tara was listening, her head tilted close to his. It struck him that he had not spoken of his daughter—apart from mouthing polite, meaningless responses to expressions of sympathy—since she had died. Even to his wife, he had said, *Please don't.*

She had a zany sense of humor, a way of pushing back her mass of curls with both hands when she dissolved into laughter. She had a temper and got into fights with him, but she forgave quickly. She wasn't pretty in the conventional sense. Her nose was too big; her chin too strong, like his. He thought she was beautiful. She was straight as a knife edge, and as sharp. She rolled her eyes when she told him about classmates who secretly met boys in cinema halls; she had no patience with subterfuge.

He would explain to her the complicated economic theories he was working on, even though she was in high school and surely did not understand. Still, she sat and listened patiently into the night. After she went away to college in Delhi, they continued their late-night conversations on the phone. His wife would come knocking on the door of his study, rumpled with sleep, complaining that he talked more to the absent Meena than to her.

Meena graduated; found a job in Delhi with an NGO that helped teens create small businesses. He was proud that he had inspired her. He showed their relatives the photos she sent, groups of girls with embroidered bags, jars of pickled chilies and mangoes.

When he started looking for a suitable match, she came down to Chennai to talk to him. There were circles under her eyes as though she wasn't sleeping well. She worked too hard, that girl. Dad, she said, I don't want that kind of marriage. I love someone.

It had been a shock. Love matches had been unheard-of in their orthodox Brahmin family. But he swallowed back his objections. Times were changing, and he was willing to change along with them if it made her happy. That was how much she meant to him, his lovely daughter.

Tell me, Amma, he said. Is it someone at work?

Yes, Meena said, her thin face flushing. I would like you to meet her.

Children. How they can tear your life apart with a single word.

At first he was sure he had heard wrong. Even after she explained, he refused to believe it. It is a mistake, he kept saying. This is not normal. You do not know what you are saying. You have fallen into the wrong company, become confused. Let us take you to the doctor.

Several times she broke down in tears, but she was also firm. This is me, Appa. I can't hide it from you anymore.

What had he said then, with his world crashing down around him? Maybe, *Disgusting.* Maybe, *You've shamed us.* He had not shouted, he knew that much. Perhaps that had made it worse, his cold, controlled voice. At the end he had said, We want nothing more to do with you. Go. Never come back.

She hadn't believed him. She had called from Delhi every night, hoping he would talk to her, until he blocked her number.

It was the police who came next, carrying the news. Death. Overdose of sleeping pills.

❧

The paramedics check us for damages, the ones that can be gauged with instruments. They tell us we're lucky. Most of what we're feeling is shock; we don't need to be hospitalized. Appropriately bandaged and medicated, we're driven to the police station, where our statements are taken. Mine barely makes sense. My mind is full of Meena, her still, pale body on the hospital gurney, her long hair falling over its edge like sorrow. *My wife clung to her, weeping,* Dr. V had said. *But I couldn't touch her. I felt I didn't have the right.*

The police must have contacted the university, because here comes the chair of the Economics Department, huffing with apologies. He's going to take Dr. V to the airport and try and get him on another flight. He glares at me as he stashes Dr. V's suitcase in his trunk. Dr. V explained to him that the accident wasn't my fault, but I've a feeling I'll be looking for a new job pretty soon.

Dr. V turns to wish me goodbye. I only have a moment.

"Thank you for telling me about your daughter," I say. I want to add something about how I feel now, not better exactly but less alone. But words would spoil it.

"No," he says. "Thank *you*." And then, "Go back to school, Amma. Don't give up."

He holds my gaze until I nod.

The chair clears his throat. Dr. V gets in the car. They're gone.

Waiting outside the station for a policeman to give me a ride, I heft my handbag, and suddenly that temple smell is all around me. I unzip the bag. The paper cone has burst. A fine gray ash coats everything: wallet, lipstick, keys, fingers. I lower my face and breathe it in, but all it does is make me sneeze.

How much do I have in the bank? How much do I have in me? Can I stick with it this time? Just thinking about the effort it'll require exhausts me, all that information I'll have to ingest and spit back out.

My head's aching like crazy, like someone's tightening a spring at the base of my skull. It's the kind of pain that requires some serious tending to. I'm out of Valium, but I still have a quarter bottle of emergency vodka in the back of my closet.

I realize that I've forgotten to rescue the stolen shawl. It's gone, towed along with the car. Like so many things in my life, I won't see it again.

My teeth are chattering. Delayed shock or withdrawal. How much longer is that idiot policeman going to take?

I consider going back into the station to complain. I'm a citizen. I have rights. But then a memory sideswipes me.

At the entrance to the temple, Dr. V informed me that we had to remove our shoes. Grudgingly, I pulled off my boots. The bricks of the wide courtyard were scorching-hot. They seared my feet. I hurried on tiptoe toward the temple door, trying to get inside the building as quickly as possible. But Dr. V called me back.

"Before we visit the goddess," he said, "we must cleanse ourselves."

There was a spigot beside the doorway, a green hose attached to it.

Dr. V turned it on. His own feet must have been scalding, too, but he aimed the hose toward me. Water pooled over my feet and under my burning soles.

That cool silver shimmer in the blazing afternoon. That small benediction. How can I forget it?

Bela's Kitchen: 2000

*T*he first time I met her was the night David left me.

After the front door clicked behind him, I needed to get out of the house. I headed to the grocery, the fancy one next to the independent bookstore where I was the events coordinator. I filled my cart with items he disapproved of. I bought ice-cream sandwiches, a six-pack of Budweiser—regular, not Light—and a family-sized package of chicken nuggets. But he had ruined me. I found myself reading the backs of the boxes, how many calories per serving, how much cholesterol. I wondered what kinds of hormones the poultry had been injected with. I pronounced the names of the preservatives—potassium nitrate, erythorbic acid, L-cysteine—as though memorizing a dangerous chemistry lesson.

I was surprised to see Lance, the manager of the grocery, working the checkout counter. His shirtsleeves were rolled up. His forearms glistened. A cashier had quit all of a sudden, he explained. He cocked an amused eyebrow at my purchases.

"What's up, Kenneth? David out of town?"

I made a noncommittal sound. It surprised and embarrassed me that he knew our food habits so intimately.

I liked Lance. David and I ran into him once in a while at a pub or a café, and he would come over to say hello or introduce the man he was with. He was good at telling jokes. Though David said he was a show-off, I enjoyed his quirky humor. But I wasn't about to discuss my situation with him.

I was no longer hungry by the time I got back to the apartment. Still, I put the nuggets in the oven. I searched in the closet for the video games I had put away soon after David moved in. I dusted off my N64 and loaded my old save from *GoldenEye*. I was pleased to discover that although I had not played for a year and a half, my reflexes were as good as ever. When the nuggets were done, I ate a plateful. It was novel, even enjoyable, to eat something that tasted different from the organic-Euro-Austin-gourmet cuisine that I had grown used to with David. After dinner, I planned to delete David's number from my cell phone. I planned to get on Facebook and change my status to single. Maybe even block him from my page. But when I fished out the phone, it seemed like too much effort. Instead, I went to the fridge and took out a Klondike bar. My mother used to give them to me as special treats during my childhood. I bit into it, hoping it would rekindle in me a feeling of goodness and self-worth. It did not.

Someone was at the door. I turned off the TV to make sure I wasn't hallucinating from loneliness. No. A key scrabbled against the lock. The doorknob rattled. There were thumping sounds, obscured by the pounding of my shameless heart. I threw the Klondike into the trash and covered it up with a used paper towel. I composed my face into forgiveness.

When I opened the door, I did not find a repentant David. Instead, there was a disheveled woman dressed in jeans and a bulky sweater. I guessed her to be Indian or Middle Eastern, in her fifties. She appeared confused. At first she spoke in a language I did not understand. Then she said, "Why is my key not fitting? Why are you in my apartment?" Her speech indicated that she had been drinking.

I informed her that this was in fact my apartment. Disappointment made my tone sharp. I banged the door shut. I heard no more sounds.

I came back to the couch and turned on *Saturday Night Live*. That was a mistake. We watched *SNL* almost every weekend, curled together under a quilt. On those occasions, David would indulge my plebeian tastes and make buttered popcorn. Today, watching alone, I couldn't keep my mind on the actors. What was David doing? Who was he with? Breaking up, he had slid his apartment key across the table and said, "Kenneth, I'm sorry, we just don't fit well together." As though we were jigsaw pieces from two separate puzzles. After I got over my shock, I thought it a plausible reason. Now, stranded inside a night lit only by the flickering TV screen, I was assailed by doubt.

David had taken his books. The few remaining volumes—mostly texts from my college years or freebies from the bookstore—lay toppled on the shelves. I had to tilt my head to decipher the titles. *Tess of the D'Urbervilles.* Ellison's *Invisible Man. Civilization and Its Discontents. Cloud Atlas.* It dizzied me.

I considered getting another Klondike, but the thought of its intense sweetness made me queasy. Already I could feel the chicken nuggets roiling in my stomach, belligerent with grease. I decided to sleep. That was what I really needed. I had work tomorrow, for which I was thankful. I reminded myself that I enjoyed my job. I liked the bookstore. I liked my boss. I had flexible hours, intelligent customers, and medical benefits. I went into the bedroom, but it was congested with emptiness. I carried my pillows and a blanket to the sofa and lay down. I imagined David. I could not stop. I pictured him with another man, pinning him down—on a rug, perhaps, or a tabletop. David was adventurous with venues. He was smiling in a way I knew well, the side of his mouth quirking up. His hands gripped the man's hair.

The mind is a treacherous thing. Before I guessed what it was up to, it had pulled me back into our early days, when we used to lie in bed after sex, fighting sleep because we had so much to say to each other.

Sometimes I traced the outline of his face with my fingertips until he laughed and said I was tickling him.

What is more painful, the misplaced past or the runaway future? I did not know.

To give myself something else to do, I went to the door and opened it. The woman was still there, sitting with her back against the passage wall. I asked if she remembered the number of her apartment. She stared at me. I repeated the question twice. At last she rummaged in her purse and came up with a sheet of paper. I saw that she was in twenty-eight, one floor below, the apartment underneath mine. Unsuccessfully, I attempted to explain this.

There was nothing to do but help her down the stairs and unlock her door. I instructed her to lock it from inside. I was not sure how much she understood. She did not look at me or thank me. I was surprised to find that I was not annoyed by this. I waited until I heard the click of the bolt.

～✦◯

I saw her a few days later in the apartment parking lot when I returned from the bookstore. She was struggling with a couple of grocery bags. When she noticed me, she looked away. This was how I knew that she remembered.

In my David days I would have ignored her. I heard his voice in my head, where it seemed to have taken up permanent residence. *Better leave her alone, Ken. It's easy to get tangled in someone's troubles but hard to cut free.*

I introduced myself and offered to carry one of her bags. Perhaps it was an act of rebellion. Perhaps I merely wanted a reason to delay my return to my apartment. She appeared suspicious but finally nodded. The bag I carried contained an assortment of microwave meals and two bottles of cheap wine. I set it on her kitchen counter and waited. For what, I wasn't sure. Her face was blotched; there were bags under her eyes. Still, I could see that she had once been beautiful. When the silence rose to a certain level of discomfort, I said goodbye. I was at the door before she asked if I would like some chai.

The apartment was full of boxes, most of them unopened. Styrofoam pellets littered the floor. She rummaged around, finally locating a saucepan and mismatched cups. The tea was pungent with strange spices, nothing like the beverage I drank at the cafés David and I frequented. Had frequented, I mean.

Her name was Bela Dewan. Her story was not uncommon, at least the parts she told me. Some time back, she had had a difficult divorce. Last week she had moved from Houston to Austin, hoping to start over. She was looking for work.

What kind of work? I asked.

Mrs. Dewan confessed that she had no degrees or training. She had been a caregiver in a preschool, but that was years ago. "All this time I was a full-time wife and mother," she said. "Now I've been fired from both jobs."

Her prospects did not sound promising. But I told her I would ask around.

～✲◟

The next time I went to the grocery, I stopped by Lance's office to ask if he was looking to replace the cashier who had quit.

"I already found someone," he said, "but if you want to come and work for me, I'll fire her right now." Was this a joke? His eyes glinted in a way that made me wonder. His shirt was partially unbuttoned. I could see the hollow at his neck, the tanned, taut skin below. In his ear, he wore an iron stud, a foxy touch. Now that David was gone, I was free to notice such things. The thought filled me with a kind of desolation.

I told him about Mrs. Dewan.

"Sorry," he said. "I don't hire people without experience." I must have looked disappointed, because he added, "I'll talk to her since she's a friend of yours. But tell her not to get her hopes up."

Gloomily, I thanked him and turned to leave. I was already thinking about other places where Mrs. Dewan might work. A hardware store? A restaurant? I was at the door when Lance said, "I ran into David last night at Harry's."

Had David been with someone else? Harry's was a dance club, so I guessed yes. Had he said anything to Lance about breaking up with me? From the curious sympathy in Lance's eyes, I guessed yes again.

"I have to go," I said.

～☙

The world never ceases to surprise. How had I forgotten that?

A couple of days later, Mrs. Dewan came by my apartment to tell me that Lance had hired her as a shelf-stocker. To show her appreciation, she invited me over for an Indian dinner.

This presented me with a dilemma.

I was familiar with Indian food, introduced to it by friends in college. I did not care for it. The curries I encountered in restaurants were too hot. The heavy sauces gave me heartburn. Even David had not been able to cure me of this culinary timidity. When we went out for Indian, I made my meal out of rice and raita, resentfully picking green chilies out of the yogurt. Leaving me, David had said, "Kenneth, you never want to try anything new." This was blatantly unfair. I had made my loyal way through any number of his concoctions, from cotija-and-chili-stuffed enchiladas to pear bok-choy soup. "Living with you," he added sadly, "is like slowly sinking into mud."

Now I decided to prove him wrong. I informed Mrs. Dewan that I would be happy to come, though I did mention that I preferred my food mild and recognizable.

The evening began well. Mrs. Dewan had risen to the challenge posed by my finicky stomach. She named the dishes in Bengali, her language, writing them down for me on a paper napkin. The triangular appetizers were singaras. They were stuffed with cauliflower. Dessert was a light caramelized yogurt, mishti doi. The chicken simmering in a mild yogurt gravy was murgir jhol. The yellow lentils were muger dal, seasoned with whole cumin. Cumin was a digestive, Mrs. Dewan informed me. "My daughter Tara—she, too, has a fussy stomach," she said. "That's how I learned to cook this way."

I wondered where Tara-of-the-fussy-stomach was at this time, when her mother could have done with some family support. I knew not to ask.

Over dinner, Mrs. Dewan opened a large bottle of wine and told me about Kolkata, the city where she had lived before marriage. Life in Kolkata seemed dangerous and exhilarating. Kolkatans loved desserts; they thought nothing of traveling across the traffic-choked city to the famous sweet shop Mrs. Dewan's mother owned to sample her Durga Mohan. Streets flooded during the monsoons, so that as a girl Mrs. Dewan had to ride a pull-rickshaw to school. During her college years, when the Naxals were in power, she had once come across the body of a young man in an alley, the word *traitor* cut into his forehead.

In reciprocation, I offered her tidbits from my youth in Waco. I went to church with my parents twice a week, listening with fascination as our pastor eloquently described the devil and the myriad snares with which he pulled us to hell. I got drunk with high school friends in the back of the Target parking lot. In my senior year, I took long, solitary walks along the rain-drenched Brazos River, tortured by the suspicion that I didn't belong. Mrs. Dewan listened, her brows creased in fascination, as though my stories were as exotic as hers. Perhaps, to her, they were.

By the end of the evening, we were pleasantly inebriated. When I was leaving, she asked if we could do this again next week.

The David-voice inside me whispered, *Careful, Ken. I'm telling you this for your own good. Leave her alone. She clearly has problems.*

To the voice I said, *Who doesn't?*

To Mrs. Dewan I said, "Love to."

I was surprised by how much I looked forward to our dinners. We met at my place one week and hers the next. It gave me a reason to clean up. I suspect it was the same for her. She still hadn't unpacked most of her boxes, but when I came over, they would be lined up neatly against the wall and shrouded with colorful saris.

After a couple of disastrous culinary episodes, we decided that she should be responsible for the food. I brought the libations. The trick was to provide enough alcohol to put her at ease without getting her drunk. I managed this by mixing her numerous weak, fruity drinks. Sometimes she gave me a glance indicating that she was on to my strategy, but she did not complain. It seemed that she was drinking less than before. Perhaps it was my imagination. These evenings, we stayed up too late. Next day I would wake bleary-eyed and require twice my usual dose of caffeine in order to make it to the bookstore. It must have been harder on Mrs. Dewan since she worked the morning shift. But I never heard Lance complain, so clearly, somehow, she managed.

I was unsure as to how to classify our relationship. We were friends, but also something else. Sometimes we played video games. (I played while Mrs. Dewan applauded.) Sometimes we watched Indian movies. (She paused them to translate; the subtitles were cryptic and mystifying.) Mostly we talked. I found myself speaking to Mrs. Dewan the way I might have to an older sister or a favorite aunt. In reality I had no siblings, and my aunt was a harridan with whom I communicated as infrequently as possible.

Often we chatted about inconsequential things. Mrs. Dewan liked to hear about the quirks of the authors who did readings at our store. I invited her to attend the events, but she refused. Crowds made her nervous. She also liked hearing about the store's latest acquisitions, though she never bought any of them. Best of all, she liked me to recount the plots of novels I had read. Her favorite genre was domestic noir. If the boyfriend or husband was revealed to be the killer, she would suck in her breath, delighted.

"I knew it," she'd say. "I just knew it!"

In return she would tell me stories she had heard in childhood, gruesome Bengali folktales filled with foolish kings who got their noses chopped off and unlucky criminals who were buried alive in holes filled with thorns.

Sometimes, as the night progressed, we would get personal. She told me more about Tara, who had dropped out of school, then cut herself off from Mrs. Dewan soon after the divorce. "She acted like the whole thing was my fault," she said, sounding astonished. I told her about Tufts, our black Labrador, and how I would come home from school and whisper into his ear the humiliations of the day. They were many, because I was a boy who attracted bullies the way garbage attracts flies.

Mrs. Dewan hadn't been able to reach Tara for years, though she had left her contact information at every address she could find for her daughter. Through the Indian grapevine, Mrs. Dewan heard that Tara had become involved with drugs. "I called her cell phone," she said, "but she wouldn't pick up. I even went to the university and talked to her classmates in case they knew anything. I was so frantic, for days I drove around the Montrose area. I never did find her. Finally, the dorm people packed up Tara's stuff and mailed it to me. That's what's in the big box in the corner, in case Tara ever comes by."

My happiest childhood memories were of taking Tufts for his daily walk, just him and me. Walking behind him, holding his leash, I believed myself to be useful. I didn't even mind cleaning up after him. Then Tufts developed cancer. The vet said he would have to be put down. I wanted to go with him to the clinic, but my parents would not let me. I was too young, they said. Later they told me he had passed away peacefully. I did not believe this.

"I sometimes dream about Tufts," I told Mrs. Dewan. "His eyes are wide, his body spasming. He swings his head from side to side, looking for me." It was something I had never discussed with anyone.

Mrs. Dewan said, "Oh, my. I have dreams like that." I waited for details, but all she said was, "My husband once poisoned a dog."

Sometimes, lying in bed sleepless, I thought about Mrs. Dewan. She appeared so ordinary. Yet she had lived a life filled with violence and mystery. Once, when she was a child, a magician—or perhaps it was a hypnotist—had tried to kidnap her. It amazed me that I had become friends with such a woman.

There were things we did not speak of at our dinners. Mrs. Dewan did not bring up her drinking problem. Or the details of her divorce. Or why she had not returned to India, where her dollars would surely have ensured her an easier life. I did not mention David's defection, or how often I found myself thinking of him. I did not describe how I had come home from college during my second semester and told my parents that I was gay. My parents had not condemned or disowned me. They had turned to me faces stricken with an incomprehension that was worse.

❧⚬

Something was wrong.

David would have caught it sooner. He was a more perceptive man than I. But even I could see that our dinners were dwindling—just a lentil dish and egg curry, the rice not basmati but generic long-grain. Mrs. Dewan spoke with her usual animation, inscribing hieroglyphs in the air with her hands. But she hardly ate anything. She said she was dieting. She wanted to lose the twenty pounds she had gained since the divorce. But one night when she was in the bathroom I checked her kitchen. The cabinets were bare except for a box of cornflakes and a few cans of beans. In the fridge were a reduced-price bag of mini-donuts and a half bottle of wine. Once when I stopped by unannounced, the apartment was sweltering; the air conditioner was turned off.

"Heat doesn't bother me," Mrs. Dewan said, surreptitiously wiping her sweaty forehead on her arm.

She was running out of money.

This surprised me. I had guessed that the grocery job would not pay for all her expenses, but I had thought she would have a sizable alimony. She had been married for over twenty years. I hesitated to ask—she had tried hard to keep her financial problems a secret from me—but finally I had to know.

"I'm not getting any alimony right now," she said. "Mr. Dewan filed for bankruptcy last year."

The situation sounded suspicious. I advised her to get a lawyer. But she shook her head vehemently and changed the topic.

I stopped by Lance's office again and asked if he could find Mrs. Dewan additional work. She was a good cook. Might his clientele be interested in a Saturday cooking demonstration?

"This woman really means a lot to you, doesn't she?" he said. What he meant was, *Why?*

I shrugged. I was not sure of the answer.

"We can try it out next weekend," he said. "I'll ask her to make something Indian, something popular. If sales go up enough, she can continue." He stared at a spot on his desk. "Do you want to go out sometime?"

My chest felt like it was too small to contain all the things knocking around inside it. Heart, lungs, excitement, a surge of blood like sorrow. The backwash of memories. Finally I said, "I'm sorry. It's too soon."

It was. I spent most of my free time at home, surfing the Net. I had a hard time sleeping. Late at night, I would go down to the gym on the ground floor and run on the treadmill until I was soaked with sweat. I tried to go out a couple of times, but it was too stressful, even when I hung with a group of friends. Their silent glances weighed on me. I wanted to denounce David. I wanted to defend his defection. Each time the door to the bar opened, my throat clenched. I feared it would be him. When it was not, I was pierced by disappointment.

I was concerned that Lance would be angered by my reply. That he would cancel Mrs. Dewan's gig. Some men would have done it. But he said, "I'll check again in a couple weeks. Maybe you'll feel different by then."

At noon on Saturday, Mrs. Dewan gave her first demonstration. I had put up flyers in the bookstore and told my coworkers, and Lance had placed announcement boards around the store. About fifteen people showed up—better than I had expected. When Mrs. Dewan emerged from the back, wearing an apron and chef's cap, she looked terrified. She stumbled over her words as she explained the dish she was cooking: chicken tikka masala. Her hand shook when she held up the bottled sauce she was using. Her accent was heavier than usual. She would not make eye contact. Things improved a bit when she began to sauté the chicken and no longer had to look at her audience. She dished the pieces into little paper cups and speared them efficiently with toothpicks. But when customers crowded around her with compliments and questions, she lost her nerve and fled to the storage area. Lance had to take over and guide people to the aisles where they could buy the ingredients she had used.

There was an event that night at the bookstore, so I had turned off my cell phone. When I turned it back on, I discovered that Mrs. Dewan had called several times. She had not spoken, though I could hear her breathing above the static. I found this troubling.

Told you, said the David-voice.

Technically, since she had not left a message, I was not obliged to call her back. At midnight I gave in and phoned.

"I am a failure," she said, in the slow, formal intonation of the inebriated. "I have let you down. Lance says I must improve my customer interaction skills."

"Please go to sleep," I said, though I knew the futility of such advice. "We can discuss this later. I'm sure we can come up with a strategy."

"I've never cooked from a bottle." She was weeping now. "And chicken tikka—why, it's not even real Indian."

I did not fully understand her grief, but I said, "Let's talk tomorrow when our brains are clearer." I was pleased at my reasonable tone because David had sometimes claimed that I was an unreasonable man.

As I was falling into sleep, it struck me, the shameful answer to Lance's unspoken question. Mrs. Dewan was important to me because she was worse off than I was. I found it easy to be reasonable with her because her life made me feel less wretched about my own.

~⌒

Over the week, Mrs. Dewan and I went over her demonstration, discussing what she did well and what needed improvement. We came up with a list of recipes that were authentic enough for her and easy enough for her audience. She practiced answering questions. She practiced accepting compliments. She practiced smiling. She watched chefs perform flashy moves on my TV and tried a couple of them herself. She did better the next weekend, and when I took a photo of her, she managed a smile. She was still timid about speaking to strangers, but there was no mistaking her talent. People loved her shrimp in coconut-milk gravy. Perhaps they responded to her shyness, too. To the fact that this was not easy for her. Afterward, they bought so many items that Lance decided to give Mrs. Dewan two sets of cooking gigs on Saturdays, and the same on Sundays. A couple of weeks later, reconnoitering again, I was pleased to see that her kitchen shelves were not as empty as before.

Lance and I went out one weekend. He came by the apartment to pick me up. On our way downstairs, we ran into Mrs. Dewan. She was on the small balcony next to the staircase landing. She liked to stand there in the evening, watching people return home. We exchanged greetings. She asked where we were going and nodded knowledgeably when I mentioned the name of the restaurant, though I was sure she had not heard of it. As we were about to get into our car, she leaned out from the balcony and shouted, "Have a good time, boys."

"Is she always this nosy?" Lance asked. "That would drive me crazy."

I considered the question. Mrs. Dewan and I had fallen into the habit of chatting on the phone every night. During these conversations, she told me about her day and asked, with great interest, about mine. I quite liked these nightly exchanges. I did not have anyone else who considered the details of my humdrum life worth such attention.

I could not tell this to Lance. "I don't mind it," I said.

"You're a good man, Ken," he said.

I accepted the compliment. It was easier than trying to explain.

We had an enjoyable time at dinner. Lance was funny, which I had known, but smarter than I had expected, more worldly. He told me about his backpacking adventures in Slovenia this past summer. "Maybe we can go together next time," he said.

My stomach gave a small lurch, part from excitement and part at the thought of strange Slovenian foods, blood sausages and whatnot. "That sounds great," I said.

Later we went for a walk along Town Lake. The setting sun had turned the water orange-pink. In the distance we could see the Austin skyline, and against it, the colonies of bats that had emerged from under the bridges. I had not been out in nature in a long time. David was more the museums-movies-clubs type. The bats milled around. I told Lance that they looked like tangled skeins of black silk. It was a poor analogy, but he laughed and said, "Why, Ken, you're a poet." Then he kissed me.

All of a sudden, my head was full of David. David rubbing my calf after I had pulled a muscle jogging, David cooking for us, holding up a forkful of fettuccine for me to taste, David reading out to me from *A Heartbreaking Work of Staggering Genius*, dissolving in laughter before he reached the end of a funny passage. I pulled away. I couldn't help it, though I was angry with my stupidity. Lance's face went dark. It stayed that way even after I apologized and he said he understood. That was the end of the evening.

⟞⟝

One night, after our weekly dinner, Mrs. Dewan said, "Kenneth, I want to show you something." She ripped the tape off a box in the corner and took out a package wrapped in a fine white woolen shawl. When she shook it out, I saw that it was a beautiful silk costume, long and skirt-like, red with a gold border and a fitted blouse.

"It's my dance costume," she said. "I couldn't bring much from India when I came to this country—I ran away from home with just a suit-case. But I made sure to bring this." She held up ankle bells on long cords. There were a lot of bells because she had studied dance for many years. "I used to love dancing. I was good at both Kathak and Rabindra Nritya. I performed in front of hundreds of people. Me. Can you imag-ine? When the auditorium went dark and the spotlight was focused on me, I felt a thrill like I've never felt since. Moving to the beat of the tabla, I forgot my life." She gave a sigh. "I'd love to wear it again, to dance so I can forget like that, even for a few minutes. But I can't fit into it anymore." She pinched at the flab of her underarm, making a face.

An excitement blazed through me. Perhaps all of us have a bit of Pygmalion in us. "You can do it," I said. "We'll make a plan."

Our plan progressed well. Mrs. Dewan went for walks, morning and evening. She cut out carbs and fats from her diet, including the donuts she was so fond of. Her dinners grew innovative, though no less deli-cious: quinoa upma, rutis made from chickpea flour, grilled masala chicken wrapped in lettuce leaf, mango glacé topped with rose petals.

"You should write a cookbook," I said. "You're so good, I bet you'd be a hit. I know a couple of publishers who might be interested. Would you like me to introduce you?"

She had a considering look on her face. "Maybe."

"You could start with a blog. I write one for our bookstore. It isn't difficult. I'll set it up for you. You can call it *Bela's Kitchen*."

She laughed. "*Bela's Kitchen*. I like that." She extended her glass. "Could you please pour me another?"

I obliged. Today our drink, which I had made, was a frothy lassi with crushed pomegranate seeds. Mrs. Dewan was making a serious effort to give up alcohol. She announced that she had lost two inches from around her waist in two weeks.

"You're doing great," I said. "I'm proud of you." I meant it.

"Now if only I could find you a girlfriend," she said, "things would be perfect."

I stared at her, dismayed. I supposed I sometimes passed, but I had assumed that she would know about me from my comb-over fade, my red Converses. From seeing Lance's arm around my shoulders when we went out. Now I saw that despite her years in this country, she wasn't familiar enough with America to pick up on the signs. I knew I should tell her, but I couldn't bear to. I didn't want to see on her the look that had taken over my parents' faces. I didn't want to lose her.

"Sorry, sorry," Mrs. Dewan said, laughing. "I'm being a nosy auntie, just like those neighbor women who used to drive me crazy when I was a girl. I won't bring it up again."

⚓︎

It had been a harrying day. Our store had booked a bestselling author and hired a large theater venue. The author, who was to arrive next week, was notorious for being temperamental. I had been fielding calls all day from his publicist about the items he required during his visit. No music in the car. Water: only Evian, with the limes cut open in front of him. For dinner before the event, Thai food, authentic but mild. He did not like air-conditioning. It made his eyes dry out.

I ventured to say that no air-conditioning in Austin in the summer was a bad idea.

"No air-conditioning," the agent repeated. "Also, no photography, no taping, no questions after the talk. And no cell phones. This one's really important. He's been known to storm off the stage if a cell phone rings."

It was my night to dine with Mrs. Dewan in her apartment, but first I needed to decompress. I threw down a stack of notes that I had to go over later, turned on the CD player, and got a chilled beer. Mrs. Dewan had recently started going to meetings, so I did my drinking before dinner. I had just put my feet up on the coffee table when she knocked. Sometimes she ran out of ingredients and came over to check if I had them. I never did, but I think it made her feel neighborly to be able to do this.

I opened the door. It was David. A thinner, more somber David. He had shaved his head. It made him look monkish and sexy. He carried two of my shirts, ironed and neatly folded. He looked nervous, which was not his normal condition. I wanted to hate him. I was halfway to forgiving him.

"I found these among my clothes," he said. "I thought I should return them."

He could have left them outside the door. We both knew that.

The world never ceases to surprise. Did I mention this already?

"Would you like to come in?" I said. My hands were sweaty. Inside my chest an ocean heaved and crashed and heaved again.

"I would," he said. I saw his Adam's apple jerk as he swallowed. "Thank you."

I was distracted by that thank-you. We had moved past the language of formality long ago. It was strange to relearn it with each other. "You're welcome," I said.

We sat on the couch next to each other, staring at the blank rectangle of the TV screen. Around us, like the soundtrack to a bad movie, rose the sounds of Simon & Garfunkel's "Bridge Over Troubled Water." I picked up the remote to turn it off, but he put his hand over mine. His nails were blunt and wholesome and familiar. It took all my effort not to turn my wrist and clasp his hand.

"How are you doing?" he asked.

"Okay," I said. He was waiting, but I didn't ask him anything.

"I'm not doing so well," he said. "I miss you." He ran a thumb along my jaw. Then his mouth was on mine. He tasted, unexpectedly, of blackberries.

After that, things moved in and out of focus. His shirt hanging unbuttoned. The dip of his navel. The slight softness to his belly, which I've always loved. His impatient hands on my belt buckle. I banged my shin against a chair and heard it topple to the floor. I don't remember how we got to the bed, but there we were, straining against each other on the blue quilt he had bought me as our first anniversary gift, whispering into each other the special names we had created for such moments.

He heard the knocking on the door before I did and stopped midmotion.

"Kenneth?" I heard Mrs. Dewan call out. "I heard a crash. I was worried because you're usually down for dinner by this time. Kenneth, are you there?"

"Dinner?" David said. "Usually?" He looked at me. "Who the hell is this woman?"

"Just the downstairs neighbor," I said. "I'll explain later." I felt absurdly guilty and annoyed for feeling this way. I pressed against David, trying to get him to continue, though I feared the moment was lost.

"Kenneth," Mrs. Dewan said, knocking again. Her voice was unsteady. "Are you okay? Can you talk? Do you need help? Shall I call the ambulance?"

"Ambulance?" said David. His raised eyebrow said, *Oh, Ken, what kind of crazy mess did you get yourself into while I was away?*

I was not sure which of us three I was most angry with. "I'm fine, Mrs. Dewan," I said, making my voice cheery and casual. "I've just been delayed. Please go back to your apartment. I'll see you in a bit."

"You sure?" She sounded calmer now, about to leave.

"I'm sure."

But David was off the bed already. "Stop!" I called. He yanked his arm away, shrugged on the robe hanging on the door hook—a green yukata, another of his elegant gifts—and strode to the door. I barely had enough time to pull on my jeans before he threw it open.

"Ken's busy right now," he said.

"Who are you?" Mrs. Dewan's voice was suspicious.

"My name is David," he said. "I'm Ken's boyfriend."

I saw Mrs. Dewan staring past him at the bedroom, where I stood half naked. In the dim light of the passage, I could not make out the look on her face before she turned away. But I saw the slump of her shoulders. I heard the heavy clatter of her footsteps receding down the corridor.

Over the next few days, I called Mrs. Dewan numerous times. She did not pick up. I sent her texts. She did not reply. I waited around the staircase to catch her, but she was orchestrating her arrivals and departures carefully to avoid me. I stopped by the grocery during her shift. Usually she would be stocking shelves or tidying up after customers. Now she was nowhere to be seen. Finally, I asked Lance. It was awkward. We hadn't spoken to each other since the botched date, only nodded across the corrugations of checkout lanes.

He gave me a look. I was not sure what it meant. Overnight, I had become expressions-illiterate.

"Maybe she's in the back," he said. "Avoiding you."

I walked to the storage area and peered through the glazed plastic sheeting into the bowels of the store. Employees scuttled around trays of bread, carts mounded with carrots and kale. I could not find Mrs. Dewan. "Excuse me, sir," a plump Asian woman in overalls said as she pushed a dolly loaded with laundry detergent past me, "customers are not allowed in here."

David and I had had a fight that night, the fight we did not have when he left.

"You didn't tell her, did you?" he said.

"You are not my boyfriend," I said.

"Why didn't you tell her?"

"What gives you the right to ask me?"

"Ken," he said in his reasonable voice, "I still care about you as a person. Whatever this codependent thing is that you have going on with her, it's unhealthy."

"Please go," I said. The traitor part of me wanted him to refuse. To insist on staying. But he left.

After four days, I stopped calling Mrs. Dewan. What was the use? *Let her turn away from who I am*, I thought. *I don't care.* But it was untrue, just as it had been untrue with my parents. I felt restless and feverish. At work I paced up and down, and people looked at me strangely. At night my head swarmed with troubled thoughts. Had I pushed Mrs. Dewan back into alcoholism? Had I, in telling David to leave, made a dreadful mistake? In my imagination, Mrs. Dewan tilted back her head and drank straight from the bottle, wine spilling redly down her chin. In my imagination, I grew old and shriveled in my empty bed as the years limped by. In the mornings, I felt hungover. A headache squeezed my brain. I took double doses of aspirin. They did nothing but roil my stomach.

In the middle of all this, the famous author arrived, sweaty and irritable. I had forgotten the limes to go with his Evian. Things devolved rapidly after that. At the restaurant I had chosen, he said, "You call this pad Thai?" Introducing him at the event, I stumbled over the name of a major prize he had won. In spite of my request to turn off phones, one rang during his talk. He threw a tantrum onstage, making certain comments about Texans. People shouted back. Some walked out. Books were not sold. I knew I would pay for it when I met with the bookstore owner the next day.

It was midnight by the time I got back. I had stopped at a 7-Eleven on the way and picked up a six-pack of beer, which I consumed in the car. My headache was so bad that even my jaw hurt. I dragged myself up to my apartment and stood outside the door, staring at the dark vortex of the peephole. Then I made my way down to Mrs. Dewan's apartment, taking the stairs one shaky step at a time. I punched the bell. She did not answer.

"Okay, Mrs. Dewan," I shouted. "This has gone on long enough. I'm not leaving until we have a talk." I sat down on the doormat and leaned against the door. It was strangely restful. I found myself drifting off. It was a sensation like falling backward. No, it was a falling backward. Mrs. Dewan had jerked open the door. I found myself lying in her entryway, staring up at her. Her face appeared, upside down. For a moment I thought she was smiling, but it was only a turned-around grimace.

"Go away," she said.

"Not until we talk," I said.

"Oh, God," she said. "You're drunk." She tried to push the door closed, but my body was in the way. Finally she said crossly, "Five minutes."

At the table she moved aside her laptop—I saw that she had been typing a recipe for singaras for *Bela's Kitchen*—and set down a large glass of ice water and a jar of Tiger Balm. As an afterthought, she brought out a packet of saltines. I ignored the insult of the saltines and drank the water in small, offended sips. The Tiger Balm smelled vile. I pushed it back at her. The things I wanted to say, apologies and accusations, crowded my mouth but refused to give themselves up.

Mrs. Dewan said, "I can't believe you'd keep such an important part of your life from me! Why did you do it? And you could have told me about David."

I searched for the right words. One of my Indian friends at college, also gay, also cut off from his family, had told me they had thought his condition—that was the word they used—a perversion.

"I didn't want you to think I was weird," I said finally. "I didn't want our dinners to stop. And David—he'd left me even before I met you." A part of my mind noted, in surprise, that it didn't hurt to say his name.

"You thought I would be upset because you were gay?" she said. "That I'd stop seeing you because of that?"

"You *were* upset when you found out," I said, with justified truculence. "You *did* stop seeing me."

"That was because you didn't trust me enough to tell me," she said angrily. "My husband, he was like that, too. Kept all kinds of things from me. Thought I wasn't strong enough to deal with them." She shredded her paper napkin into furious strips. "And this after I'd opened up my life for you, told you shameful things I hadn't ever discussed with anyone. You thought I was such a petty, prejudiced person? That's what you thought about me?"

She started on another napkin.

"I'm sorry," I said. I was no longer angry, just tired. "After I told my parents, my mother couldn't look at me. When she served me dinner, she squinted down at the plate. When she asked about my classes—the only safe subject she could come up with—she stared at a spot on the wall to the right of my head. It made me feel . . . lopsided. Finally, I stopped coming home."

Mrs. Dewan was silent. Then she leaned forward. For a moment I thought she would take my face in her hands, as one might with a child. Instead, she whispered, "I've kept things from you, too. Do you know, I caused the deaths of two, maybe three, people. People who loved me."

I must have stared. She shook her head. "I'll tell you, but not tonight. Tonight we need something different." She took away the saltines and brought rice and fried okra in two small bowls. Left over from her dinner, I guessed. I fell upon them as though I had not eaten in days.

She watched me indulgently. "Don't eat so fast," she said. "You'll get a stomachache. I'll be back in a few minutes."

She ducked into her bedroom.

Her cell phone, which she'd left on the dining table, rang, making me jump.

"It's probably Lance, with a last-minute schedule change," Mrs. Dewan said from the bedroom. "Could you pick it up for me?"

Lance. My insides lurched at the possibility. But it was a woman, most likely conducting a survey of some kind. I asked her to hold, but she hung up.

"Really!" said Mrs. Dewan. "These salespeople! You'd think they'd let people have some peace and quiet this late at night."

When she came out of the bedroom, she was wearing her dance outfit. The gold threads caught the light as she walked toward me. There was something otherworldly in the way she moved, the way she lifted her arms and spun around, the red-and-white silk blurring like an undulation of fire.

"You can fit into it!" I said.

She laughed, her face mischievous, merry like a girl's. "Surprised you, didn't I? I cheated and let out the sides. I figured it'll never fit me otherwise. I didn't want to waste any more of my life waiting."

How had I imagined I could be Pygmalion to a woman like this?

She put on some music. Drum and flute, I think. She played it soft, because it was dreadfully late, a time when all good men and women, or at least the practical ones, had gone to bed. Then she danced for me.

Medical History: 2015

Patient's Name
Sanjay Kumar Dewan

It was his grandmother who gave him the name (which meant victory), holding him wrapped in red malmal cloth for luck. There was a celebration feast in Ranchi, where his father was a teacher in the city's best school. A hundred guests were invited because he was the first son.

He's not sure how he knows this. An old photo maybe, or a story, or merely a craving inside, because his grandmother died within the year, and his parents in a train crash when he was five. So much for the luck of red malmal. He was brought to Kolkata to live in the reluctant household of his uncle, where he became Sheno, the name usually coupled with an invective, son-of-a-dog-Sheno, burnt-face-Sheno, brainless-ape-Sheno, haramzada-Sheno, and followed by a clout to the ears. But he survived it, so perhaps there was luck after all, tucked like a stolen rupee note into the waistband of a ragged pajama. More luck came with Bishu, his friend who softened his name to Shonu and saved his life. In college he dived into the danger of Communist politics, became a hero, you might say. Car-

ried a Nepali kukri, bought secondhand in Chora Bazaar—not that he ever used it. On its blade was a dull stain that he liked to think was blood. Sanjay-da, his juniors called him, their eyes lowered in respect. He was Shona to his sweetheart Bela, who flew to him from India, straight as an arrow. He would have done anything for her then. But he lost her somewhere in Texas—or was it the love that went missing? To his daughter Tara, he was once the world. Now he's a blocked number, an erased name, a swiveling away of the shoulders should they chance to meet. Ah, enough of that. To his professional contacts he's Jay; to his bar buddies he's J.D. On the carpet in front of their fireplace, his current girlfriend grabs fistfuls of his hair and screams, bucking as she comes, *Jayman! Jayman!* Like he's some kind of superhero. From Sanjay Kumar in Ranchi, India, to Jayman here in Oakland, California, it's been— pardon the pun—quite the ride.

But today Sanjay is stuck in the doctor's office—a new doctor, since he goes through them quickly—filling out this idiot form, because last night he had a breathing episode.

The office is generic, nothing to write home about. (But even if it was, where is the home he would write to?) Pukey pastel colors, the mandatory mid-sized aquarium, carpet chosen to camouflage accidents of various natures, an odor like resignation, patients at various stages of decrepitude slumped in their chairs, careful not to make eye contact, as though you could catch something that way.

Today's Date
July 13, 2015

Something about this day nags at him like an ache in a phantom limb. It's not just how old he's become, sixty-plus, though that astonishes him from time to time, as though he were the victim of some trick, the pages of the calendar flipping fast, then faster, like in TV cartoons. This morning, for instance, he'd looked in his bathroom mirror and was shocked by the baggy-eyed apparition confronting him. His girlfriend didn't make things any better, emerging from the shower right at that moment, all perky breasts and cacophonous concern. *Oooh, honey bear, you look like death warmed up. Do you feel okay? I'm going to call the doctor's office right now. No, don't even try to talk me out of it.*

He'd glared at her, recognizing anew their age difference. A younger Sanjay would have decimated her with sarcasm. But today his brain was working at glacial speed. The best retort he could come up with was, *Don't call me honey bear.* His only victory: he refused to let her drive him here.

Now he remembers. It's the fifteenth anniversary of his divorce.

It was a day he had waited for with fierce eagerness, though it is hard to remember what exactly he had hoped would happen. That he would float into the sky, untethered and shiny as a helium balloon? That he would shed his polite, discolored smile and emerge more dangerous and attractive than he'd ever been? That he would take off for a sunset on a tropical island with a special someone? It hadn't worked out like that, though there had been a woman. (Her name? Nope, it's gone AWOL.) They'd flown to Vegas for a weekend where they drank too much and won an indecent amount at blackjack and then lost it and more elsewhere. Somehow they ended up at a police station, an inch away from being slammed in the locker, except he'd been able to talk his way out of it. He was good at that.

But the resentment he'd longed to escape settled back on his shoulders all too soon, like ash on the overcoat of a man watching in fascination a building going up in flames. Later, he brushes and brushes it, but the coat is ruined.

And the revenge he had hoped to exact? That he got, yes. But it cost him.

Date of Birth
October 7, 1950

Funny to think that for years he didn't know when his birthday was. They didn't celebrate it in his uncle's house, and even as a six-year-old he knew not to ask. There were parties for his uncle's two daughters, giggly round-faced girls whose features he has forgotten. But the food he remembers. Sugary twists of jalebis from the street-side shop. Singaras stuffed with spicy potatoes. And rice pudding with raisins and almonds as a once-a-year treat because his uncle wasn't a rich man. One time his aunt gave him some, after the girls' friends were done eating. Sitting here in the doctor's office, he can still taste those delicious, grudging spoonfuls. He got them because she was superstitious and believed it would bring her daughter bad luck otherwise. *Have you seen how he watches them eat?* she had hissed to her husband. *Have you seen his eyes?* His uncle told her not to be ridiculous. *He's just a kid.* But he was too tired, after a long workday at the post office, to argue further with her.

That night, the dream was born. He, Sanjay Kumar, would grow up and make a mountain of money and throw an enormous party for himself on every birthday. Lying on his lumpy mattress in the dank room he shared with Gopal the servant, he imagined it: mutton pastries from New Market, shrimp cutlets from Bhabanipur, three kinds of ice cream from Magnolia's, a Flury's fruitcake big as a table. Foods that he'd only heard of. Places of myth festooned with stars. There would be an acrobat, a clown, even a dancing bear, why not. He would invite his uncle and his cousins and especially his aunt and force them to eat until they got sick from it, the too-rich food and his too-much success.

As you might imagine, that never happened.

Other things happened, though, almost as impossible.

In America he found out he had a nose for sniffing out the best deals. He became scandalously successful, though sometimes this meant he wandered into less-than-legal alleyways. He bought the bigger house on the hill, the sports car, the tailored suits, the club memberships. His life would have been a cliché, if it hadn't been for baby Tara. She wanted her father, only him. He was the one who crooned her to sleep, off-key, though Bela was the better singer. When she was restless with the colic, he walked her up and down for hours. One night she had the stomach flu and threw up on his only designer jacket. Bela was horrified—*Oh, God, it's the Valentino*—but he didn't care. When Tara pushed her mother away and clung to him instead, it made his chest swell with secret victory.

But back to his birthday. Once, early in their marriage, he had mentioned to Bela his cake-less childhood. He had regretted it immediately, hating the way pity had clouded her eyes. But it was too late.

From then on, his birthday became their family's biggest celebration. Bela made him cakes from scratch, layered with fresh strawberries and buttercream, embellished decadently with coconut-almond frosting. She cooked dinners over which their guests sighed in envious pleasure: an Italian feast, all the way from antipasti to gelato; a Hawaiian luau, complete with roasted pig and leis. Oceans of wine and vodka and gin and scotch to toast him with, and for his fortieth birthday, a chorus girl dressed only in colored feathers. As good as any dancing bear, wouldn't you say?

Only, it wasn't.

It's hot in this room; he's sweating into his collar. He considers telling the plump blonde behind the glass-walled counter to turn up the air conditioner. But just as he pushes himself to his feet, she gets up and disappears into a hidden corridor, as though she knew what he was about to ask.

Which of the following conditions are you currently being treated for or have been treated for in the past?
Heart disease/murmur/angina

He pauses at this one. *You don't have a heart, you bastard,* Bela had screamed at him when he moved out of the house. Would that qualify as a disease? Over the years other women have accused him of similar things. Even Bishu had stared at him toward the end, his brows scrunched up. *You've changed, Shonu. What's happened to you?* But Sanjay-Shonu-Shona, well on his way to emancipation by then, had smiled like he didn't know what Bishu was talking about.

Sometimes his heart murmurs to him. *Tara*, it says. *Tara-Tara-Tara.*
He's generally dexterous at ignoring things he doesn't want to pay attention to, but his heart, it knows how to get beneath his skin.

Puns. They'll be the death of him.

Shortness of breath

Yes, this is the one he's here for, the way it comes upon him unexpectedly when he's playing blackjack, or talking to his broker, or messing around with his girlfriend, or paying her bills (younger women are expensive), or giving in to rage. Yesterday, after he received the call about Tara from the private investigator, he had to lie down. The breathlessness pounced upon him, worse than ever before. He's not scared of much. But that desperate hunger for air, that feeling of spiraling into blackness: okay, he admits it, it was terrifying.

He knows what the doctor will say. He's heard it before. *Quit.* All those cigarettes, especially the nonfiltered ones in India Bishu and he shared because that's all they could afford, they've ruined his lungs. He's damned if he'll give them up, though. He's not sure he can. Faithful, uncomplaining, they've been with him longer than any human in his life.

There's got to be another solution. There always is. That's the motto he's lived by, and except in one thing, it's served him well.

He looks around the room with some satisfaction. Even with all his troubles, he's better off than most of the sad sacks sitting in this room waiting to die. He'd bet his last dollar on it.

Describe any current or past medical treatment not listed above.
Malaria

He remembers the torn mosquito net, dug up from some rag pile by his aunt. She smiled as she handed it to him, relieved because now she wouldn't have to buy a new one. *Be sure to use it. We don't want you to get sick.* By now he was good at hearing the unspoken words: *And cause us even more trouble and expense than you have already.*

Obediently, he attached strings to the loops at the corners and hung it up each night in the downstairs room. There were already nails in the wall for tying the strings to, put up by the servant, Gopal. Gopal, who resented him because he'd had to give up his spot on the wooden takta-posh for Sheno-the-usurper, and now Gopal was forced to make his bed on the damp concrete floor. That first night Sanjay heard him grunting and breathing hard, straining, then crying out in a way that made Sanjay pull his covers up over his frightened head. In the morning Gopal looked at him with narrowed eyes and made a slicing motion across his throat. But he need not have worried. There was no one in that household to whom Sanjay could have told anything.

That's why he didn't complain when the mosquitoes (particularly prolific that year because of the rains) made their merry way in through the rents in the net and raised swollen bite-bumps all over his legs. Or when the fever came upon him one evening and his teeth chattered so loudly that Gopal complained that the noise kept him up at night. Sanjay didn't mind the fever too much. It transported him back to their garden in Ranchi, his mother snipping marigolds for their altar. He could smell the wild acrid flowers. In the morning he felt like a wrung-out mop rag, too exhausted to get ready for school, or even to climb up the stairs for breakfast. His aunt sent down barley water and aspirin via Gopal, along with instructions to rest. Translation: *Don't get near my girls and make them sick, too.* No one came to see him.

Except Bishu, the neighbor boy with whom he played street football, who shook his shoulder and called his name. Shonu, Shonu. Or did he fever-dream that, too? In that dream other people appeared, leaning over his bed, people he barely knew, like his history teacher Lal Ratan Babu, and a strange man with spectacles and a stethoscope. And next to them his tired-eyed uncle, first blustering, then meek and dwindled. Sanjay's head was steadied; he was forced to swallow pills that left bitterness etched on his tongue; a needle poked his arm; a thermometer was thrust into his mouth; he smelled, one last time, the marigold smell of his mother. Then Gopal, sobered by this brush with death, was holding up his head not ungently, making sure he drank his barley water. The bottom line: he survived.

Was that good luck, or bad? Once he thought he knew. Recently, he's not so sure.

Last tuberculosis screening?
May 1971

So it says in the records, but that's actually a lie. In fact all his papers are a lie, concocted in a dingy back room in Kolkata off of a dangerous alley by a man with a squint. He's never had a screening. Wouldn't Uncle Sam have a cow if he knew!

In 1971, Sanjay had had to go into hiding. The Naxals had had a bitter falling-out with CPI (M). As a student leader, he was an easy target. He remembers those days, shunted from host to reluctant host, hiding under beds, terrified every time someone knocked on the door. He didn't even dare to phone Bela to let her know he was alive. Then one day, like magic, Bishu called him from America. How did he even know his phone number? *Go to Barabazar, Shonu. Look for Sarfaraz. Give him my name. Tell him I'll make sure he gets the money.*

And just like that, abracadabra, chi-ching-fank, he was on his way to America, armed with fake documents and a fake job offer. When the plane took off at Dum Dum Airport, he shook with exhilaration and terror and an illogical longing for the city that had brought him little except trouble. It felt as though someone had reached into him and was wresting out his heart. In later life his sorrows would be deep-drawn and bone-aching sad, but never like this. Perhaps only the young can feel such exquisitely intense pain.

On the flight, he was stuck in an uncomfortable, last-minute middle seat. He leaned toward the small oval of the window, wanting to look down at Kolkata one last time, the city where Bela lay in bed. What would she do when Bishu's friend delivered his note to her? Would she find the courage to leave everything she knew for the sake of love? The fat man in the window seat grinned unsympathetically. *Nothing to see*, he said, pulling down the shade. *Two a.m., everyone sleeping.*

Something's wrong. He forgot to check the clock when he came into the doctor's office, but he'd bet his bottom dollar that he's been waiting for over an hour now. Why are none of the other patients concerned? Don't they have a life? Well, he, Sanjay Kumar, has places to go and things to do, and he's getting ready to give someone a piece of his mind.

Do you wear a seat belt while driving? Do you wear a helmet while riding a bike?
Yes

He's not stupid. He chooses his risks and pleasures, weighs them against each other. Most of the time he gets the formula right, though the divorce—that hadn't quite turned out the way he thought it would, had it?

Have you ever had a sexually transmitted disease?
No

And he never plans to. He's told his women, including his current girlfriend, that they have to take a test up front, or else it's no go. He's fair about it; he offers to take a similar test himself. If they're not okay with this, well then, it's so long farewell auf Weidersehen goodbye. A clean and simple system. It works for him because he knows how to enjoy people without getting mawkish about it—a good skill to have.

He just wishes he'd learned it earlier in life.

Do you drink alcohol? How many drinks per week?

He's going to ignore this one. What kind of fool counts his drinks?

That would defeat the purpose of drinking, which is to float above consequence, or at least create a brief belief that such a thing is possible.

What directives do you have in place for the end of your life?

He ignores this one, too. In fact, he's done with the entire bloody questionnaire. He walks over to the receptionist, who's back behind the glass wall, fiddling with something on her computer. He bangs the clipboard down on the countertop and gives her a feral grin when she jumps.

"We'll call you just as soon as we can," she says in answer to his query. He's willing to bet they've been specially trained to talk to patients in this neutral-as-oatmeal tone. Especially when they've made them wait beyond reason. He stomps his dissatisfied way back to his seat. If they don't call his name soon, he's walking out.

About that unanswered question: he's got an excellent directive in place, but he isn't about to tell anyone about it. *Loose lips sink ships.* That's one of his favorite sayings. He'd taught it to Tara when she was little, and it had become her favorite, too.

For a while, he'd been going to the doctor, to several doctors as a matter of fact, with gaps in between so they wouldn't get suspicious. He complained to them about pain, about his inability to fall asleep. Lies, every one of them. He slept like a buffalo after a long day of tilling fields. Snored like one, too, according to his girlfriends. The doctors gave him pills, which he stashed away safely in different parts of his house, to be used all at once when he really needed them. But then he did some research and realized they might not be enough. He wasn't going to gamble on this one. He contacted a man who had connections in Mexico. Now he has enough Nembutal to send a horse to heaven. Sanjay Dewan is not going to end up in a wheelchair, eating mush and peeing his pants and being pushed around by an ugly bitch of a nurse with a mousetrap for a mouth—like the one who's just entered the waiting room to make an announcement.

The doctor has been delayed at the hospital, says mousetrap-mouth.

One of his patients is in the ICU. Life-or-death. They're not sure when he'll be able to get to the office. If your problem isn't urgent, we suggest you reschedule.

Three patients zombie-shuffle to the counter.

Sanjay considers it, too. But then he remembers how it felt last night, an evil genie grinding his lungs under its heel. He thinks of his girl-friend's face, the bumblebee questions she'll ask. She'll probably drive him right back.

He'll wait another half hour.

Here's another question, just when he thought he was done. He's not sure where it came from. Maybe it emerged from behind the water cooler? It hangs eye-level in front of him.

Name one human mystery.

That's not difficult:

Why people do things.

After he had recovered from the malaria, he asked Bishu what had made him come to check on him. What made him go, that same day, to their history teacher and tell him what was happening. What made him describe Sanjay's condition with such vivid distress that a concerned Lal Ratan Babu made a trip to Sanjay's house and demanded to speak with Sanjay's uncle.

Bishu shrugged his shoulders. He wasn't a big talker, those days. *I don't know.* He kicked his patched old football at Sanjay so they could play some more before it got dark.

I don't know. Wasn't that the truth.

Years later, a cannier Bishu, revisiting the incident, would come up with a shitload of motives. Just like Sanjay could, if asked why he had wanted Bela to run away from home and join him in America. Or why he quit his perfectly nice computer programmer's job to take on a life of investments so risky that for years they teetered between flush and broke. Why he decided to divorce Bela. Why he has the PI keep tabs on Tara. But the truth is, he doesn't really know why he did any of it.

Here comes another question, twisting lazily in midair.

Describe an incident you regret.

Regret is an idiotic emotion indulged in by masochists, and he for sure ain't one.

Except there was this one time.

Soon after he decided to get the divorce, even before he told his wife, he drove up to the university where Tara was studying. He wanted Tara to know first. He wanted to explain to her why he was doing it. He wanted to make sure to get her on his side before Bela poisoned her mind with lies and tears.

He took Tara out to Niko's. Personally he would have preferred a fancier place, but it was the girl's favorite restaurant. One of these days he was going to work on her taste, but today he just wanted her happy. He let her order everything she wanted: stuffed grape leaves, hummus, moussaka, gyros, baklava, the works. She loaded up her plate. She was chattering away, excited, waving her fork, talking with her mouth full. It was almost the end of her first semester of college; she had settled in; she liked her professors. *My roommate's a pain in the butt, though. I can't wait until next year, when I can move out and get my own place. You said I could, right?* Now she was describing a psychology class, some experiment about delayed gratification with children and a cupcake. It didn't make sense. His head was too full of his own words, how to phrase them. He interrupted her. Started on the speech he had rehearsed in the car.

She put down her fork. She pushed back her chair. He thinks there were tears in her eyes, but maybe it was the glitter of rage. *You're leaving us?* Her plate was full of food. She'd had only a few bites. *Are you having an affair?*

Sit down, he told her. *Don't be melodramatic.* He considered confessing that there was another woman, but that wasn't the real reason for the divorce. The real reason was more complicated. It was because Bela had betrayed him already. That was why, each morning when he awoke and looked at her placid, sleeping face, he felt like he was drowning in sawdust.

Instead, he assured Tara that he wasn't leaving her. *You're my sweetheart baby and always will be.* But she walked out midsentence. He remembers her plate, the red-brown moussaka bleeding into the creamy hummus. She'd arranged the dolmades in a neat heap, a small green mountain. She liked to save them until the end because they were her favorite.

He wishes that he hadn't been in such a hurry to talk, that he'd waited until she'd finished her meal.

They'd met again on the day when he was moving out of the house. Bela had forced Tara to come home from college, hoping that her presence would make him change his mind. Hah! To think he was going to let Bela manipulate him like that! Tara hadn't said a thing, though Bela had cried and carried on enough for all three of them.

Their last conversation took place on a day when he'd followed Tara to her job. She'd dropped out of school by then and was working in that iffy thrift shop. She'd turned to face him outside the graffitied entrance. She wore clothes that were too loose for her, in shades of drab. She'd lost a lot of weight. A ring pierced her left eyebrow. He couldn't take his eyes from its small, violent shimmer.

"Baby," he said. "I love you." When she didn't respond, he said, angrily, though he knew he shouldn't, "It's not all my fault. Ask your mother. Ask her. She betrayed me a long time ago."

She looked at him, her eyes opaque and disbelieving. "If you follow me again, I'm going to call the police." Her voice was newly grown up, emotionless as paper.

What is something that makes you feel guilty?

Where did this one come from? Sometimes when he can't breathe right, things begin to blur. Is that what happened here? No matter. He answers it quickly:

Nothing.

A lie, of course.

After that confrontation with Tara at the thrift shop, he'd backed off. But he couldn't stand not knowing, so he hired the investigator. Paid him religiously for years, even through the lean times. Followed his daughter's life that way. It was about as satisfying as a starving man staring at glossy food photos.

The news was not encouraging. Tara got into bad company. Drank. Did drugs. She moved in with a loser, some kind of masseur, then moved out. The investigator thought the guy had cheated on her. Sanjay wanted to kill the bastard. Things got worse. An abortion. Two years later, a car accident. He longed to help, but he could do nothing except watch from the sidelines and agonize. And send her checks.

She never cashed them.

Then—amazingly—not too long after the accident, she straightened herself out, went back to school, graduated, found a decent job. How did *that* happen? Even the investigator couldn't figure it out. She even reconciled with Bela. That was a low blow, when Sanjay had been the one who wanted her the most, who'd been ready to give her everything she could possibly want.

Tara got married. Had a kid, who was ten now. Slowly, slowly, Sanjay allowed himself to relax, one muscle at a time. He started carrying, in his wallet, courtesy of the PI's zoom lens, a photo of the boy, whose name was Neel. Pulled it out to show to his friends like a real grandfather.

A month ago, abruptly, Tara quit her job. Or maybe she was fired. Now she was seeing a shrink.

He paid the PI a chunk of money to find out why.

The man was good at what he did. But finally, yesterday, he had called Sanjay to say that he couldn't get hold of Tara's medical records.

It would have been bad enough had Sanjay known what was wrong. Not knowing was a hell of a lot worse.

Later that night, as he was trying to make it through the worst breathing episode of his life, it struck Sanjay that although he didn't know what exactly Tara's problem was, the cause was blinding-clear: Her father, her guide, the one person she'd depended on, had abandoned her. He had made himself the center of her life, and then he'd left.

The light in the office is very dim. Maybe they've turned it down to save on electricity? It's grown cold, too. Shivery-cold. He's had it! He's not waiting around in this godforsaken place any longer, answering more of these weird questions. He pushes past a uniformed woman who's trying, what audacity, to stop him. He's going to get in his car and go home. Tomorrow he'll find a different doctor, one with a better notion of punctuality and a normal medical questionnaire. If he walks slowly, he should be fine. Level 4 of the parking structure, space 434. He remembers it perfectly. Yes sirree Bob, his heart might be flip-flopping like a beached fish, but his mind is a scalpel.

What is the nature of life?

He wasn't going to answer any more questions, but this one—he's ready for it. He's been over it many times, lying awake in bed alone or with a sleeping stranger's arm (the same thing) draped heavily across his chest.

Life is lines of dominoes falling.

One thing leads to another, and then another, just like you'd planned. But suddenly a domino gets skewed, events change direction, people dig in their heels, and you're faced with a situation that you didn't see coming, you who thought you were so clever.

The first falling piece is etched in his memory.

It was a few months after Bishu's divorce. Sanjay and Bela hadn't moved to Texas yet. They were still living in that dingy apartment in the Bay Area, and Tara was a baby. Sanjay had come home in a good mood that evening, though he has forgotten why. He'd opened the door, whistling, and seen them together on the couch, his wife and his best friend. For a moment, it made him happy.

It had always troubled him that Bela never liked Bishu. Things became worse one year back, after the incident with the tenant. Bloody redneck. Wouldn't pay rent. Wouldn't move out of their house. The house that was Bishu and Sanjay's one-and-only, in which they'd sunk all their savings. Things got hairy. They couldn't make the mortgage. The bank sent them a warning. It looked like they were going to lose the house. Finally, Bishu poisoned the tenant's dog and everything worked out.

When Bela discovered what had happened, she threw a fit. She wanted nothing to do with Bishu, never see him again. Of course, Sanjay couldn't give in to a ridiculous demand like that, not after all that Bishu had done for them both. They had a fight, a big one. Bela didn't talk to Sanjay for days. She would lock herself in the bathroom when Bishu came, leaving Sanjay to stammer out excuses.

But now they were sitting close to each other, Bishu's arm around Bela's shoulder, talking in low voices. Baby Tara—she was maybe eight months old then—was balanced on Bishu's knee.

When she noticed Sanjay, Bela jerked away with a start.

"My mother's sick." She pointed to an open aerogram on the table.

Maybe she was telling the truth. Maybe Bishu had only been comforting her because he found her crying. Maybe he, Sanjay-Shonu-Shona-Sheno, was overreacting. There were crumpled balls of Kleenex strewn on the floor.

Bull, said the voice in his head. The way she'd pulled away, the way she'd raised her startled eyes to him, Sanjay, standing in the doorway, then glanced down: That wasn't sorrow. It was guilt.

The next week, he came home from work one evening to find that Bela was gone. But her car was in the parking lot. Where could she be? He paced the balcony for an hour, worrying, wondering if he should call the police. Then he saw Bishu's car drive up. Bela spilled out, laughing in a green silk sari. Sanjay hadn't realized how pretty she'd grown in the last few months, having shed all her pregnancy weight. Bishu leaned into the back and picked Tara up from her car seat. She patted his face with her palms, babbling baby talk. Bishu smiled and nuzzled her neck. It made Sanjay furious. Ashamed, too, in a strange way. He stepped away from the balcony before they could see him. Went into the bathroom. Only after he heard them enter the apartment did he come out, flushing the toilet needlessly.

Bela looked at him with wide eyes. "Sorry we're late. We got caught in traffic."

"Where were you?"

"I went to the temple in Livermore. It's my father's death anniversary today. I didn't feel comfortable driving alone all that way, and I know you don't like to go. So I asked Bishu-da."

He stared at Bishu, who had insisted, all through college, that religion was the opium of the people. Who had never set foot in a temple in India.

Bishu gave a shamefaced shrug.

"I couldn't let her drive all that way with Tara all by herself," he said. "Could I?"

Yes, you could, Sanjay wanted to shout. Instead he said, "Would you like some tea? I picked up that chai masala that you liked so much last time."

Later, when they were alone, he said to Bela, "You never visited the temple on your father's death-day before this."

"People change," Bela said, shooting him a cool, unreadable glance from beneath her lashes.

What did she mean? Was she hinting at something? Now she lifted her chin, as though daring him to hit her. He didn't know what to do, so he grabbed the baby, who was in her lap. Tara, startled, started to cry. A look flashed across Bela's face, clear enough this time: fear.

This, he thought. *This would be the way to punish her.*

He swung Tara up, turning around and around and making airplane noises until she gurgled with laughter. He changed her diaper, which he usually shied away from. When it was bedtime, he said, "I'll take her." He stood at the crib, making little finger-circles on Tara's back until she fell asleep.

Bela watched him warily from the door of the bedroom, a frown gouging her forehead.

He did this every day, for a week, two weeks, until Tara refused to go to sleep without him. Until she became his. And—though he hadn't quite thought through this part—he became hers.

Over the next month, it seemed like he saw them together, Bela-Bishu, all the time. Sometimes Bishu would already be at their apartment when Sanjay returned from the office, claiming that his shift at the Indian motel where he worked as a manager was over early. That was a lie. Sanjay knew that Bishu worked the night shift because it paid more. He must have left the desk in charge of the cleaning lady, bribed her a few dollars and slipped out.

He said nothing about this to Bishu. He was always cordial to him, more polite than ever. But he avoided all conversations that leaned toward intimacy. Sometimes Bishu would look at him with a perplexed frown. But Sanjay deflected this successfully with an innocuous smile.

The days he couldn't come over, Bishu called. If Sanjay picked up the phone, Bishu would ask a few cursory questions; then there would be an awkward silence because he had nothing more to say to him. Bishu, his best friend, his brother. "Can I talk to Bela?" he would ask. They would be on the phone for half an hour, Bela laughing as she described Tara's antics in unnecessary detail. Sanjay sat nearby, staring at his copy of *Business Week*, turning the pages as though the words he read made sense.

The worst was when Bishu rang the doorbell late at night, bearing gifts. Hotel candies or soaps for Bela—cheap stuff that she exclaimed over fatuously—or a balloon for Tara that she'd bat at over and over. *Biku-Biku*. That's what she called him, short for Bishu Kaka. She'd put her small fat arms around his neck when he picked her up, while Bela smiled indulgently. It destroyed Sanjay to watch the three of them together like that.

Can you blame him for writing the anonymous letter to the owners of the motel that led to a sudden night-check when Bishu wasn't there, that resulted in him losing his job? Bishu looked for other positions, but word had sped along the motel owners' grapevine in California. He tried for other kinds of work, minimum-wage clerking at stores, night watchman jobs. He listed Sanjay's name as a reference. Strange, no one would hire him.

Desperate, his savings dwindling, he was forced to start looking out-of-state. Finally, with Sanjay's help, he managed to land a manager's job in a motel in a small town in Utah. He hated the place. He would call them each week and complain bitterly about the terrible winters, the weirdos who came through, the crippling loneliness. "I miss you folks," he'd say to Sanjay, who made sure he was the one to pick up the phone. "Is Bela doing okay? Can I talk to her?" When Sanjay made excuses— Bela was out, or asleep, or in the shower—he'd say, sadly, "How's my Tara-baby? She must be getting so big. Being away from you-all is killing me."

Perhaps it wasn't an exaggeration. In two years, Bishu would be dead. When he received the phone call from the motel management, because Bishu had listed him as next of kin and beneficiary on his life insurance, Sanjay was torn between relief and shame.

The first weeks after Bishu left the Bay Area, Sanjay watched Bela for signs. But she went about her daily chores cheerfully, humming as she vacuumed or folded clothes. If anything, she seemed happier, even, than she had been before. He would come home at unexpected times, trying to catch her out. Would she be in tears? Would she be talking to Bishu on the phone? But all he ever found was her taking a nap or watching *Sesame Street* with Tara. Sometimes the Indian woman who had moved into the apartment below would be there. She had a baby, too. Sanjay would come home to find the babies crawling around on a bedsheet while the two women drank tea and munched on chanachur. They would look at him curiously and a little disapprovingly, as though wondering what he was doing home in the middle of the day.

Months passed. Bela remained serene, glowing, Madonna-like. When Bishu phoned, she did not ask to speak to him. When Tara turned one, she went back to her job at the child-care center, taking her daughter with her. Work suited her. Gave her confidence. At dinnertime, she served, without apology, boiled rice and dal, prepared quickly in the pressure cooker. She interrupted Sanjay's news-watching with anecdotes of things that had happened at Tiny Treasures.

It bewildered Sanjay, how well she hid her sorrow at Bishu's absence, and, later, at his death.

One night, several months after Bishu's death, Sanjay lay in bed unable to sleep. Childhood memories of Bishu pressed against his skull until his head hurt. Beside him, Bela's breathing was rhythmic and untroubled.

That was when the truth struck him. Bela had never been attracted to Bishu. She had only pretended, in order to make Sanjay jealous, to create a rift between them, to make sure that Sanjay drove his best friend away. She'd even used Tara as a weapon. She must have planned this for a while, perhaps since the dead dog incident. He'd thought she'd forgotten it, but she'd never forgiven either of the men.

Rage seared Sanjay's veins like poison. He couldn't breathe. This was a greater betrayal than if she'd actually cheated on him. He jerked upright, his body at once hot and cold and shaking, like the time when he'd had malaria. How dare she manipulate him this way? He was going to choke the lying life out of her, never mind what happened to him after that. He looked down at his hands. They were flexed and ready.

He was this close to doing it.

Then he heard Tara in the crib, murmuring as she shifted, snuffling in her sleep.

He forced himself to breathe. For her sake, he forced himself to lie down.

A better punishment: he would divorce Bela, leave her to flounder in loneliness, the way Bishu had, in snow-choked Utah. But not now, not until his daughter was grown up. He wouldn't jeopardize Tara's future, take the chance of losing even a little bit of her. No messy joint custody for him. He would wait, patient as a heron by the water, waiting to swoop ruthless upon the right moment, when Bela had grown too dependent to manage without him. Meanwhile, he would love Tara fully and fiercely. He would make himself indispensable in Bela's life, would make her believe that he adored her. Then when he left her, Bela's life would be shattered.

He didn't know then that the long interim would be studded with moments when the light would be of a certain quality, dust motes dancing in it as when they had been in Kolkata, and Bela, smiling at him contentedly as she pasted photos into an album or concocted a special dish for his dinner, would look so like the girl he had loved in college that his truant heart would twist, murmuring, *Maybe you're wrong*. Or, *Stop, it's not too late*. But of course it was.

～✦◯

It is dark in the car inside the parking garage, and strangely cold, far too cold for Oakland in July. No matter. He zips up his jacket and rests his forehead on the steering wheel. A few minutes to recharge; then he'll start for home. The dominoes are falling in beautiful sweeps of black and white, as they did that night when he lay next to his lovely, unaware wife. Watching them, he sleeps.

A Thousand Words: 2020

I stand in this unfamiliar kitchen, wrestling with a stubborn acorn squash, because my mother has decided that as her last meal before she's jailed she would like Bengali pumpkin curry.

My mother is given to exaggeration. It's not really her last meal. We'll have several meals together through the weekend while I pack her things. And it isn't jail but Sunny Hills, a decent, if not lavish, senior facility in Austin. After her second fall, the one that fractured her leg two weeks ago, her doctor called me and said she couldn't live alone anymore. I took a week's emergency leave and flew down from San Jose to persuade her to move to a facility. I would have preferred one closer to me, where I could have kept an eye on her more easily. But she told me right away she wasn't leaving Texas. Bela Stubborn Dewan, that's my mother.

I'd been nervous about coming out here. I'd never spent an entire week alone with my mother since the divorce. The few times we'd met, on occasions of family importance, my husband and son had acted as buffers. Otherwise it was emails or duty calls, brief, pragmatic exchanges of information, mostly to prove to each other that we were doing just fine.

"What will I even say to her?" I had wailed to Gary as he dropped me off at the airport. "I'm afraid she'll bring up sad, sad things from the past, and we'll end up having a fight."

"You'll do great," said my sweet accountant husband, who believes that with assiduous goodwill, the books eventually balance out. He handed me my carry-on bag and kissed me goodbye. "Just remember that it takes two to tangle."

"Tango," I said grumpily. "It takes two to *tango*." I wanted to add something about his misplaced optimism, but right then one of those airport cops blew shrilly on her whistle and yelled at him to move the car.

Struck by last-minute panic, I called Dr. Berger, my therapist, from the airport gate, but she wasn't of much help, either. "Keep in mind that this is harder for your mother than it is for you," she said. And then, "Maybe being alone with her will give you an opportunity to work out some of your issues."

I told her I greatly doubted that. Besides, I didn't want to work out any issues. Not with my mother, at least.

All week I've been ferrying my mother to retirement homes around the city. It's been hard, with her leg being in a cast. Each time she's given the place a cursory glance and said, "I hate it." A couple of times, she refused to even get out of the car. Inside my head, I chanted Gary's parting advice like a frantic mantra and kept my mouth shut, but I wasn't sure how long I'd be able to manage that.

Sunny Hills was clearly the nicest among the facilities we could afford. The private room we looked at opened out on a pleasant courtyard lined with flowers. It was more expensive than we had budgeted for, but when I saw that it had its own kitchenette, I said yes.

"I hate it," my mother said.

I was ready to scream. Then I had a better idea. "You'll just have to come back to California with me, then," I said in my sweetest voice. "Remind me to book your ticket as soon as we get home."

She seemed to deflate. She allowed me to push her wheelchair into the office without making a fuss. Once in there, she signed the forms silently. When the manager asked if she had any questions, she shook her head. In the car she closed her eyes. I hadn't realized how much weight she'd lost. Her eyelids were creased and delicate, tissue-thin.

I expected to feel victory, or at least relief. I was entitled to it. But I only felt like there wasn't enough air in the car.

❧

I've managed to hack the squash into jagged halves. But scooping out its stringy, seed-filled entrails is proving to be a challenge. After that I must peel and steam it until it's soft but not mushy. I must sauté it until golden, thicken it with a flour-based sauce (no lumps, my mother has warned), and garnish it with coriander leaves chopped fine enough to suit her standards.

I really don't have the time for this, but having won the war of Sunny Hills, I feel I should concede this battle. I confess: I am a disgrace to my family. My mother has several successful cookbooks and a popular food blog, *Bela's Kitchen*, now well into its second decade. My grandmother Sabitri's desserts were legendary in Kolkata—so I've been told. No wedding in my great-grandmother Durga's village was considered complete without her special malpua, golden-fried and dipped in rose syrup, sprinkled with crushed fennel seed. Me, I just want to fix a meal, chopping block to dining table, thirty minutes max.

"Don't put yourself down," Gary tells me. "You're a fine cook."

"I forgive you for lying," I say.

My mother once announced, "Tara, you have no ambition." We were rolling rutis in the kitchen. I was twelve years old, and my rutis refused to come out as round as she wanted them to. I pointed out that they still puffed up when she roasted them on the skillet. Wasn't that good enough?

"No." My mother was easygoing about many things, but not the preparation of food. She took my rolled-out rutis, the ones that were waiting to be cooked, and mashed them back into dough. "Do them again."

"Hitler!" my father said, swooping into the kitchen like a savior angel. He led me away to play a board game. I loved him because he always took my side.

My mother was wrong. I do have ambitions; they're just not the same as hers. I want to be able to hold on to my job, bland as it is, in the human resources department of my company. I want to be the kind of mother Neel will call from college. The kind of wife Gary will never want to leave. I have one ambition, in particular, that only Dr. Berger knows about: I want to cure myself of the disease hiding inside me like a canker curled up in the heart of a rose.

"Tara," my mother calls from the bedroom, "I'm hungry. Is the pumpkin curry ready? Did you use the recipe I told you to look up?"

I scowl at the shiny hardcover I'd pulled down from the shelf, *Everyday Delicacies of the Bengal Countryside*, by Bela Dewan. I had, indeed, looked up the recipe. It spanned three entire pages and asked for twenty-seven separate ingredients. It would require severe modification. "Curry's not done yet, Mom," I say, trying to keep the exasperation from my voice. "If you're really hungry, I can give you some cereal."

"It's noon." My mother's voice is affronted. "Normal people don't eat cereal at noon. You haven't even started the curry, have you? I would have smelled the frying spices. . . ."

I consider reminding her that I'd been occupied all morning in sorting through the many closets in this house. But I exert saintlike control over my vocal cords and say, instead, "How about a cup of tea, then, with a couple of those cranberry-and-white-chocolate cookies that I picked up for you from San Francisco?"

There's a pause. But finally my mother, Bengali in her food habits if nothing else, can't resist the offer of cha and mishti. "Be sure to use the Darjeeling," she calls out. "Brew it on the stove, not in the microwave. And take out the good gold-rimmed cups. No point saving them, now that I'm going to jail."

Our delayed lunch is a startlingly pleasant meal. Rice, Bengal gram lentils with coconut, and curried squash. The squash has turned out well, which I didn't expect, and my mother compliments me on it. That, too, I didn't expect. Is she delirious with hunger? But no. She wants this weekend to be free of conflict—as do I. A visit we can remember without regret. God knows we don't have many of those.

We make cautious conversation, sticking to nonflammable topics. I ask her about the book I'd taken the recipe from, published roughly ten years ago. It was her second cookbook, her most successful one. The publisher had arranged a tour for her in seven cities.

"Seven cities!" I try to imagine her rushing from airport to auditorium, holding forth in front of gaggles of strangers. "Were you nervous?"

"Terrified," she says. But a smile flits across her face.

And suddenly I'm sad because there are chunks of her life that I know nothing about. There was an entire decade after her divorce when we didn't communicate. My doing, mostly. I can admit this now; Dr. Berger and I have been working on accepting responsibility.

Maybe it was good we weren't in touch. In those days I wasn't a nice person to be around. I hurt people who got close to me. And I hurt myself.

Once my mother asked, "Why were you so angry with me after the divorce? I wasn't the one who wanted it, you know that."

I didn't reply. I didn't want to talk about it. Plus, I wasn't sure of the answer. Perhaps it was a displaced rage. Perhaps the person I was really angry with was myself.

Also this: The one time since the divorce when I'd reached out to her, the time I'd needed my mother most, she hadn't been there for me. She'd already moved on with her life. Was it any wonder that, for years afterward, I'd done my best to avoid thinking about her?

Neel's birth changed things some. A couple of weeks after he was born, I was nursing him. He wasn't too good at latching on to my nipple yet. Every couple of minutes he'd lose it and make urgent snuffing sounds as he nuzzled around for it. It was funny, really, so I don't know why I found myself weeping. Maybe it was postpartum hormones. I held him to me and cried like I'd never cried before. It didn't make up for the things that were snatched from me, or the ones that I'd thrown away, or the people who had shrugged me off like a threadbare sweater. It certainly didn't make up for the baby I'd scraped out of myself. Nothing would do that. But when I stopped, something was different. When Gary, who had been wanting me to make up with my mother, found her address through the Internet, I allowed him to send her a photo of Neel. And when she called a few days after that, I didn't refuse to speak to her. We talked about safe things: Neel and Gary, her books, my job, her arthritic knee, my sore nipples. Then and later, we stayed away from the things we really needed to say.

❧

My mother's napping. I hear snores from the bedroom, though should I mention this later, she'd totally deny it. I'm glad she's getting a bit of rest. The cast tires her out but makes it hard for her to sleep at night. I've made her leave the door open and instructed her to call me when she has to use the toilet, but if I don't watch out, she'll try to maneuver her walker in there by herself.

I'm sleepy, too. I'm not used to eating such a heavy meal in the middle of the day. I long to stretch out on the sofa, wrapping myself in the red quilt that's lying there. Then, with a stab, I recognize the quilt. My father had brought it back from a business trip he took to New England long ago. Ironic, how objects remain in your life long after people have exited.

I start to empty out the family room cabinets. My mother the arch-squirrel has quite a stash: old receipts, packets of Floralife flower food, barf bags courtesy of American Airlines, music tapes that are useless now that technology has moved on, dusty crime thrillers that I can't picture her reading.

As soon as I get home, I'm going to clean out my junk so Neel will never have to go through this dismalness.

In one of the cabinets I find a stack of photo albums, fat hardcover tomes of maroon and green, embossed in gold. I remember them from my childhood. My mother loved photographs and took them at every opportunity, a strange obsession in someone who rarely alluded to her own past. My father would scour the stores before Mother's Day to bring her special albums, their metal cases engraved with her name, their covers inlaid with glass so a favorite photo might be displayed. My mother has instructed me clearly: The albums are to go with her to Sunny Hills. All I have to do is put them into a packing box and label it accordingly.

I know I shouldn't open them. There are a hundred other things to take care of. I must have everything ready by Monday morning, when the movers will come, along with the Salvation Army folks, the cleaners, and the realtor. I must settle my mother in Sunny Hills by midafternoon so that I can catch my evening flight back home.

Even as I think this, I'm sitting cross-legged on the floor flipping the stiff cardboard pages.

The books are jumbled and in no chronological order. The first one is filled with pictures I sent to her, mostly of Neel. The next one opens onto scenes of my mother at various culinary events: demonstrations in bookstores or clubs, talks at larger venues, some onstage. I try to judge her age by the photos. Here's one of her standing in front of grocery shelves arranged with Indian wares—lentil sacks, jars of pickles, spices in bright cardboard packets—stirring something in a wok. She wears a bunchy white apron and a chef's hat and looks out at the camera with a smile that's nervous but pleased, as though the photographer is someone she likes. Who could it be? The photo seems to be from three or four years after the divorce, a period she doesn't talk about. I turn the pages. The audiences grow larger. Here's one with her on a stage, holding up a new book. I guess it to be from her mid-fifties. She's wearing an embroidered Indian top with pants—very fusion—and has lost a lot of her post-divorce weight by this time. She has also bobbed her hair. The style suits her, and she angles her chin confidently as though she knows this. On the next page is a close-up of the same event. Once again there's that look on her face, a sparkly mix of pleasure and shyness, almost girlish. I'm intrigued enough to put the album aside. If she's in a forthcoming mood this evening, I'll ask her about the photographer. I wonder if he's the same man who picked up the phone when I called her all those years earlier, that fateful night before my abortion. I wonder if he'd made her—for a while, at least—happy.

The next album documents my history. On the first page is a class photo, labeled in my mother's handwriting: *3rd grade, St. John's Elementary.* I'm squinting at the camera, head tilted. Big grin, missing front tooth. Cute, if I say so myself. A few pages are dedicated to pictures of me in T-shirts imprinted with the logos of various recreational teams to which I must have belonged. In some, my right foot is on a basketball; in others, my arms are outstretched, fingers held up in the victory sign. Looking at them makes me chuckle, but there's an aftertaste of guilt. So many photos, so carefully preserved. How absurdly central I'd been to my mother's life.

I linger on a photo where I'm clutching a trophy to my chest, grinning maniacally. There's something odd about this picture. It's long and narrow, not the regular rectangular shape. Also, it's slanted at the edge, as though someone had cut away part of it. I turn the page, then another. There are several similarly lopped-off photos. In between, there are gaps as though entire photos have been ripped out of the book. It hits me that there are no pictures of my father here.

I turn to a different album, then another. Some are filled with my baby pictures from early in my parents' marriage, when they lived in California. My mother carrying me, drowsy-eyed in a blue-hooded onesie (she hadn't figured out the American color-coding system for babies yet), the requisite Golden Gate Bridge looming behind us. A birthday where I'm kneeling on a chair, trying to blow out two candles on a homemade cake. My first day of preschool, with a large red backpack, the photo slightly blurred because I'm too excited to stand still. Then we're in Texas: a trip to Austin, where I straddle a cannon outside the capitol; in our backyard pool, I swim elated in a tiger-print bikini my father had bought me over my mother's protests; at my graduation, I hug my best girlfriends—all now swallowed by time's darkness—group-smiling in the belief that our real life was finally about to begin. Every photo is meticulously fatherless. I imagine my mother after the divorce, bent over the albums with the kitchen scissors, cutting him out of our lives. Snipping late into the night, she is a figure at once piteous and triumphant.

But haven't I, too, done the same? I blocked his number. I instructed the bank so he couldn't transfer money into my account. Even when I was so short on cash that I didn't know how I'd pay next month's rent, I took nothing from him. I sent back his letters unopened. Later, when I had less energy to invest in such things, I tossed them in the trash. That's how much I hated him.

"Did he think I'd let him absolve himself so easily?" I tell Dr. Berger.

She says, "You blame him for your troubles. That's understandable. But did your own weaknesses play a role in your problems?"

Yes, they did. Still, for years I couldn't think of him without feeling my face heat up, my hands begin to sweat.

After his death last year, his lawyer phoned me. He'd left all his life insurance money—a substantial amount—to Neel. I was too furious to speak. Finally I said, "I don't want it. Donate it to charity." But canny devil that he was, my father had thought of everything. The money wasn't mine to dispose of. It would be given to Neel as a lump sum when he turned twenty-one.

We've been having some big fights about that money, Gary, Neel, and I. I want Neel to give it away. It's tainted money, I tell them. They think I'm being ridiculous.

"It's bad enough that you never allowed Neel to see his grandfather when he was alive," my usually mild-mannered husband says. "Now you want to take away his inheritance?"

"It's like that man is reaching out from the grave to tear my family apart," I tell Dr. Berger, who blinks patiently.

"Do you think that perhaps you are exaggerating?" she says.

Here's a slim album I don't remember seeing before, pushed to the back of the cabinet. With its faded silk covering and tassels it looks exotic, non-American. Opening it, I'm assailed by a smell that plays hide-and-seek with me. Then I remember. On a hot afternoon years ago, I'd smelled it in a temple. Scent of benediction and catastrophe. I was in a car accident later that day. The details have faded, but I remember it was a bad one, the could-have-been-killed kind. It shook me up—pardon the pun. After that, somehow, I began fixing things in my life. Dr. Berger says being close to death will do that, but I'm not sure catalysts of change can be so easily identified.

There's a sentence, embossed in gold, on the inner cover of the album. *A Picture's Worth a Thousand Words.* It pulls me back into childhood, when my mother often quoted such sayings at me. *Two Wrongs Don't Make a Right. Beggars Can't Be Choosers.* And the one with which she woke me in the mornings: *By Delay Nectar Turns into Poison.* They used to drive me crazy. My father had his sayings, too, though his possessed more zing: *Whoever Owns the Stick, Owns the Buffalo. Loose Lips Sink Ships.* Or *Traitor Vibhishan*, which meant the enemy at home was more dangerous than any stranger.

Could sententiousness be a cultural gene? If so, was it lying inside me, too, waiting to explode?

Dr. Berger says I worry too much. She has gifted me a plaque with a Mark Twain quote: I'VE LIVED THROUGH MANY TERRIBLE THINGS IN MY LIFE, SOME OF WHICH ACTUALLY HAPPENED.

Opening this album, I'm surprised and delighted. It's filled with black-and-white pictures from India, attached with little brown photo corners to pages that are thick and soft. Here are glimpses into my mother as a girl, snippets of the life she's withheld from me all these years. In a rush of excitement, I call out to her to wake up and see what I've found.

"What is it?" my mother says. I can hear her scowling. She comes out to the family room, yawning, making a big show of limping as she drags her walker over the tiles.

I hand her the author events album. "Who took this one, Ma?" I ask, pointing to the photo of her smiling in the grocery store.

She peers at it. "That would be Ken. He was my neighbor when I first moved to Austin. I was going through a bad time then. He helped me turn my life around."

Yes, he must have been the man who picked up the phone when I called the night before the abortion. So one could say he turned my life around, too—though maybe upside down would be a better term. I still wonder, sometimes, what would have happened if my mother had picked up the phone that night. I'll never mention it to her, of course.

I push aside my useless resentment of Ken. *It was a long time ago*, Dr. Berger would say. *Move forward, Tara.*

"Tell me more about this mysterious man," I say.

My mother glances at me, her eyes mischievous. "He was a wonderful man. I've never known anyone quite like him." She laughs at the look that must have taken over my face. "No, not *that* kind of wonderful. He was like a son to me, always there when I needed something."

She looks sideways at me to see if I registered the dig. Then she turns serious. "I wouldn't be where I am today if it wasn't for him. I'd probably be dead."

From her tone, I can tell she isn't exaggerating. It shuts me up.

"He moved to Mexico some years ago with his partner, Lance," she says, surprising me again. "I was happy for him, though of course I miss him terribly." She's silent, remembering things I'll never know. And I'm silent, trying to take in this new, open-minded woman.

Then she breaks into my reverie with an exaggerated mother-sigh. "If he'd still been here today, I bet I wouldn't have to—"

I interrupt masterfully. "Look what else I've found, Mom." I hand her the Indian album.

My strategy works.

"Goodness, this old thing!" she says, abandoning her walker and her grouchiness as she sits down on the sofa to flip through the pages. "Why, I can't remember the last time I opened it. Here's our apartment in Kolkata, and the balcony on which my mother grew jasmines. It used to be my favorite place."

I peer over her shoulder at the photo. In it, my mother, a teenager, wears a sari and has her hair in looped braids tied back with ribbons. She's perched on a stool, her elbows resting on the railing of a tiny balcony not much bigger than a bathtub. She's looking down at something. What is she watching so intently? I try to guess, though most of what I know about India is from books and movies and the Internet. Perhaps there were children sailing paper boats in the gutters after rain. Perhaps there were lovers making their surreptitious way to the cinema. Perhaps a tram was set on fire during a bandh.

Or was she hoping to see my father?

My mother squelches my fantasies. "I was waiting for the jhal-muri man. He made the best puffed-rice snacks. It's the one thing I've never been able to replicate. Probably the special taste came from Kolkata dust! Oh, look, here's our store."

It's a modest rectangle of a shop, DURGA SWEETS etched on the glass-front, collapsible gate raised to the top. My schoolgirl mother stands in front of it, wearing a pleated uniform skirt and looking vaguely bored. It strikes me that she, too, had been central to her mother's life.

"You'd never know it was one of Kolkata's most famous sweet shops," my mother says. "The bigger confectioners were always trying to steal my mother's recipes. It wouldn't have done them any good, though. It was my mother's special touch that gave the sweets their unique flavor. In Bengali we call this haater-gun."

"Did you like visiting the shop?"

"I loved it when I was little because inside it always smelled of sugar and saffron and chocolate, like a festival. But once I got older, I started hating it. It stole my mother from me. So many nights, I fell asleep on the sofa waiting for her to come home. . . ."

I know the feeling. When I was little, I used to wait for my father in the same way. His business deals often took place late in the night, and I'd fight with my mother if she tried to put me to sleep before he returned. Forced into bed, I'd pinch myself to keep awake until he came in to kiss me good night.

"The shop made us grow apart," my mother was saying. "That's why, once your father was earning enough, I quit work so I could be at home with you. I paid for it, of course, when the divorce happened, because I was good for nothing."

I stiffen. This is when the accusations start. I heard them all, over and over, in the months following the divorce.

"She really believed I was responsible for her difficulties!" I tell Dr. Berger. "She blamed me for them!"

"Yes," Dr. Berger says. "People tend to do that." She looks at me and raises an eyebrow. Then she adds, "Have you ever told her how you felt about this?"

I draw in a deep breath. Today. Today I'm going to tell my mother how I feel about this unfair blaming.

But she's distracted by a picture of herself in an elaborate costume. "We were performing a dance drama of Tagore's in college," she explains. "I was Shyama, the heroine who saves the hero from death and is then abandoned by him."

The moment's gone. I'll have to find another opportunity. I peer at the elegant young woman dressed in glistening silk and ankle bells, her hair braided back with silver ribbons, her tragic, painted eyes. I would not have recognized her as my mother.

"You don't know this," my mother says, "but that's where your father first saw me. Onstage. Maybe the woman he fell in love with was never me. It was Shyama. . . ."

Two of the pages are stuck together. She tugs at them gently. They separate and a photo falls to the floor. I pick it up. It's older than the others, a formal, sepia-toned composition. In it a young woman—not my mother—stands looking directly at the camera, dressed in widow's white. Her hair is pulled back in a matronly bun and her face is grave, but it shines with unintended beauty. She holds on to the shoulders of a girl of about twelve who stands stiffly in front of her, wearing a ruffled frock and looking equally grave.

"Oh, this photo!" my mother says in a strange voice. "I'd completely forgotten about it."

"Is that girl you? And is that—Grandma?"

My mother nods. She turns the photo over. On the back there's a faded ink-stamp that reads, *With the Compliments of Amrita Bazar Patrika.*

"What does that mean?"

"There was a big story about her in the paper," my mother says, "along with this photo."

"About your mother? What did she do?"

"She sued the company my father worked for after he died in an accident. They wanted to hush it up, but she demanded compensation. It was quite unheard-of in that time, a widow, all alone, taking on a major company."

"Did she win?"

My mother shrugs. "I was too young to understand what was going on. And my mother—she was a very private person. She never talked about it afterwards. They must have reached a compromise because she got enough money to start the sweet shop. I don't know how she would have survived otherwise, with a child to take care of." She pauses. Then she says, awkwardly, "Thank you. I would never have found this photo on my own. My mother hated having her picture taken. She considered it a vanity unfit for a widow. It's the only one I have of her."

I pick up the picture and peer at it. My grandmother looks out at me, her gaze lovely and cryptic. It bothers me that I know so little about her. I search the photo for clues to her character. Is she pressing down on her lip to keep it from trembling? Or is it a sign of determination? Is she holding on to the little girl for her own comfort, or to give her motherly support, or to make her behave with proper dignity? I want to keep staring until the photo yields its secrets to me.

Maybe now that her own end flickers like a shadow in the corner of her eye, my mother will be ready to tell me more about my grand-mother.

"Mom," I begin. "Did Grandma—"

"Let's look through my clothes, shall we?" she says, cutting me off. "Here, give me the photo." She holds the photo delicately by its edges so as to prevent finger-smudging.

"Mom." My voice shakes. I'm nervous as a girl. "Can I keep it?"

My mother replaces the photo in the album and snaps shut the cover. "Tara! I've just found it. I want to keep it with me for a while, look at it. You'll get it soon enough, once I'm dead. Come on, now. I have some nice saris that I won't wear again. I want you to take them." She rises and makes her lurching way into the bedroom.

But I hang back. A familiar tingling begins in my hands and rises into my wrists, my forearms. I feel feverish and shivery. I want that photo. I want it so badly that my mouth goes dry. I must have it.

This is my secret.

In the last few years, with therapy, the episodes had been less fre-quent. I'd been sure I was getting better. But today it's as though I lost my footing and tumbled all the way down a hillside into the dankest ditch. Through the pounding in my head I hear Dr. Berger say, *Stop, Tara. You don't want to steal from your mother. You don't need that photo. All the things you've stolen, has even one made you happier? You're stronger than your craving. Walk away from it. Walk away now.*

She's right, of course. With my kleptomania, it helps if I remove myself from temptation as quickly as possible. Distract myself with something else. But I can't. It's not just the craving. It's also a sudden anger. I could have known this woman, visited her, loved her and been loved in return. I might have been able to turn to her when everything in my life started to go wrong. Perhaps things would have ended up dif-ferently then. My mother kept me from all that.

"Tara," my mother shouts. "What's keeping you?"

I force myself to control my voice. "Coming, Mom."

I lean over the album. I snatch my grandmother up. I hurry to my bedroom, slip her inside my carry-on, and cover her with T-shirts. Elation and guilt thrill through me. I feel like I'm going to throw up.

~+~

It's late at night. My mother has gone to bed. I can't sleep, so I'm in the garage, dividing things into piles. *Throwaway. Giveaway. Keep. Unsure.* My body is still jangling from the theft. Little sounds make me jump. My breath feels jagged in my chest, like I'm coming down with something. My head aches, though I've taken a double dose of my mother's ibuprofen.

For dinner we had canned soup and toast. I could tell my mother was disappointed. She'd wanted us to use up all her fresh vegetables. She hated waste, especially of food. But that's all I was capable of putting together. I would have killed for some vodka, but my mother doesn't keep alcohol in the house. The way I was tonight, that was probably a good thing. Flashes of pain pulsed behind my eyes. When Gary called my cell phone the way he does every night, I ignored it. I responded to my mother's questions with monosyllables, mumbling about a migraine. When she complained about her leg, how the pain keeps waking her up at night, I didn't respond, though I could see she was hoping for some sympathy. It's often this way after one of my lapses. I felt worse than usual because my mother had just given me three beautiful silk saris, her most expensive ones, plus an elegant white woolen shawl, which looked at once familiar and magical, an object out of a dream. I don't think I'll ever use them, though—they're not exactly my thing.

"Send me a photo when you wear them," she said as she handed the bundle to me. Then, because she's who she is, she sniffed and added, "If I'm still alive, that is."

I've made it to the corner of the garage. Another hour and I'll be done. Another two days and I'll be out of here with my stolen photo. I haven't decided what I'll do with it.

Everything else I've stolen, I got rid of. It started with a stuffed raccoon I took from my boyfriend. (Or was it earlier? I forget.) I let the raccoon float away into the ocean. From the thrift store where I worked, I took a Jesus statue. Left it at a bus stop. With time, it got easier, though perhaps *easier* is not the word I'm looking for. When I went back to college, I stole textbooks from other students and stamped envelopes from the department where I worked. I stole pen-holders from my professors' offices. Plaques. Things I didn't need. Things I wouldn't use. Sometimes I threw them in the first dumpster I came across. When I was dating Gary, I stole his college jersey, three novels, his spare keys, and a box of Clif Bars. I did this even though I was in love with him.

At the various jobs I've held, I've stolen coffee mugs, staple removers, cushions, wall hangings, even photographs and kiddie art off of my coworkers' desks. I once stole a rabbit paw. I'm good at it. I came dangerously close to being found out sometimes—those were the most thrilling moments—but I always believed I'd never be caught. When people started looking at me funny, I quit my job and moved on.

Then a colleague brought in a glass paperweight, one of those antique ones where, if you shook it, snow fell slow and silent over a tiny Eiffel Tower. Her dead aunt had left it to her. She held it cupped in her palms and told us in a breathless, teary voice about how she would play with it when she went to visit her aunt. She looked so happy, remembering, that I had to have it.

I took it one afternoon when I thought no one was around. But someone must have seen me. When I got down to the lobby, the security officer made me empty out my purse. Other employees stopped to gawk. My boss was summoned; there was talk of notifying the police. I was blamed for other things that had gone missing, even those I'd had nothing to do with.

The security officers accompanied me to the house. I was terrified my family would find out, but providentially, Gary was still at work and Neel at an after-school game. The officers searched, but there were no stolen goods. I'd thrown them all away long ago.

I lost my job, of course. But my boss, who'd been fond of me, said she wouldn't put anything in my employment file if I started therapy. Thus, Dr. Berger.

It took me a long time to find work again. I had to tell my poor trusting husband a slew of lies. I thought the ordeal had cured me, but it wasn't so. Over the last couple of years, I've started stealing again, no matter how much I hate myself for it afterward.

Dr. Berger says, Stealing doesn't bring back whatever it is that you feel you lost. Think about it, Tara.

She says, Why are you attracted to self-sabotage?

I don't know, Dr. Berger. Is it because it takes less courage to hurt oneself than to hurt others?

There's a big box in the corner, sealed. I'm surprised to find my name on it, and our old address from when my parents were married. It's battered, as though it's made it through several of my mother's moves. For a moment I'm confused. Then I see that it's from my dorm, postmarked from the time when I dropped out of school. I'd walked out with a backpack, leaving everything else behind, as though in doing that I could shrug off my life. I remember a message from my mother on my cell phone, saying the university had mailed my things back to the house. I hadn't responded. I'd been sure she would have got rid of them by now. But she hadn't. Nor had she opened the box to pry into my life. She'd carried it patiently with her, apartment to apartment, year to year, hoping I'd come back to her.

I carry the box to the throwaway pile, but then I pull at the packing tape. I want a glance at my old self, the Tara who would never have dreamed of stealing anything. The brittle tape comes off easily. Textbooks, outdated clothes, music CDs, a jumble of Sharpies, strips of Pepto-Bismol crumbled into pink powder, an alarm clock, bottles from which the perfumes have long evaporated, a favorite blue comforter that my mother gave me so I wouldn't feel homesick.

The girl I'd been, I can't feel her in any of this.

I throw the box on the pile. It tilts. Items spill onto the floor, clatter-

ing. I swear. More work for me now. Squatting, I start to stuff everything back. Then I catch sight of a large sealed envelope. It doesn't look
familiar, unlike the rest of the junk in here. When I pull it out of the
box, I see row upon row of Indian stamps. Someone spent a lot of money
to mail this to me. The sender's name is Bipin Bihari Ghatak. I have no
idea who he might be.

Inside is a thick stack of papers. The sheet on top, written in a
cramped, meticulous hand, says, *Your grandmother spent the last hours before her heart attack writing this letter to you.*

My grandmother. I imagine her sitting cross-legged on a marble
floor, pulling a low rosewood table close to her. I see her unscrewing a
fountain pen. She looks a little like old Mrs. Mehta, a woman I'd once
known. Mrs. Mehta had told me stories about the stars. She'd gone with
me to get my things out of my cheating boyfriend's house. She wrote to
me twice after she went back to India, lovely, meandering, melancholy
letters in which she she invited me to come and live with her. I reread
the letters thirstily and thought about it. But I didn't have the courage.
Then I moved, and moved again, leaving no forwarding address, and I
lost her, too.

I'm afraid the letter will be in Bengali, which I can't read, but it's in
English. My hands start to tremble. When I was young, I asked my
mother many times about my grandmother. But she never liked to talk
about her. I knew Grandma passed away around the time of the divorce,
but I didn't have any details, and later, when my mother and I started
speaking again, I'd been reluctant to bring up a topic that would surely
have been painful for her. Perhaps, finally, this letter will help me parse
the mystery that is Sabitri Das.

> *Dearest Granddaughter Tara,*
>
> *Your mother informs me that you do not wish to continue with
> college. I am very sorry to hear this and hope you will reconsider. It
> would be a criminal waste if you do not avail yourself of the opportu-
> nity life has given you.*

How would my grandmother have known about me dropping out of college? Did my mother and she discuss me? I feel a twinge of anger but drop it. It was a long time ago, and besides, I'm curious.

But the letter is confusing. Page after page is a variation of the same theme. Had my grandmother developed dementia in her old age? I shuffle the pages of clichéd advice, disappointed, glancing through them one last time before I stuff them into the box.

Then I come across this:

> . . . at that, I stopped. Perhaps a part of me believed that, charity case that I was, he had the right to command me. But a part of me wanted to stay because he was young and handsome and had been chivalrous. My heart beat unevenly as I turned to face him, and not just out of fear.

Somewhere in there, my grandmother had started telling me a story. Her story. The story I'd been longing to know since I saw her photo. No, I'd needed to know this story all my life, though I hadn't always been aware of the needing. My breath comes fast as I retrieve the sheets and spread them out on the garage floor. I try to put them in sequence. It takes a while because nothing is numbered. I'm longing to read, but there's something I must do first. The universe has given me an undreamed-of gift. I must reciprocate.

I go to my bedroom and retrieve the sepia photo from my carry-on. It isn't easy. I take a deep breath and hold it. I bite the inside of my cheek until I taste blood. Twice I turn back. But finally I manage to walk with the photo to the family room, stepping carefully in the dark. I'm going to put it back in the album.

Dr. Berger, it's the first time in my life that I'm returning what I've stolen. I think you might call this a landmark moment.

I maneuver gingerly between unfamiliar pieces of furniture, banging my knee a couple of times in the process. But I don't want to switch on a light and wake my mother, who's sleeping with her door open. I don't want to field a host of awkward questions. I feel around on the coffee table for the album, but I can't seem to find it. Damn. Could my mother have taken it into the bedroom with her? I feel around some more and knock over something loud and metallic.

"Who's there?" my mother calls in a startled, quavery voice. I'm startled, too. Her voice sounds very close—much closer than the bedroom. I hear a sharp clapping sound, and then I'm blinded by the blaze of a table lamp directly in front of me. Double damn. She has one of those clap-activated switches.

My mother sits up groggily, feeling around on the table for her glasses. She must have woken up and come out here to try and find a more comfortable position on the sofa. On the side table, in front of which I'm standing, is the photo album. So near. But there's no way I can replace the photo without my mother seeing it.

"What are you doing, Tara?"

"I—I was sorting through your things in the garage. I came in for a drink of water." Even to my ears, my voice sounds squeaky and suspicious. I try to hide the photo behind my back, which of course draws her attention to it.

"What's that in your hand?"

I offer up the photo, feeling much like a four-year-old caught with my hand in the cookie jar.

My mother stares at it, then at me, anger replacing the surprise on her face.

"You were taking it? After I'd told you no? Taking my mother's picture, which would have given me a little comfort in that mausoleum?"

"Actually, I was putting it back," I say. But there's guilt in my voice, and with her infallible mother-instinct, she hones in on it.

"You couldn't wait a few months, until I was dead? You had to steal it now?"

Maybe it's that word, *steal*. Maybe it's the pent-up stress of the entire week. Maybe it's the weight I feel because I'm putting an end to my mother's independence. Something breaks inside me.

"Yes," I shout. "I steal. That's what I do. That's why I keep moving from job to job. I already got caught once. I'm sure I'll get caught again. My husband will come to know. My son. But I can't stop."

She shrinks back from me. The horror—or is it disgust?—on her face is like red pepper rubbed into a wound. It forces me onward.

"Do you want to know why I steal? I take things that I should have had but didn't get. Things that mean happy memories. Things that stand for love and commitment. But sometimes I steal things that mean nothing. I steal them because there's a big hole in the middle of my chest and stealing fills it up for a moment."

"Why the photo?" Her whisper is shaky now, as though she is afraid to hear the answer. As she should be.

"I stole the photo because *you* kept her from me all my life."

And suddenly she's furious. "How dare you accuse me! What do you know of how carefully I had to walk the razor's edge with your father? Do you think I didn't miss her? Didn't want her to come to America and be with me when I was so lonely that I wanted to die? Didn't want to see her holding you when you were born, as you were growing up? But he wouldn't let me."

At the mention of my father, I find myself beginning to shake. God, that he should have such a hold on me years after I promised myself I wouldn't care! My words come from somewhere deep down that I'd forgotten about—or forced myself to forget. *Why don't you ask her?* he'd said at our last meeting outside the thrift store where I'd been working at the time.

"Don't blame my father," I say. "None of this would have happened—not the divorce, not all the disasters afterwards—if you hadn't betrayed him first."

The words sound ridiculous as soon as they're out of my mouth. I wait for her to laugh an incredulous laugh of denial, to scoff at me for trying to change the subject, to accuse me some more of thievery. But she looks down, defeat evident in the slump of her shoulders.

My mother? She was unfaithful, too? What kind of stock do I come from, then? What twisted genes have I passed on to my son?

She averts her eyes, reaches for her walker, and makes her lurching way to the bedroom. The door closes behind her with a small, final click.

I've ruined everything.

❧✦❀

After I replace my grandmother's photo, because I can't think of what else to do, I go back to the garage, to her letter. All night I read my grandmother's adventures. Her words enter me like spears. They hurt, but also for a while they make me forget my own problems.

Her dreams were audacious, unseemly for the daughter of a poor village priest. People around her were determined to crush them. The rules her mother wanted her to live by, proverbs for good women, were too simple for her. She could not accept them.

> *Good daughters are fortunate lamps, brightening the family's name.*
> *Wicked daughters are firebrands, blackening the family's fame.*

There are secrets in this letter, things she has told no one: How she lived, a poor guest in a rich Kolkata home, swallowing humiliation daily for the privilege of education. How she fell into forbidden love and for that crime was thrown out into the night; how in desperation she beguiled my grandfather; how she got back at her onetime hosts but learned that revenge exacts its price. How the problems between her and my mother began, with words of deadly innocence spoken in a car, and a slap that echoed through the years.

❧✦❀

It's morning by the time I finish reading and rereading the letters. I'm exhausted. My eyes are rough and burning, scratchy with sand—as though I've traveled halfway across the world without stopping. But I'm strangely comforted, too. In the context of my grandmother's life, mine seems a little less desperate.

But no, I'm not finished. There was something else Grandma Sabitri had learned, the most important of all. It was the last thing she wrote for me before she died. In truth, she wrote it for my mother as much as myself, and thus I must share it with her before I leave.

I knock on my mother's door. I know it's not going to be easy.

"Go away," she says, her voice muffled.

I turn the knob and enter.

"Didn't you hear me?" she says. "Go. We have nothing more to say to each other. Fortunately, after today, we won't have to see each other again."

I hand her the letter and tell her where I found it. I hear the intake of her breath. I wait.

"I didn't know," she whispers to herself as she reads. "Oh, God, I didn't know." I think she has forgotten my presence.

～•◦

My mother's on the last page now. She's crying—ugly, racking sobs that make it hard for the words to push through.

"When you told me you were dropping out of college, Tara, I didn't know what to do. I'd dropped out of college myself—so many of my problems stemmed from that. I didn't want the same thing to happen to you. I guess that's when people call their mothers—when their world is falling apart. I told your grandma that she must write to you. Get you to change your mind. That it was her duty. I was so focused on my own pain, I didn't even think how much my news might distress her. Oh, my poor mother, all my life I've given her only trouble. Even as a child, I was sullen and difficult. I blamed her for my dad's death. And even more for my baby brother's. I felt it was her job to keep him safe. I didn't know then that mothers can't necessarily save their children, no matter how much they want to.

"After I talked to her, all day I paced the house. I called you, but you didn't answer. I called your father. He had already changed his number. My body felt like it was burning up. That night—probably just as my mother was having her heart attack—I took sleeping pills. I was planning to take the whole bottle, but halfway through, I lost courage. In any case, I passed out. Didn't hear the phone when it rang. The next morning, I woke up on the bathroom floor, dry-mouthed, my head feeling like it was about to split open. I wanted to crawl into bed and never get up.

"But I dragged myself to the phone and checked for messages. I was hoping you'd called back. But the messages were all from my mother's phone. I skipped them. I couldn't bear to listen to her scoldings, telling me once again that I'd messed up.

"The messages weren't from her, though. They were from Bipin Babu, our old manager at Durga Sweets, the only one who was there for her in the end. By the time I realized this, everything was over, even her ashes scattered. Tara, I'd killed my mother!"

She rocks back and forth, her shoulders shaking. I hold her as best as I can, and think how near she herself had come to death because of me. Dr. Berger, I, too, am entangled in this web of sorrow and responsibility. Pain makes us crazy. All we want is to throw the live coal of it as far from us as we can, not thinking what we might set afire.

My mother clutches at the collar of my shirt. I rub her back and feel her tears on my neck. It's been decades since our bodies have been this close. It's an odd sensation, like a torn ligament knitting itself back, lumpy and imperfect, usable as long as we know not to push it too hard.

In a while, my mother sits up.

"I did betray your father," she says. "But not in the way you think. Perhaps what I did was more shameful. I'll tell you about it before you leave. It's only right that you should know. But first, will you read me the rest of the letter? My eyes hurt."

She holds out the page.

"Yes," I say.

Before We Visit the Goddess

But that moment in the car wasn't the happiest moment of my life. Just like it hadn't been so on the starlit terrace. . . . My happiest moment would come much later. . . .

One day, in the kitchen at the back of the store, I held in my hand a new recipe I had perfected, the sweet I would go on to name after my dead mother. I took a bite of the conch-shaped dessert, the palest, most elegant mango color. The smooth, creamy flavor of fruit and milk, sugar and saffron mingled and melted on my tongue. Satisfaction overwhelmed me. This was something I had achieved by myself, without having to depend on anyone. No one could take it away. That's what I want for you, my Tara, my Bela. That's what it really means to be a fortunate lamp.

Acknowledgments

It takes villages upon villages to birth a book. I would like to express my heartfelt thanks to the following people who helped me through the complex process of creating this one in particular, where I dared to try many new things.

My agent, Sandra Dijkstra (who has been with me since the very first book), and her wonderful team, especially Elise Capron and Andrea Cavallero, for their unflagging support.

My editors at Simon & Schuster: Millicent Bennett, for her excellent critical eye, and for praising and pushing me in turn as needed, and never accepting second-best. And Emily Graff, for generously sharing her insights with me and for championing *Goddess* in-house and out in the world.

My amazing writers group—Zack Bean, Nicholas Brown, Will Donnelly, Irene Keliher, Keya Mitra, Oindrila Mukherjee—for their careful, kind, and honest reading and rereading of drafts, for pointing out what I was too close to see by myself.

Friends Robert Boswell, Sreya Chatterjee, Auritro Majumdar, Punam Malhotra, Alex Parsons, Roberto Tejada, and Elizabeth Winston, for providing information and encouragement, and patiently going over details in the stories and correcting them when needed.

My three men, Murthy, Anand, and Abhay, for being my best cheerleaders and for understanding all those times when I needed to recede into the fictional world.

Acknowledgments

Those who have passed away but whose blessings are still with me: my grandfather Nibaran Chandra Ghosh; my mother, Tatini Banerjee; and my mother-in-law, Sita Divakaruni.

My spiritual teachers, from whom I'm learning how important it is to approach the world with compassion: Baba Muktananda, Swami Chinmayananda, Swami Tejomayananda, and Swami Vidyadhishananda.

Thank you, all. Truly.

About the Author

Chitra Banerjee Divakaruni is the author of sixteen books, including *Oleander Girl*, *The Mistress of Spices*, *Sister of My Heart*, *The Palace of Illusions*, and *One Amazing Thing*. Her work has appeared in *The New Yorker*, *The Atlantic*, and *The New York Times*, and has won, among other prizes, an American Book Award. Born in India, she currently lives in Texas and is the McDavid Professor of Creative Writing at the University of Houston.